USURPER

WILLIAM D. HOY

Published by:

OMNIBOOK Co.
99 Wall Street, Suite 118
New York, NY 10005 USA
+1-866-216-9965
www.omnibook.org

For e-book purchase: Kindle on Amazon, Barnes and Noble
Book purchase: Amazon.com, Barnes & Noble, and www.omnibook.org

Omnibook titles may be purchased in bulk for educational, business,
fund-raising, or sales promotional use. For more information please e-mail
admin@omnibook.org

contents

CHAPTER 1

Trenton, New Jersey, 1850. Morning rush in the middle of town. A nicely dressed young man in his early twenties hurrying down the wooden planked sidewalk weaving in and out of the crowded side walk.

"Good morning, sorry, excuse me, pardon me," Antonio is saying as he cuts in front of a slow-moving man. Women pushing baby carriages, couples walking together, a few dogs running loose, people taking, slow walkers or going to work. The good-looking guy named Antonio Ferretti on his way to work, and he's running a little late. He's dressed in his work cloths, a pin-striped suit, tie, black shoes, and wearing a bowler hat. Walking fast, he quickly approaches a busy cross street; out of the corner of his eye, he sees a fast-moving horse and buggy approaching the intersection.

"Oh god," mumbles Antonio as he quickly stops almost falling off the sidewalk in front of the horse and buggy rushing by. Controlling his balance, he's breathing heavy, thinking about what could have happened to him—a total annihilation could have happened. Almost losing his hat as he adjusts it, straightening himself up, he adjusts his hat once more, trying to compose himself as he takes a quick look around to see if anyone saw him. He's thinking that everyone must be watching him, as he almost got run over by a horse and buggy. Looking both ways to make sure nothing is coming in either direction, he and the rest of the crowd step lightly into the smelly, muddy road soaked in horse dung, as they all tiptoe to the other side of the street. Getting to the other side, he takes off in a hurry dodging walkers. After hastily going a couple hundred feet passing several businesses, he stops in front of a business window with large words written across it saying, "Buy Cheap Land Out West," in small lettering, printed underneath, "Real Estate." Briefly looking at himself in the reflection of the front window, making sure he is presentable, he opens the door and enters the business.

Entering a small room, he hangs his hat neatly on the hat rack at the door, glancing at the clock on the wall, and heads to his desk. Quickly sitting down, he looks off to his left at the desk next to his, where his friend Nolan is working. He asks, "Did I miss my appointment?"

Nolan replies, "No, no one has come in."

"Is the boss in?"

"You're lucky," Nolan says, "he won't be in today."

In a sigh of relief, Antonio starts bringing out of his desk drawer a few black and white photo brochures of land for sale in California, laying them so they can be seen by a customer. Just as he finishes laying them out, suddenly the door opens and in walks a sophisticated, rich elderly woman named Ms. Esmerelda Forty. She's fancying a rich-looking bonnet, a full dress with lots of flowers, and a brightly colored parasol.

"Good morning, Ms. Forty," Antonio immediately says as she quickly walks up to his desk and sits down in the chair in front of his desk.

"And good morning to you, Mr. Ferretti." She begins to apologize as she removes her gloves.

"I'm sorry for being late, I was just so busy. I had to stop by the florist and order some beautiful red roses on my way here for a small gathering of ladies I'm having over to my house later this afternoon, you know, a few bakery things and tea, they go so well together. I have been so busy since I was in here the other day. Oh Lord, I hadn't had the proper time to ask about the purchase of the property, but today is the day."

"Oh, that's all right, Ms. Forty. I was just finishing up a few sales I wrote yesterday."

Ms. Forty, says, "Last time when I was in here, you showed me some lovely photos of that beautiful land out in California, and you quoted me some amazing prices."

"Yes, I did," he said as he opens up a few of the brochures on his desk.

Antonio says, "Here's the pictures I had shown you last time so she can see them again," as he points to them in front of her, as she looks at them.

"Ms. Forty, the prices I quoted to you the other day will not last long, and any day I will have to ask for more money. A lot of people are buying them."

"Stop, stop, young man," she says as she holds her hand up in front of his face.

"I told you last time when I was in here. I have to talk with God and have been too busy to ask if I'm doing the right thing." She starts putting her gloves back on. She's starting to raise her voice as she says, "He will tell me if it will happen. So I will be back tomorrow, and we will talk then."

Antonio, starts to think that maybe Ms. Forty has changed her mind and all of his efforts will be in vain. Suddenly, she stands up from her chair, as she slightly straightens her dress. "I must go now, Mr. Ferretti. I will return tomorrow." She turns and walks out of the office heading up the sidewalk toward the church as she's holding her parasol above her head.

Antonio is sitting at his desk with a depressed look on his face, thinking he has lost the sale.

Spending all this time on this customer, and not making a sale, he's sure his boss will not be happy with him. Suddenly he jumps to live, as his snaps his fingers with an idea, pulling open his drawer on his desk as he starts to rummage through it looking for something as he's mumbling something like, "white collar."Nolan looks over at him with an amused look.

"You have an idea?"

"Yes," he says out loud as he holds up one of those white stiff collars a Catholic priest puts around his neck when they are wearing civilian clothes.

"I have this crazy idea, and I hope it works."

"What do you have, oh, yes, I know what it is. But how are you going to use it?" Nolan asks.

"I'll let you know later tonight over a beer." He grabs his hat and rushes out of the office, heading up the sidewalk toward the church where Ms. Forty was heading.

Antonio enters the doors to the church, hangs up his hat, and heads over to the corner, pretending to be looking at something on the wall. As he's standing, they're trying to feel comfortable, as he's adjusting his eyes to the dim light, thinking about what he's going to attempt to do as he glances around trying to locate Ms. Forty. Many people moving around, about a dozen sitting on the back benches saying their prayers or just resting in a blessed place.

As he scans around the room to locate Ms. Forty, trying not to be conspicuous, when he suddenly sees her sitting in the end of the last row of benches not too far from the confession booth. As she sits, he notices she keeps glancing at the confession both seeing when it will not be occupied.

After several minutes pass, a woman departs, and a minute later, the priest departs as well.

Antonio starts to get a bit nervous as he waits, watching, wondering what Ms. Forty is going to do.

"She's going to do it," he quietly says to himself as Ms. Forty gets up from the bench and heads toward the confession booth, enters, closing the door behind her.

Suddenly Antonio's breath stops, his feet are not moving. He asks himself, "What am I doing?"

Somehow after a few seconds, he feels his feet moving toward the booth. He can't remember how he got to the door, as his hand opens it. He takes a quick look around, making sure he is not seen, and ducks in and sits down. Trying to control his nerves, he fumbles in his coat pocket and pulls out his white collar and puts it on, twisting his neck around as he adjusts the collar.

Feeling in his other pocket, he brings out a large unsightly used handkerchief, wadding it up in his hand to disguise his voice. Feeling a bit light-headed, he opens the sliding door, trying not to look into the mesh even though neither the priest nor the confessor can see each other. He's trying to build up nerve to say the first word. He remembers what the priest said to him when he was younger and getting into trouble just like the other young boys, sweating, hoping the punishment will not be bad as he sat in the confession booth.

Now grown-up, he is here and he has to say something. Nervously putting the handkerchief up to his mouth, "When was the last time you confessed?" he manages to say, hoping the nervousness won't come through his voice.

Ms. Forty begins, "Let me see, I have had some thoughts that might be troubling in my decision. I haven't sinned or that is I don't think I have. I have a question, to make sure I won't sin."

"Oh, tell me your troubles," Antonio replies, surprised by her answer.

"I have been looking at some property for sell in California. The wonderful salesman has shown me beautiful pictures of the property at his office. I love the property, and *oh*, it's a good price. I may use it as a wedding gift for my grandson. I want to ask God if this is a good idea before I do anything."

"I see," Antonio replies as he's trying to give her an answer. Then he decides to use this approach.

"This question is a bit out of the ordinary that I get, my lady. So let me ask a few questions. Do you like the salesman?"

"Yes, he seems to be honest and trustworthy."

"Do you like the property that's for sell?"

"Yes, I love it. I just wished I would be able to see it before I purchased it. The salesman told me they are selling fast, and I might lose my chance of getting it if I wait long. Also, the wedding will happen next month, timing is not on my side."

"It sounds like a nice present. Is the price appropriate for you?"

"Oh yes, money is no issue. I just want to be sure I'm doing the right thing."

"Well, with what you had told me, I think God would give you the blessing to purchase the property. Property enriches a person's life, giving them a chance to prosper."

"Thank you so very much," Ms. Forty says.

"I think you need to say ten Hail Marys just to satisfy your soul. You possibly had some misgivings, and your thoughts need to be cleansed."

"I will," she says as she opens the door and goes over to the bench and sit to say her Hail Marys.

After waiting a few minutes, Antonio nervously puts his handkerchief back into his pocket after wiping his face and hands covered with sweat. He peeks out the door, and Ms. Forty has gone.

Looking closely out the crack of the door, Antonio making sure a priest is not close by or may be heading to the confession booth where he is at. He has to get out now. He opens the door, keeping his head down as he quickly heads to the exit. Just before he exits the church, he moves to the corner of the alcove and clumsily removes the white collar, putting it back into his pocket, and getting his hat.

+ + +

That night, Antonio very excited as he meets up with Nolan at their favorite watering hole for several beers.

He explains in details to what he had done and how extremely nervous he was. He's not sure wearing the white collar helped him. In a confession, both person neither see each other.

Maybe it gave him an emotional support. He didn't put it on until he got into the booth. He tells Nolan that while talking with Ms. Forty with the handkerchief stuck in his mouth, he sort of felt like he was a real priest. He feels that when people talk with priests, they can tell all their secrets, lies, and feelings without being hurt. He hopes that he did not do any damage in her belief.

"Don't worry about it," Nolan says.

"No one is going to tell her. Do you think she will buy the property?"

"I got a real good feeling she will, just keep your fingers crossed. If she buys the property, that will be the first I have sold in a month."

As the two young men sit talking and drinking, several older businessmen they know sit down at the table next to them ordering up several drafts. One of the men is tall, and the other businessman is short and porker. After talking for a while, the tall man lays down on Antonio and Nolan's table the *Trenton Examiner* newspaper.

"Turn to page 11," he says as Antonio thumbs through the pages to eleven.

As Antonio looks at the page as the man continues, "A Bishop Mangini in Denver, Colorado is running an ad in the newspaper and is desperately looking for Italian priests, he even put in his mailing address in the paper.

The bishop says, "There is an enormous amount of Italian immigrants moving out west, mostly doing hard work on the railroad. It appears that this Bishop Mangini is in dire need for priests and has to run an ad in the *New Jersey Examiner*."

The porker businessman says, "Yeah, and there are a lot of gold miners digging for almost anything out there.

The tall man says to Antonio and Nolan, "Think about what I'm going to tell you. When you are in church, and the donation plate passes by, almost everyone deposits some amount of money in it. Some of those plates are almost overflowing with money. Have you ever taken a close look at those plates when they're taken around the corner and disappear in the back? They are loaded, sometimes almost running over. I remember one time when I went to church, one of the plates was so full, they had to get another empty plate to continue passing around for donations.

"Have you noticed there are envelopes in the plates, well I'll tell yah. People put in promissory note pledges, and sometime that is a lot of money. The parishioners will come into the office of the church during the week and give them money. Now mind me, I'm not saying anything bad, or insinuating anything about the church. But they get a lot of money every service."

"Yeah, really interesting, you're right. I've seen the money in the plates," Antonio says as he's listening to what the man is saying.

The porker businessman says, "If I was young again and had another chance, I think I would be a priest. I would be a hell of a lot better than I am today," as he washes down the last word, finishing up his beer with a long swallow. Both businessmen finish their beers as they bid to the two young men a good night and leave.

The tall businessman says as he hands the paper to Antonio, "Here, you can have the paper, son, I'm finished with it," as they head home, and Antonio folds the paper and lays it on the table. The two young men are getting close to the bottom of their glasses as Nolan says to Antonio, "That article in the newspaper of where a bishop is looking for priests looks like a good thing, but we are not priests."

Antonio smiles and looks at Nolan. "I got this idea yesterday when I was at church with Ms. Forty. I'll let you know in a couple of days what I'm thinking about. I was just wondering, tell me, do you think that Bishop Mangini out there in Denver, who's in a desperate need for priests, would be asking for credentials or proof of schooling? By looking at this article, it appears there is an air of desperation out there."

"I don't know anything about being or training to be a priest," says Nolan.

"I was thinking," says Antonio as he's finishing up his glass of beer, "way out west, there are almost no rules. I read about it every so often in the newspaper. Maybe it could happen in the church as well, no rules."

"Maybe, I'm not familiar with anything that happens way out in nowhere land," says Nolan as he drains the last drop down his throat.

"Humm," says Antonio as he continues.

"This is just a hypothetical idea, just pretend that I write a letter to the bishop who ran that ad in the newspaper, and pretended I'm a priest. What do you think would happen if after I got out there, someone found out I was an imposter?"

Nolan, looking very serious now, says, "I don't know, maybe it might work. But how are you going to be knowledgeable about prayers, the right hymns to sing, the right prayers, perform a communions and burials?

What if the church finds out, will they put you in jail or might even kill you especially out west, where there are no laws? And one more serious thing," says Nolan, "no fractionation with women."

"Now thinking about it, this is what I was going to tell you in a couple of days. I can start going to the churches around here, making notes. I'll get a Bible and a hymn book from one of them. I remember a few things from when I use to go to church with my parents until they got divorced."

"That's a possibility, but once you start your impersonation, you just can't quit because it gets rough. If you get caught, the parishioners or the Italian immigrants of the church might do harm to you. Drag you through the streets by horse, or maybe hang you from a tree."

"Yes, I thought about that. I would have to leave town very fast."

"Ya, you're right about that."

"How is your horse riding?"

"I've never been on a horse."

"If you decide to go through with this crazy idea, I think horse riding would be a good idea."

"Ya, you're right, maybe we can ask around when we're in here for our next beers."

"Or maybe," says Antonio thinking about what they have been talking about,

"I could stay here earning pennies, selling property out in the wild west, not even sure if the properties exist."

+ + +

The next morning, Antonio arrives at the office early, looking forward to Ms. Forty's visit. He has all the brochures out on his desk and the contract ready to be signed. An hour has passed, and Ms. Forty has not arrived at the office, as Antonio sits wondering what has happened to Ms. Forty.

Maybe she has a meeting at her house and she's stopping at some store to buy things. She didn't tell him when she was going to stop buying, if she has decided to buy the land. As he glances at the clock on the wall, he starts to think that maybe in the confession booth he said the wrong thing to Ms. Forty and she changed her mind.

"No, that didn't happen. She was very joyful and said her Hail Marys, I'm sure everything I said was correct."

"Hey Nolan, did Ms. Forty come in early before I got here and I missed her?"

"No," says Nolan, "she hasn't been in, and there wasn't a note on the door either. I hope she hasn't changed her mind."

"Strange," mutters Antonio, "I thought for sure I had convinced her."

"She must be running late," comments Nolan.

"Yeah, I was thinking the same thing."

Another half an hour passes.

Suddenly the office door opens, and in walks Ms. Forty, with smile from ear to ear. She walks briskly up to Antonio's desk and sits down.

"Good morning, Mr. Ferretti. It's such a wonderful and beautiful day, isn't it?"

Antonio's still recovering from the sock of seeing Ms. Forty come in so quickly, with such a dazzling persona about herself.

He responds, "And a good morning to you as well, Ms. Forty."

Before he could say another word, Ms. Forty begins, "I spoke to God yesterday, and I got his blessings. So I thought about it last night and have decided to buy three parcels today if that is all right. You did such an excellent job in explaining about the new land, it's so exciting," and she giggles.

"Well, well," says Antonio, getting caught off guard, looking for the right words to say, as he's shuffling through his papers looking for a new blank contract.

"I'm very happy you have decided to buy three parcels. We have to look at the map so you can pick out the other two parcels.

"I'm sure my grandson will be excited. So I stopped by the bank on my way here and got enough money for all three parcels, that's why I'm late." As she's talking, she begins to dig into her large bulky purse, pulling out bundles of banded paper currency stacking them on Antonio's desk. "There's one stack for each parcel," she says.

Antonio is shocked in disbelief as he sit there for a few moments staring at Ms. Forty, and then looking at the three rows of stacked bills.

"That is great, that's great," Antonio repeats his words, glancing over at Nolan as he motions for him to come over to his desk.

"Ms. Forty, this is Mr. Nolan, my associate. He will count the money as I prepare your contract."

Antonio pulls his desk drawer open and brings out a blank contract.

Nolan, holding a pencil and a note pad, he said, "Nice to meet you Ms. Forty," as he sits down at the desk and begins to count the money.

The contract is signed by Ms. Forty, Antonio and Nolan witness the signatures. "I will have my boss endorse the contact, and you can come back in two days and pick up your copy and the property is yours."

CHAPTER 2

For the next couple of weeks, Antonio tries to think up ideas on how he's going to convince Bishop Mangini, or anyone else, that he is a priest. He wants to answer the ad that the bishop in Denver, Colorado, ran in a New Jersey newspaper, but what is he going to say? How can he be addressed as a priest, without any experience, no schooling records, no graduations from any institutions? One afternoon on his day off from his real estate sales job, Antonio walking down the street, with his troubled thoughts, passes a church, and he notices the large front door is slightly ajar.

Not really thinking about anything or what he's going to say, he approaches the church, Slowly he pushes open the door, he glances around in the dark room, and calls out, "Hello, hello, is anyone here?"

No one answers as he enters through the door. He slowly starts walking to the left side of the dark room, as he remembers where most offices are normally located. Trying to adjust his vision to the dark room, he gets to the corner of the room and sees a flickering glow from a light illuminating from around the corner. He approaches and sees an open door where the light's coming from and figures this must be the office.

Standing at the door, he looks into the gloomy office.

"Hello, hello, is anyone here?" he says as he notices dark shadows moving like someone's twisted faces moving on the wall, giving an idiosyncrasy feeling from the occasional flicker being produced by the kerosene light. The smell of oak, mahogany, and salmon wood fells the air, a low *clunk, clunk* sound came from the old grandfather clock ticks in the corner of the room. As Antonio stands motionless, he is trying to decipherer his heartbeat from the old clock's beat. Standing motionless in the doorway, he thinks he heard something from behind him. As he jumps to the side, nothing is there.

He glances around looking for the priest, but no one is there. He gets a bit nervous standing and waiting. After several minutes waiting, his nerves are beginning to take over. It is so quiet, he now can hear his heartbeat loud and clear.

Then he nervously takes several steps up to the front of the large mahogany desk. The desk is a monster, covered with several stacks of papers, several ink wells with writing pins stuck in a jar. The large kerosene lamp covers one large spot on the left side of the desk; Antonio could feel the heat on his face from the lamp.

Slowly Antonio becomes inquisitive, as he looks at everything laying on the desk from an upside position. As his eyes scans the top of the desk, he suddenly sees a stack of blank church stationery with the church's name and the priest's name printed on them. Antonio thinks it's OK, there would be no harm if he borrows a few sheets of stationary from the church to write a letter to the bishop in Denver. He is not stealing anything; it's all about the church. Pausing for a moment, he takes a quick look around then reaches down and picks up several sheets of stationary paper, and slips them inside his shirt. Besides the blank sheets were a small stack of envelopes, picking up a few, slipping them under his shirt as well. Suddenly he has become nervous, thinking he has stolen something from a church. He turns around taking a quick look around, making sure there is no one coming, and quickly walks out of the office heading toward the front door.

He's almost to the front door when he hears a man coughing several times from the back of the room. He's really scared now; immediately he thinks that he needs to run so he won't get caught. Strangely, something comes over him and surpasses his urge to run as sweat breaks out on his forehead. He continues to walk out of the church and will continue to walk fast down the street for a couple blocks, making sure no one is following.

✦ ✦ ✦

For the next week after work, Antonio sits at his kitchen table in his apartment and keeps trying to compose a letter to the Bishop Mangini in Denver. He has limited drinking for just a couple of nights with his friend Nolan so he could work on the letter. He fabricates few stories, telling Nolan he has other things to do so he can have the time to write his letter. He doesn't want to tell Nolan of his plan just yet, until he has it pretty much completed. The evenings he has set aside, he writes over and over, and nothing appears to his liking. He doesn't want to write too much about himself as a priest, maybe Bishop Mangini might detect something suspicious and deny his letter. Maybe he can write in a way to see if the bishop will be interested in a young priest.

He continues writing, changing the wording often until it starts to make since.

As he's thinking about this fantasy adventure, if he gets it, then he stops, and says to himself, "Will they pay for my train ticket?"

"Yes," he says to himself as he continues.

"Of course they should pay, they are in desperation for priests."

+ + +

Several hours later as he becomes comfortable with the letter, he decides he has to improve his writing skills, which he didn't get in school. But now he's working for a real estate company, selling land out west, being forced to write professional documents such as contracts and other important papers. So he gets some scrap paper and old newspapers to practice his writing. He decides to give himself the name of Father Mariano Luca, the priest with his name on the stationary from the church he borrowed the stationary from.

Looking at the first name Mariano, for a moment, that's printed on the church's stationary brought back memories of his younger life. Focusing on the name, he remembers back when he was a young boy living in New Jersey. His parents knew a handsome young priest at their church, who's first name was Mariano, but they never got to know him personally. He gave nice sermons and connected with the parishioners, and that was all. He had such a wonderful personality; many people came to the church as it seemed to be growing with popularity. Shortly later, Antonio's parents got a divorced, and his father left home, and he stayed with his mother, who moved back with her mother in a different town, never returning to listen to Mariano. "I wonder what ever happened to Mariano?"

+ + +

Couple days later in his room, Antonio says with satisfaction, "This letter will convince Bishop Mangini." While admiring his penmanship, he holds it up getting a better look at it. That evening, as Nolan and Antonio were having their beers at the favorite watering hole, Antonio tells Nolan his secret he has been working on. Nolan was a bit shocked on what Antonio has been doing.

"Have you thought about what might happen to you if you get caught?" Nolan says.

"What implications with the church and what will the police do? What kind of police do they have there, are they called sheriffs? You know, you are going to be in the Wild West. Are there cowboys and Indians? Do you think the church has a headquarters somewhere and have a list of all the priests in the United States?"

"I don't think so," replies Antonio.

"Are you sure about that, don't they have to know where they are at?" says Nolan.

"There must be thousands of churches I guess, and some churches might have several priests."

"Yes, I have thought about it, and no one is going to find out."

"Well, of course, I'm your best friend and your drinking buddy, you don't have to worry about me."

"Thank you, that makes me feel good. And you are by best friend as well, and I trust you with anything," says Antonio as both men make a toast with their beers to friendship.

"Thinking about your new name, Father Mariano Luca, does have a nice ring to it. But in private I will still call you Antonio."

"I will be maybe, two thousand miles away from here, way out in the Wild West, where there is hardly any law. I really doubt very much the bishop will know Father Mariano Luca in Trenton, New Jersey."

"Do you know everything that a priest does in church, maybe a wedding, and oh, how about a funeral?"

"Yes, I thought about that. I'm going to start visiting churches and take notes on what the priest does and says. I'll get myself a Bible and a hymn book and make notes at each service I go to."

"Yeah, due you think it's going to be too much to learn?"

"Well, it's worth a try, maybe I'll learn something. Ha, ha."

"I'm just trying to think about how much money will I be making. I guess it depends on how many parishioners will be coming. I was thinking, I remember one church I went to that had a lot of attendance, the donation plates that went around were almost full when they were taken into the back."

"Yeah, you're right, it's a long way from here, and I hope you make it big."

"I'll tell ya, when I get some extra money, I'll send you a train ticket."

"That sounds great, that's a good idea."

✦ ✦ ✦

Back in Antonio's apartment, he's finally written the letter and ready to copy it to the stationery he got from the church. Not taking any chances of making a mistake, he writes the letter on an old piece of newspaper several times, making sure his penmanship looks right, no mistakes in spelling. After several practice runs, he is ready to write his letter.

Clearing everything off his kitchen table, he positions the blank sheet of paper with the church's letterhead and Father Mariano Luca on it, at a comfortable angle to write at the right angle. He puts the ink well off to the right side of the paper, precaution for ink drops, when dipping and removing the quill. He begins to write, every several words he blots the fresh ink, making sure there are no smudge marks. Then he realizes that he must be very careful about moving his writing hand over fresh written words to avoid any smudges, so he lays a piece of paper lightly over the new writings. As he's getting close to the end of the letter, he starts to get a bit panicky thinking he cannot make any miscues as he's getting so close to finish. He stops writing and decides he must take a break, or he's going to mess it up. He gets up from the table and walks around the room, trying to clear his mind, then snapping his fingers. "I need a beer," he says. So he goes over to the drinking salon, and there sits Nolan. "Hey, my friend," he says to Nolan as he walks up the booth Nolan is seating in and goes over to the counter. He tells the bar tender, "Two drafts," and pays for the drinks. He gets the to two drafts and walks back to Nolan's booth and puts them down. "I had to get away for a while. It was getting nerve-wracking. I just knew I was going to mess up, and I would have to start all over. I only have three blank sheets to work with, and there is no way I'm going back into the church and get any more."

"Well, Father Luca, you seem to be almost in over your pretty head," says Nolan, giving Antonio a smile. "But I must say, you are gutsy, and determined to do it."

After both friends drink their new glass of beers almost to their bottoms, Nolan says, "It's my turn," as he starts to get out of the booth to get two more beers."No, no, Nolan, I have made up my mind, I want to finish the letter tonight and mail it tomorrow. If I procrastinate too much longer, the bishop might get his quota of Italian priests and I'm out of luck. I'll see you tomorrow and will give you the update. I won't be into work either."

✦ ✦ ✦

Antonio gets back to his room, recharged now after having a beer and a small conversation with his friend Nolan. He goes to his kitchen sink, gets a wet towel, and mops his face several times to get a fresh feeling. He sits down in his chair, taking a look as his masterpiece as he reads it over. He reaches over, picks up his quill, dips it in the ink well, and begins to write. After several minutes, he is finished. Yes, he has finished his letter to Bishop Mangini, and he has not made any mistakes; the letter looks like it was written by a professional writer.

Sitting back from the table, he takes a deep sigh of relief. He has finished writing the letter, happy he didn't make any mistake. Now he'll leave the letter on his desk for an hour, making sure the ink is completely dry.

Getting up in the morning felling very fresh, knowing that he has finally finished the letter, he addressed the letter to Bishop Mangini and walked to the post office and mailed it.

CHAPTER 3

Antonio, in his plan to be a priest, must learn what a priest does at church services. He can still remember some of the things the priest did at the services during the short period of time he went with his family, but he couldn't remember what specific pages to turn to and what phrases to speak about. He needs a list and locations of churches within walking distances from where he lives. So he gets a simple map that the city had made for people to find businesses and to get around town without getting lost. Now his plan is starting to take shape. He will visit the churches only to find out what time they will have their services. If they have two or more, he writes all the information down. Once he has all the information, like days of service, the days and times. Now he is ready to start visiting all the churches on his list. He needs to start visiting the churches and make notes and what pages to turn to. Now with the completed lists, he's ready to make his visits.

The first church he visits is just down the street from where he lives. He doesn't take any notes; he just wants to listen and study what the priest is doing. The next week, he is back to the same church with his Bible, hymn book, and a pencil in his hand at the beginning of the service.

The priest instructs the parishioners to turn to a page in the Bible for a prayer. Antonio turns to that page and marks the page and underlines the passage. Feeling a bit conspicuous making notes in the Bible, he tries to mask his work so he won't be noticed. If a parishioner glances his way as he's writing, he tries to turn a bit so not to be seen writing in a Bible. Then through the service, he begins to notice several people making notes in their Bibles as well for future reference, but not for the reason he's making marks, he's thinking. So now he's feeling more comfortable about note-taking. When the priest tells the parishioners they will sing a song, he gets the church's hymn book out and underlines the passages and page numbers.

The following Sunday he brought the bible and hymn book he borrowed from the church, just like almost all parishioners had done, making notes, underlining paragraphs, and emphasis about what the priest was talking about, carrying both books as he leaves the services.

+ + +

After a while going to several different churches, he starts to enjoy the service, the priest and their sermons, the great feeling he has when he leaves. Each church he visits, the priest has different pages, different prayers, different hymns, and almost all of them are slightly different from each other. He even shook hands with the priest as he is leaving, "Thank you, Father, for a wonderful sermon. I got a lot out of what you said."

"Thank you, my son, I hope you come again," he is told by several priest as he left their churches. One time as he was leaving, he tried to respond back to a priest, wishing him a wonderful day, but an older woman cut into the conversation, though he wanted to ask the priest about something. Antonio walks on out of the church thinking how rude the woman was.

That night Antonio decides he needed to start visiting other religious churches and choose another denomination to expand his knowledge as a priest. He puts together a list of several address for the local churches and starts going to their services. He is really starting to enjoy the different services and making notes in his Bible as well, leaving the service with both books, the Bible and the hymn book, tucked under his arm full of notes as he shakes hands with the priest after the service.

One day as he is going by a church, he senses they are conducting a funeral; he needs that information for his notes. He cautiously enters the church trying not to be noticed, sitting in the last row in the back of the church. He watches the priest conduct the funeral service and what he is doing, as he tries to remember so he can write it down in his Bible later. There are many parishioners who got up in front and talk about the deceased, their personal interaction with him in life. The priest interacts very well with each person who has something to say.

Everyone is saying many wonderful things, and what he has done for them. Then a strange thing happens, a man whom no one knows gets up

18

in front and tells nasty things about the deceased. He goes on telling how cruel the deceased was to his family, and may his damned soul rest in hell. After the man tells his story, instead of seating back in the audience, he leaves the room.

This unusual thing has gotten a lot of people in the audience upset, as they talk about the man's demeanor and his disrespect for the dead.

+ + +

Another day as Antonio is not too far from a church, he notices a lot of people dressed all up and knows there is going to be a wedding. As he starts to enter the church, a well-dressed man at the door tells Antonio he is not invited by looking at his appearance, and stopped him.

The man says, "Excuse me, sir. Are you on the wedding list?"

Feeling slightly embarrassed for the stop, Antonio answers back, "No, I'm not, I just thought I would like to watch the wedding."

"I'm afraid you will not be able to come in if you're not on the list. There's also a dress code for the wedding."

Antonio nods his head. "Sorry, I didn't know." He continues walking down the street as he watches more people arrive and go inside the church.

+ + +

Antonio at his apartment continues to read all the underlines in both his Bible and the hymn book; soon he begins to find himself memorizing some of the hymns. He practices reciting the passages from his Bible and sings the hymns until he has almost mastered them all.

Every couple of days, he stops by the post office, asking the counter clerk, "I know this is beginning to sound dumb, but have you received a letter for Mariano Luca?"

"No, sir, nothing has come in," replies the postmaster.

+ + +

A couple weeks pass, and as Antonio and Nolan one night are drinking their beers at their local watering hole, Nolan asks, "Maybe the bishop didn't get your letter?"

"I'm sure he got the letter," Antonio replies. "Thinking about it, if the bishop decides he doesn't want me, there's not much I can do about it."

"Yeah, you're right, just wait and see, I guess."

Two days later, Antonio stops by the post office, before he asks if he has a letter, the postal worker with a vivid memory of Antonio says, "Yes, sir, your letter has arrived for you from a Bishop Mangini, in Denver, Colorado." The clerk goes into the back room; after several minutes, he returns with the letter, handing it to Antonio, who's so excited, he wants to share the excitement with Nolan. He races over to Nolan's apartment, and both pals want to open the letter together for the big surprise. They decide it will be best that they open the letter while they have a beer to celebrate.

Both men go to their drinking salon to celebrate. They got themselves a table, a couple of beers. As Antonio lay the letter on the table, they both look at it as if it's going to change into something.

"Damn," Antonio says as he takes a sip of beer starting to look nervous.

"Do you think it's for real, really? There is my answer, lying right here on the table in front of us of a letter I wrote to a bishop in Denver, Colorado, to be a priest in one of his churches. I'm not a priest, and I haven't had any training. What was I thinking when I wrote it? I'm just thinking, what I'm I going to do if he says yes. Here's the answer, right here in front of us."

Antonio makes a facetious comment, "It'll probably start off with, thank you for the interest, but no thanks, you are too young, or maybe you need gray hair." He laughs.

Nolan says, "Yeah or, he'll start off, we are looking for an older priest with all the credentials and so on."

"Well, here it goes," says Antonio as he rips open the end of the letter. Looking at the letter for a moment, then he begins to read out loud.

Dear Father Mariano Luca,

The letter reads. "Father Mariano Luca. I hope this letter finds you in good health and in high spirits. Thank you so very much for your lovely letter, responding to my advertisement in the newspaper. Yes, we are in desperate need for Italian priests. It would give me tremendous admiration for you if you would come to Denver, Colorado. It will be rough for you at the beginning, but you will quickly acclimate to the environment, and the way of life, with the help of God. We will not be able to pay for your trip to come here, but we will pay you back after your arrival. If you decide to come, write and tell me when you will arrive, and I will have you picked up at the train station by my personal driver, Christopher. I do hope you will find compassion in your heart and make the challenging trip, and may God bless and be with you on your journey.

Cordially yours,
Bishop Angelo Mangini

Antonio, not moving his hands as he continues holding the letter, not saying a word, his face flushed in appearance.

"That letter sounds powerful, and with a lot of meaning. It is written directly to you, Father Luca," says Nolan, taking a gulp of beer, not noticing Antonio's demeanor. Then Antonio snaps out of his trance and says, "Wow, when I started to read the letter, something strange came over me. I felt so odd, it's hard to describe. I felt like something in the words that was sending me a message, like it was calling me. In reality I didn't expect a letter looking like this letter. Unknowingly this is what I have been waiting for, I will be going to Denver as a priest."

+ + +

Several weeks later, Antonio and Nolan have their last drink at their favorite drinking salon.

"Tomorrow, I will be on the train to Denver, Colorado. I've got everything. Oh, thanks for the help in getting the old priest clothing."

"I got my neighbor and had her sew up the pants and jacket so they will fit. There was a patch we had to replace."

"I owe you, my buddy, for everything you done for me, all those crazy things we had done. And I will miss you and your stories, but I'm not going to miss selling properties out in the Wild West. If things change, and you decide to come out west, drop me a letter, and I will have something set up for you when you arrive. And that is a promise."

"Good luck, my friend, Father Mariano Luca," Nolan says with a big smile. "It's going to be hard for me to say your name next time we meet."

They both toast to their friendship.

CHAPTER 4

After Antonio purchased his train ticket to Denver, Colorado, under the name of Father Marino Luca, he now prepares to sit for a long time waiting in this giant, cavernous room of the Grand Central Station, New York. Every day, thousands of people rush through this enormous station catching their trains going everywhere in and around the city, as many are leaving the city, as thousands are coming into the city. As he patiently waits, studying notes he had written in his Bible, a pretty twenty-year-old girl walks up to him.

"Excuse me, Father, I couldn't help noticing you," she says as he closes his Bible and looks up at her.

"You see, I saw you seating for quite a long time. Father, do you mind if I can join you until my train arrives?"

"Yes, yes, please do so," he replies.

She pauses for a moment before sitting, as she looks closer at the father.

"Thinking about it, you look very much like the handsome priest I had at my parish back in Genoa, Italy."

"Oh, we'll thank you for the lovely comment, but I haven't been to Genoa. I have heard it's a charming town."

"Yes, now I'm on my way to Chicago, where I'm going to get married. I received a letter couple months ago with a wonderful marriage proposal. He's a very nice man. He owns his own printing company and is making good money."

"Congratulations, I'm sure you're going to have a wonderful life in Chicago," he says as he's focusing on his style of talking like a priest.

A luggage porter walks up, wearing a red working cap, dressed in black pants and coat, pushing a large four-wheel wagon. "Father, will you be needing some help with your luggage?"

23

Father Luca replies, "I don't believe my train has arrived yet. It's on track 9A for Denver."

The porter pulls out a pad from his coat pocket with a questionable look on his face, and thumbs through several pages.

He reads from his small pad, "Father, in one and a half hours, your train will arrive on track 5. These tracks and trains are always changing, you have to be careful you don't get on the wrong train. I will be back in about forty-five minutes and assist you."

"Thank you."

As the father waits for his train, he notices a young boy walking around through the busy crowd, dressed something like all the porters, but his clothes look more theatrical in appearance as he's holding a long wooden pole with a chalkboard sign on top written in calk. As the boy walks around, he is calling out, "Train schedules for arriving trains, train schedules for arriving trains."

Father Luca mumbles to himself, "That's a good idea about the portable sign, telling people what tracks they can pick up friends from arriving trains." As he sits there, he is amazed with disbelief as he looks at the large, cavernous building, with its interesting painting and sculpturing that ordains its walls and the beautiful marble floor and walls.

Then the young female sharing his bench says, "Father, my train has arrived and I must board it." She is very excited as she reaches down and holds the father's hand briefly. It was so nice talking with you, and I'm sure you will enjoy where you are going." She disappears in the crowd. Father Luca watches her disappear into the crowd as he briefly thinks she was such a beautiful girl. He quickly changes his thought and focus on being his holiness.

Sometime later, the same porter walks up to Father Luca pushing his wagon showing a little wear.

"Father, your train will be arriving shortly. It will be on track 3. May I assist you now? In a few minutes, there will be several trains arriving almost at the same time, and I will be extremely busy and may not be available to assist you." Just then a man and woman rush up to the porter. "We need your help now. We are late arriving at the station, and we are going to miss our train."

Calmly, the porter replies, "Sir, I'm helping the father to his train. If you will look around, there are many porters who can help you to your train."

"I need your help now!" the man barks at the porter."That would be all right," says the father. "I can find another porter."

"No, Father, I said I would help you to your train, and that is what I'm going to do. Sir, please excuse us," he says to the upset couple as he starts piling Father Luca's baggage on the cart.

"That would be an excellent idea, bless you," replies the father as he stands and starts to organize all of his baggage.

The man and woman run off into the crowd yelling for a porter.

The porter begins loading Father Luca's baggage onto the pushcart, and they both start heading to track 3. As they begin walking toward the tracks, the porter says, "Father, I got the track change a few minutes before I got with you. It's amazing how often they change tracks. Sometimes I often wonder how a train passes another train when the other train leaves a station an hour before the other train leaves, and how often the tracks changes to where a train is going to park." The porter continues talking as they head to their track.

As they walk towards the track, Father Luca says, "You are doing such a hard job of assisting me with my baggage. I want you to have—"

The porter puts up his hand to stop Father Luca. "No, Father, I appreciate what you want to do, but I owe plenty to God. This is my way of catching up on what I have missed. I need to go to church more often, but in my situation, work comes first right now. Someday, will make up for the lost time."

"No, I must insist," says Father Luca as he stops walking.

"I want you to have this blessing of God." He hands the porter a few coins. The porter extends his hand and excepts Father Luca's coins and slips them into his pocket.

"Thank you so very much, Father," replies the porter as they both start walking again, as they continue to talk.

Father Luca has boarded the train and been guided to his seat. He's sitting next to a window, watching all those busy people rushing to board their trains. The porters are the hardworking laborers at the Grand Central, as they struggle meeting the short time frame they have between trains. At times they are overwhelmed especially if several trains arrive and depart at the same time, creating an avalanche of bags to haul crashing down on them. There's one baggage in particular that is a headache for the porters to move, and that's this behemoth wooden box that's heavy, and hard to lift; it's called a trunk. The name steamer for this trunk came from somewhere probably ocean traveling.

Luca fixes his eyes on this particular porter as he struggles with two heavy cases as he finally gets them on his pushcart with one of the family member's assistance. He pushes the cart through the crowd as the family of seven trails behind him. The group passes by the entrance to the car the family is going to as the porter pushes his cart toward the baggage car.

"The poor soul," Father Luca mutters as the family boards the train, the dad giving some kind of hand signals to the porter. Father Luca slightly shakes his head as he couldn't understand what the man was doing. The family boards the train, not giving the hardworking porter a penny for his hard work. Then he switches from the porter and begins watching the busy circus outside his window as he begins to daydream, probably from exhaustion from his from New Jersey to here. He begins to think, *So many people, so many ethnics all traveling in so many directions. How can all this happen at one time? The railroad will be the mode of travel for everyone, and the horse and buggy will someday be obsolete. I wonder how crowded will it be in Denver?* Suddenly Father Luca is brought out of his dream stupor when a young lady nicely dressed in her late teens asks, "Excuse me, Father, is this seat saved?" She points at the empty seat facing him by the window. He looks up. "No, no, it's empty. I believe it is not reserved. You may sit here," says Father Luca as he pulls out his Bible from his satchel and begins thumbing through half a dozen pages and begins to read more of his notes.

She sits down and looks through her handbag looking for her train ticket. Shortly later, the conductor comes walking down the corridor as he announces, "All aboard, Chicago bound, finals destination Denver, Colorado."

Several minutes later the young lady says, "Father, it's such a beautiful day."

Father Luca looks up from his Bible and removes his small spectacles, the pair Nolan, his friend back in Trenton, had given him for his appearance to look like a priest. Suddenly, the train jerks several times as it slowly begins to move. "Ah, it appears we are on our way. Yes, it's a wonderful day for a lifetime of adventure," Father Luca says.

"And what could that be, Father?" she says. "Are you going on a long trip?"

"Yes, a very long trip," he replies.

"Oh, same for me, Father. I'm on my way to the midwest part of America, Denver, Colorado. I will be staying with a friend of mine. I think I might be a school teacher. You know, they are short on school teachers there."

"That's amazing. I'm going to the same place, Denver, Colorado," he replies with a smile. "And yes, I imagined they are short on teachers and schools as well."

The young lady begins, "But first, I will make a visit to Chicago, I think about four or five weeks. I have several friends living there, and they want to show me the town before I continue on to Denver. I'm sure they're going to try and convince me to stay there. But I want to go to Denver, I have made up my mind." She stops talking as she seems to be thinking about something as she stares out the window. After a couple minutes, she begins talking again, "That's wonderful, maybe I can come to your parish after I get settled in Denver."

"That would be delightful, but I haven't been assigned one yet. I have a meeting with Bishop Mangini shortly after arrival, and he will assign me to a parish. Oh, by the way, what is your name? When we meet the next time, I wish to address you with your given name."

"That would be lovely, my name is Adela Finnly. I'm looking forward to our next visit." She pauses for a moment. "Father, have you come a long way?"

"Yes, I came from New York."

"You must be tired."

"Yes, I didn't get much rest or sleep on the train."

"Excuse me, I didn't mean to disturb your rest."

Father Luca smiles as he leans his head back and closes his eyes. A couple minutes later, just when he dozes off, he hears a male voice, "Tickets, get out your tickets," the conductor calling out as he's coming through the train checking and punching tickets. Father Luca hands the conductor his ticket. "Father, you will not be changing trains when we get to Chicago. This train continues with no transfers. The train will stop in Chicago for one hour for loading and unloading. There will be a lot of passengers getting off, and many more getting on." He punches Father Luca's ticket and hands it back to him and continues checking everyone's tickets walking down the car.

+ + +

For the next several days as the train travels to Chicago, Father Luca sits comfortably as he reads his Bible and hymn book, focusing on how to be a priest. Occasionally his mind begins to drift forward to his arrival in Denver, as he writes notes to himself trying to imagine what he is going to talk about with Bishop Mangini. He rolls through his mind trying to come up with an answer of what could be the pressing issue for Bishop Mangini to advertise in a newspaper seeking a priest. Maybe there has been problems and his priest or priests had to leave, or worse, got killed. Then his eyes get tired as he lazily watches the beautiful landscape fly by, relaxing his mind, almost falling asleep.

As Father Luca rests, he begins to think about what he has endured. Eating in the busy, crowded dining car, nights sleeping in the shaking sleeper car, and cramped quarters in the restrooms bring back memories of America as time passed slowly. "The train is arriving in Chicago," the conductor announces as he walks through the train.

"Father, just stay where you are," says the conductor as he walks by. The car he's sitting in suddenly comes to life. Passengers all over the car begin gathering up their belongings, making sure they leave nothing behind, appearing in the car coming from all over the place, people he hasn't seen on the train since they started the trip. "Amazing," he says as he watches the commotion. The train rumbles into the terminal, its brakes making loud hissing noises as large clouds of steaming blowing out, then a small jerk and the train has stopped.

Passengers poured out of its doors, and the army of porters pounce upon the train, busy unloading the luggage out of the baggage car, transporting into the terminal with owners moving behind through the congestion. Porters in the train hurry around cleaning, sweeping, taking out used linens and bring cleaned linen for bedding, towels, table cloths, preparing for the new passengers. Then suddenly the gates open as new passengers scurry aboard the train all looking for their seats, opening up and getting things out of their cases, getting out their books, or just walking around getting familiar with the setting. In the rush of madness, as men taking off their coats and women with overtops as they crowd the isles looking for a spot to hang them.

Everyone is joggling around trying to find a hat rack for their hats. The inside porters are busy helping passengers, some are ordering something to drink. After little over an hour, the train has resupplied its food, water, and fuel and all passengers aboard who are heading to Denver, Colorado.

As the train travels cross country, Father Luca watches the beautiful scenery, keeping his leather satchel close to his side with all his prayers, hymns, and verses, which he reviews every once a while.

Then he falls asleep again from the vibrations from the train as it rumbles on.

Finally, after several days, the train pulls into Denver, making its first of two stops. The first stop is located in the middle of the bustling town where most of the passengers depart. Half an hour later, the train continues on to the second stop on the other side of town, in the more rural, undeveloped area of town where it's still part of the Wild West. Father Luca's eyes closed, resting as he seat comfortable in his seat as the conductor makes his way through the car. "Second stop in Denver coming up, be there in ten minutes."

"Father," the conductor says as he stops by his seat, "this is your destination. You can exit out the door to you rear." He continues through the car.

Father Luca gathers all his belongings and prepares to exit the train. The sun's shining, it's a nice morning. The train comes to a rigid stop, blasts of steam shoot out from under the train.

The porters on the train is busy as they start to unload the baggage from the baggage car for the passengers exiting the train. There's another porter on the dock dividing the baggage up on the landing where they will be loaded off into the wagons or carriages picking up the passengers.

A female passenger come's up to the porter. "Can you carry my bags over to my carriage?"

"Yes, ma'am," replies the porter as he picks up her three bags and heads to the edge of the loading dock.

A few minutes later, the same porter come up to Father Luca. "Father I have put all your baggage right over there." He points at the stacked baggage.

Father Luca, wearing a wide brim hat to protect his fare skin from the bright sun, says, "Thank you so much, it was such a pleasure riding the train."

"You are very welcome, and have a wonderful day," replies the porter as he busily move more bags onto the dock from out of the baggage car.

As Father Luca waits, he notices a one-horse carriage pulling up to the passengers loading dock, and an older Italian man in his fifties get out and comes up the steps and approaches him.

"Hello. Are you Father Luca?" the man asks. "Yes, I am."

"My name is Christopher. I work for Bishop Mangini. I'm here to take you to Bishop Mangini's villa."

"Wonderful," replies Father Luca.

Christopher starts loading all the baggage into the carriage and assists Father Luca into the carriage.

CHAPTER 5

Bishop Mangini smiles as he says to Father Luca as they stand in the illuminated foyer completely surrounded by windows at the bishop's villa. A crafted flower garden with many variants in bloom in the front surrounded by tall trees.

"I'm glad your trip was uneventful. I'm so happy and relieved that you could come to Denver. I'm a little disappointed that no other priest responded to my plea. I got a few inquiries, but they all declined."

"There is just one small thing I wanted to say. When I first met you as you got out of the buggy, you seemed so young to be a priest. But since we are short on Italian priests, age has no meaning here in the Wild West. I and the church welcome you with open arms."

Father Luca didn't really know how to respond to the statement coming from the bishop. Did he suspect there is something that is not right? He just hopes the bishop doesn't suspect anything.

He just knots his head and continues to smile and says, "They come young nowadays don't they."

After a few minutes, neither man said anything, as Father Luca walks around looking at the decor of the bishop's villa.

Then Bishop Mangini asks, "You didn't lose any baggage?" as he's pouring boiling water into Father Luca's cup of flower peddles.

"Well, there was a problem."

"Yes," acknowledges Bishop Mangini.

"You see, one of my bags didn't make it here with me."

"That's terrible," replies Bishop Mangini with a tone of sadness.

"It must have been put on another train in Chicago, or maybe even New York. I didn't have to make a transfer, but the baggage handlers must have moved it when passengers were getting off or on the train. The porters are wonderful, but sometimes they are swamped, and the passengers are not understanding and are inpatient at times. For my train

31

trip, the shipping company was careful with my luggage, except for a few scratches and a handle on my large case, which was removed, or pulled off, probably because it's an old bag."

"Oh, how terrible," says the bishop with a concern look as he hands Father Luca tea with saucer to him.

"I was thinking, maybe I may have overloaded it and was a bit heavy." Both men laugh.

"About your lost bag, I hope there weren't any valuables in it."

"Just clothes, nothing I can't replace. I did register a complaint with a lost bag department with the station when I arrived here in Denver. I don't think they will recover the bag. The distance coming from New York is tremendous, thousands of miles. The bag is gone."

Both men continue sipping their tea as they sit down.

"You may never see that bag again."

"Yes, I know, no telling what part America it is in. I hope the new owners of my clothes wear them well."

Bishop Mangini pauses for a moment, looking up toward the ceiling as he reminisces his past.

"I saw the same thing when I came across the big ocean a long time ago. Sometimes thinking about it, it seems like it was a hundred years ago." He chuckles to himself.

"The hardship people experience will not stop them. Some have lost everything with famine, war, corrupt government, and some just want to start a new life with the opportunity to succeed and raise a family and to get a job and raise a family."

"Yes, I truly understand. I'm ready to start work."

"Good, we are in dire need for you to start work in an area we call Little Italy, on the north side of town. This area of Denver is a bit rough, but there's always a way for improvements. We don't have a church yet. It may take some time before we get one. There's not a lot of money around here to pay for services, but there are a few wealthy families around who are willing to help, but they need an assurance of success. There is a large building in the center of our neighborhood that we call the mercantile building, which is our general store that sells mostly things for the farm and the homes. The owner of the building is a big man named Ethan, a real nice guy. He lets the town use the building for our monthly town hall meetings. Now since we have a priest, he will let us use it as a house of prayer. We'll make a visit in a couple days after you get settled in."

Both men sip their teas for a few minutes.

"This tea tastes wonderful," says Father Luca.

"Thank you for the compliment. My driver, Christopher, makes the tea. He uses the rose pedals from my garden. He blends all sorts of colors, which has different pleasant smells and tastes. After drying them out, they are ready to drink."

Both men continue sipping their teas.

"Now, for the good news," Bishop Mangini begins.

"The railroad has been building their railroad not too far from Little Italy. The train company needs a lot of labor workers, and they hire those without experience. The pay is very low, but at least it's a job. The downside of this is there's many accidents and many are fatal. We are experiencing a lot of homeless people with nothing, and many orphan children."

Bishop Mangini watches Father Luca with sort of a curious look as he starts to talk about the many orphan children in town. He is a bit concerned if young Father Luca has that compassion for homeless and orphaned children. Does the father have the experience he's looking for? "Mr. Notary," Bishop Mangini continues, "a wealthy businessman and realtor, has expressed interest in helping the church with the children. There's not a lot of adoptions for the children. He has talked about some ideas that he would like to work on to help the orphans. We will have a meeting with him one of these days and talk about it."

"That sounds wonderful. I'm looking forward to the visit," replies Father Luca.

"I'm going to have you stay here on the compound in the guest house until you get settled, which may be a couple of weeks, or maybe longer, we'll see about it. I will have Christopher show you around and get you settled in. Tomorrow, we will take a ride around town so you can see what's out there."

Bishop Mangini steps out of the room briefly and finds Christopher.

"Christopher will show you around the compound, and if you need anything, I mean anything, please do not hesitate, call Christopher and he'll help you. Now remember, if Christopher can't help you, please contact me. We will have dinner at five o'clock."

+ + +

For the next couple days, Christopher drove Bishop Mangini and Father Luca around in their buggy all over the area, as they talked about their future plans for the neighborhood.

Several days later, a bright sunny morning, Father Luca enters the dining room for breakfast and sits himself at the table.

A couple minutes later, Christopher enters the room caring a coffee pot. "Good morning, Father Luca, hope you slept peacefully."

He pours Father Luca a coffee. "What breakfast appetite do you have for this morning?" he asks."Let me think," Father Luca pauses. "Yes, I will have a poached egg and toast, and a refill on the coffee."

"Coming up," says Christopher as he leaves the room. A few seconds later, he is back out with the coffee pot.

Bishop Mangini enters the room and sits down at the table. "Father Luca, sorry for the delay. Been writing a few thoughts in my journal, and I got caught up on time and look at me, I'm late."

Christopher enters the room carrying the coffee pot and pours the bishop his coffee.

"Bishop Mangini," Father Luca says, "I just sat only a couple minutes ago myself."The bishop nods his head as he takes a long sip from his hot coffee.

"Father Luca," Bishop Mangini begins, "today we will visit the merchant building. Like I said before, this building sells almost everything that is used to farm and needed in a house. Since we don't have any large building, that is where we have meetings to deal with any town problems and church services. We don't have a priest, but Ethan, who owns the building, fills in as our priest. He's not real good, but he tries and that is what counts."

+ + +

Both men finish their breakfast and are on their way in their buggy driven by Christopher. The buggy is equipped with a surrey top to protect the men from the sun as they head downtown.

Father Luca and Bishop Mangini arrive in front of the mercantile, and Christopher ties up the horse and helps both men out of the buggy.

"Father, watch your step," says Christopher. "The first step you need to put your foot on is hard to see. We had it installed because it was too difficult getting in and out of the buggy."

"Thank you, Christopher," replies Father Luca as he gently gets out of the buggy.

As they get out of the buggy, several townspeople walking by noticed Father Luca and begin to get curious because of his age. Within a couple minutes, there are eight or nine townsfolk, mostly women converging around both men as they enter the building. As they enter the building, several women shopping in the store has introduce themselves to the young, handsome priest.

"Hello, nice to meet you," Father Luca kept saying as he met a couple dozen more people within the first half an hour at the mercantile.

"Father Luca, it's nice to meet you," says Ethan as he suddenly appears in front of Father Luca. Ethan, a big burly Irishman with a firm handshake that weakens any man's grip, introduces himself to the father.

"Father Luca, my name is Ethan and I'm the owner of this place. Everyone calls this place the mercantile building, and I have been trying to guide the townspeople in the direction of our Lord.

It's been tough, and just too many questions. Thank God, you are here."

"You are very welcome," replies Father Luca.

"Ethan, you have done a wonderful job. All you have to do, just talk from your heart, and people become friends."

"Thank you, Father."

"Oh, Ethan," Father Luca says, "your store is very interesting. You sell everything here in your store?"

"Yes, Father, everything you see here I sell."

"Very interesting, Ethan," says Father Luca. "I just haven't seen a store with so many bags of grains, potatoes, clothes, tools everywhere, and even candy on the counter."

"Yes, Father, that is licorice candy in that jar." He opens the lid and offers to Father Luca. "Please, it's a gift, I want you to try one, you will like it," says Ethan.

"Well, if you say it's good, I'll try one small one." Father Luca takes it out of the jar. He pauses for a moment as he looks at the long black candy hanging from between his fingers.

"Is this tar?" the father commented, a puzzled look on his face.

"Oh no, it's soft and sweet with a unique taste."

Father Luca bites a small piece off its end. "Yes, you are right, it tastes very good," he says as he begins to chew.

"I must try it again on my next trip," he says as Bishop Mangini stands with a smile as he watches Father Luca eating the licorice, interacting with the new people of the town.

A middle-aged man comes up to Father Luca and says a few words in Italian. Surprisingly, Father Luca replies back in Italian. Briefly, they exchange a brief conversation and the man leaves.

"That was nice," Bishop Mangini said. "You told that man you will be having a service here next week, good. We can start preparing for the service this afternoon. I will let Ethan know. Oh, I believe there are about a dozen Italians who live in the area who don't speak English. Hopefully we can get them to come if we have an Italian-speaking priest. Maybe we can have a short service afterward. We can talk about that later."

"Good to know, Bishop Mangini," replies Father Luca. "I will add in a few Italian words into my sermon. If there is enough nonspeaking English parishioners, I could have a service in Italian."

"I'll have to check that out, I think Ethan would be able to give me that information."

CHAPTER 6

It's Sunday morning, the sky is bright emerald blue, a slight wind blowing as it whips up a dust devil in the middle of the dirt street. The buzz around town is there's a new handsome young priest named Father Mariano Luca, who just arrived in town and will be giving his first church sermon on Sunday at the mercantile building. It's early before service as a crowd of townspeople dressed in their Sunday best mingling around in the building, trying to find themselves a place to sit for the first church service in their town. Many townsfolk are arriving in carriages, a few arrive on horseback, some are walking, others tying up their working wagons at the hitching posts in front of the building.

Stacked everywhere in the building are burlap bags of wheat, barley, beans, potatoes, corn, farming tools big and small leaning against the walls, some are hanging from the ceiling that made movement a bit of a challenge for the guests. Stretched out on wire hangers, a few rabbit furs hang on the wall with a pile of hay bales near the back entrance. The stale air stifled with a musky smell of cow and horse, except a few chickens in the corner of the building pecking at the floor, picking up loose seeds. Ethan has opened up the double doors in the back of the building to get fresh air inside.

"Ethan, where is everyone going to stand, and the seats for the elderly?" a woman asks as Ethan and several of his workers move several bags of potatoes around on the floor. "Good morning," Ethan greets Mrs. Silverwood. "I have decided we will make a few benches in the front two rows, using these bags of potatoes with several wooden planks connecting them together where the elderly will sit. I have plenty of everything. I have piled several bags of corn with a cow hide cover for Bishop Mangini, just to the right of the planks. He will have a perfect spot and be very comfortable. I suppose the rest of the guest find themselves a place to sit where they can."

"Wonderful," Mrs. Silverwood replies, as she continues walking around the large room scrutinizing the placements of where people are going to sit. She is known in town as the nosy woman with the big nose.

"Oh, by the way, Mrs. Silverwood," says Ethan, "I decided to have Father Luca stand on a couple apple crates for his sermon. It's probably best he stays on them. I don't want him falling off. I'll be close by just in case he needs assistance. With so many people I expect to show up, they might not be able to see him from the back of the room if he gets off the crates. I have some things hanging on the wall, and I can't be taking them down every time we have a service."

"That's a good idea, but maybe you need to talk with Father Luca, he might have other plans. Most likely he won't change anything. It is his first service, and I'm sure he will be nervous, just like everyone else," she replies.

"Good point, I'll talk with him as soon as he arrives. It will only take a few minutes to make any changes."

As time moves on, more and more people are arriving for the service as a few are still shopping in the mercantile. Most of the people are families, a few single men and women arrive. Father Luca has been given a small spot behind the service counter, where he is sitting, going over what he is going to talk about. The sermon will not be lengthily. Most of what he's going to talk about are his plans for establishing a church in the city and a little about himself. He plans on visiting and meeting and shaking hands with every person who came to the service.

Ethan walks around in the building trying to organize everything. He goes to the front of the building telling everyone to find themselves a place to sit or stand, that the church service will begin in several minutes.

"Sit where you can find a place," he is telling everyone. A few minutes later, everything got deathly quiet as Father Luca makes his way around several piles of bags of turnips, holding his Bible as he walks toward the apple crates. Ethan, a very big man looming a foot or more over the height of Father Luca, puts out his big hand and assists Father Luca up onto the rickety crates.

"Is it stable?" Father Luca asks. "Yes, Father, I tried it myself."

"You did?" he says with a surprise look. "Then it should be sturdy and ready," he replies with a smile.

Several young women are smiling as they quietly whisper to each other while they watched the handsome priest get up on the apple crates, then immediately someone starts to clap their hands. Then another person joined in clapping, and before anything else could happen, everyone begins clapping their hands for the respect of Father Luca, their first priest in their town. The clapping continued for several minutes as Father Luca turned and smiled at his parishioners, then glanced down at Bishop Mangini sitting comfortably on his big pile of corn bag, who gave his big smile of approval. He says, "Bless you, Father Luca, my son."

"Thank you very much, thank you very much. Bless you all," said Father Luca, as he kept saying over and over again as he looked and tried to make eye contact with every person in the room.

"God bless you all," he kept repeating in between "thank you very much."

After some time, the clapping slowed down then stopped. Father Luca composed himself. "Good morning, what a wonderful day it is."

He begins his story about himself coming all the way out to the middle of America, the Wild West, from New Jersey, and about writing Bishop Mangini, who helped him get there. He realizes that he looks very young to be a priest, but he had the will and the drive to be what he wanted to be, that he believes in himself. As he was talking about the trip to Denver and his desire to be a better priest, he saw many people nodding their heads, showing the pain they had endured when they came as well, all immigrating to America.

"We all made it as God watched over us, regardless of your age or reason for your coming. We suffered and experienced the pain and we made it," he says. Pausing for a moment, he looks at the faces of the parishioners, and sees their pain. "Everyone has endured pain in some way or another, and God is ready to help," he says.

Father Mariano Luca and his well-kept secret of being Antonio Ferretti from Trenton, New Jersey, is slowly eroding from his mind.

Father Luca opens his Bible and reads a few lines he had underlined, then he turns several pages and begins to read some other lines from a service he went to in New Jersey, then reads several other lines, then he closes the Bible.

"My people, my family." He pauses as he looks around the crowded room, at faces that shows the hard life struggling for survival. He says, "Today's service is going to be short. After service, I want to shake hands with every person who are here today and talk to them. It does not matter how long it will take, I'm here for you. I will not be able to say goodbye, as you exit our temporary church, because we don't have the space."

"Please, will everyone bow their heads," says Father Luca as he says a prayer he had underlined in his Bible and follows with "Amen." Then he begins, "I want to thank Ethan very much for allowing so many people to squash into his business this morning. Hopefully he will be in favor of having other Sunday services here for a while."

"Thank you, Father," says Ethan as he says. "Those were nice words, and yes, we will have services here again, hopefully next Sunday. I need to talk with Father Luca to see if it would be possible. In the meantime, I need to organize my merchandise a lot better before the next service. Bless you. Listen up, everyone, I have an important announcement. If there are some strong men here who would like to volunteer for next Sunday, come here two hours before service and give me a hand in arranging a few things so we can have a pleasant church service. I would appreciate it. Thank you."

Father Luca raises his voice for another announcement so to be heard over the noise of everyone talking. "Please, everyone, before leaving, we have something to drink and a lot of wonderful homemade pies on the service corner, all donated by the women's auxiliary. I will see you next Sunday service right here, God bless you all."

Many parishioners crowd quickly around the service counter, sampling the pies and drinking the sprints, talking among themselves, hoping to meet and talk with their new priest.

+ + +

A couple days later Bishop Mangini and Father Luca make a visit to the mercantile building to have a meeting with Ethan about having future church services at his building on a temporary basis.

Bishop Mangini insisted there has to be a signed agreement between both parties and a small financial payment to Ethan's business for the utilization of the building. In the agreement, Ethan agrees to have in place temporary seating for the elderly and merchandise organized in a manner to accommodate the folks coming to the service.

After all three men agreed to the agreement, Ethan says, "Father, I have been thinking about something that's been on my mind for the last couple days with some intense scrutiny, and I love the idea I have in the corner of my building, behind the service counter, a small room that I don't really use. I use it to keep things in it that I really should have out on the floor in the public for customers to buy. I want to give it to you, Father Luca, so you can use it as your office for the church. When the town builds a church, you can give it back to me when you move into the church. I have a couple old tables and a few chairs and a very old filing cabinet you can fit into the room. Please, I won't except anything from you except the Word, thank you." He smiles at Father Luca.

"I really don't know what to say," Father Luca says as he puts out his hand for a shake from Ethan. "Thank you, oh so very much, and may God bless you," Father Luca says as he shakes Ethan's hand and continues shaking for some time.

"I will have one of my workers clean out the room and put in the furniture. Next time you come, it will be ready for operation."

Bishop Mangini follows as he shakes Ethan's hand, thanking him for his immense generosity to the church.

"Thank you very much, Ethan. I realize we don't have a church at present, but with the help of God, we will have a church one of these days. God bless you and your family."

"Oh, Bishop Mangini," says Ethan, "before you and Father Luca leave, I just briefly want to add on something to our brief conversation about the possibility of having in the near future, a church in our town. Please let me know about a day's notice before you return to your new office. I know of a wealthy businessman, a Mr. Notary who has spoken to me several times this last year about investing into our town. Him and his wife are well-liked, and they both have concerns about the growing population of orphan children living in and around town. Many of them lost their fathers to accidents working for the railroad. Their mothers could not take care for them with no money, and some left town leaving the children behind."

"That is a wonderful idea," says Father Luca.

"In a couple days, yes, next Thursday, I think we can make it. We will be working on the service for next Sunday." He looks at Bishop Mangini, who gives a nod for yes.

CHAPTER 7

Bishop Mangini is sitting in an old chair across Father Luca at his desk in his new office in the mercantile buildings. Both men are talking about what they had drafted up for the upcoming service for Father Luca on Sunday.

"Excuse me," followed by a knock on the wall," a man's voice came from their open door of their small office.

"My name is Mr. Notary." A short man, slightly bald, a bit on the chubby size, dressed in an expensive tailored pin stripped suit is standing at their open door.

"Hello, Mr. Notary?" he asks.

"Yes," replies Mr. Notary.

"We were expecting you. My name is Father Luca and this is Bishop Mangini."

"Yes, nice to meet you. I know of Bishop Mangini. We have talked briefly before, it was some time ago."

"Here please sit down," says Father Luca as he slowly navigates a chair around his desk for Mr. Notary.

"Thank you, Father," Mr. Notary says as he looks around at their crowed office.

"Not too much room to move around in here," Father Luca gives a chuckle as he sits.

"It's the best we have right now." Father Luca smiles.

"Do you mind me smoking?" Mr. Notary gestures to the two men. Both Father Luca and Bishop Mangini nods their heads of approval.

For the next several hours, all three men talked business. The first part of the business was Mr. Notary's concern about the orphaned children.

He paused for a moment as he takes a drag from his cigarette.

"When I walk around town, mostly at night, I see these children doing odd jobs for some of the business owners. They're small and ignorant to the likes of people who abuse them. Sweeping and mopping floors, hauling trash, clearing tables, cleaning horse stables, and more, and they are paid hardly nothing. If they complain, they are kicked out or get beaten up. If they were grown adults, they wouldn't do that work for what the children are paid. I've heard, so I can't collaborate this story, they are used in some of the gold mines hauling rock out of the tunnels. These kids hide during the day. I know of a place on the other side of town in the red-light district, where there are very young girls, they are children, as prostitutes working on a bar. These children are having sex with a full-grown men. What is going to happen to them when they grow up, if they grow up? Some of these children have parents, but they have no money. They encourage the child to work. I don't understand what is happening to the human race around here."

"Yes, I have heard of such places. There's no help, everyone gets paid off, there aren't any objections."

"With the help from the church, and I'm not talking about money, I would like the help from the church spiritually in support for the town. I have a large house with many rooms and plenty of space. My wife and I had two children, but they got married and are gone, and we would like to help these homeless orphaned children. My wife would like to work with these children, helping them through life to grow up and be someone. I have made a lot of money in my life, and now we are not getting any younger and want to give back in some way. With the help from the church, we would like to have a small classroom in our home. On a temporary basis, mind you, my wife and I can bring in about four children into our home, feeding them, clothing them, and they sleep in our house. My wife has some school training from where she and her family lived in Philadelphia before I met her."

"That is a wonderful idea you have. I have never met any man more generous than you, Mr. Notary," comments Bishop Mangini.

"And I think it could be accomplished with some hard work and volunteers from the community. It's something we can talk about after service on Sunday. We can organize a committee, who can start things. We will put up a notice on the bulletin board that we made, at the entrance to this building. Interested people can stay for a meeting after the service."

As the men were about to finish their meeting, Mr. Notary says, "There is one more thing I need to talk about. I hope I'm not taking up too much of your time," he asks the men?

"No, no," Bishop Mangini and Father Luca respond almost at the same time.

"The town needs a church, and now we have a priest. I think the time is right to talk about a church."

"That is another wonderful idea you have, Mr. Notary," replies Bishop Mangini.

"But at this time, we have no money for a church. Now this last week, we had our very first service here in the mercantile building, and ahh."

"Bishop Mangini, I want to explain something, I'm not that good with words. The idea is in my head, but the words don't exactly explain my thought. What I meant is that I would like to pay for the church."

Both Bishop Mangini and Father Luca stopped talking as they both sat motionless, stunned for a few moments, as they gave a quick glance at each other.

Father Luca slightly cleared his throat. "Mr. Notary, you just said you wanted to fund a new church here in our town?"

"That's right. I have been thinking about this for a long time, but the timing was not here. I hope I'll explain it right this time. I will fund a simple church, nothing expensive, everything can be done by volunteers. There will be a tarpaulin used for the roof to keep the sun and light rain off the parishioners. Simple wooden walls with doors, floor, and windows. With heavy rain, thunderstorms, or cold weather, we'll continue to have service right here at the mercantile building. After building the simple church, if you may, things can be repaired for a small cost, which will not be a big factor. After it's finished, we can start planning for a bigger stone church. I figured the simple church will start to draw people to our church, and we will get more parishioners, and with that we'll bring in more donations."

"So what you are saying is, you will fund a temporary simple church while we collect money and donations to build a much bigger church built of stone, which will withstand the length of time."

"Yes, Bishop Mangini, you are right."

"It's a lot of money to spend, even if it will be a temporary church," says Bishop Mangini as he sits back into his chair, thinking. "Why would you want to invest all of your money into a temporary building, I mean a church?"

"I just knew you were going to ask me that question," Mr. Notary replies.

"I had to ask you that, it's a lot of money."

"My reason, yes, I was born in this area about fifty miles from here, and my parents struggled to survive raising seven children. I saw a lot of immigrants come to this hardworking land, and the railroad and mining helped a lot of people to survive. There were a few miners who became wealthy and wanted to stay and started to build expensive homes. Yes, I made my fortune in real estate, although I struggled and almost didn't make it. Finally, with some luck, I sold a few properties to those rich families who made their wealth from mining gold, and then to their friends. Also, some of the executives in the railroad bought land around here and started to build. Before I knew it, more and more people were asking me for properties, and it just continued selling and made a lot of money. My parents never got to the day of not working hard, they died early, you might say they worked themselves to death. There was no church, or priest, around here. My two surviving brothers who stayed here helped, and we buried both of our parents, two sisters, our younger brother who died of that horrendous disease that came through here, killing a lot of people. We buried everyone up on the hill on the outskirts of town where everyone was buried in those days. After our simple burial, I swore I would help to get a priest or a church here. I have a parcel of land that's not too far from here, it's large and we can build a small church on it, and then build a bigger one when we get the money, staying on the same property. I would like to donate the land to the church, where we can have the new church built. Now I have the money, and maybe I can help some of the unfortunate people here who have nothing, and give them hope on a Sunday with a prayer. It does not have to be Sunday, anyone can come to the church any day, just a place of where they can come and pray for hope."

"Amen," says Bishop Mangini.

"That's wonderful, you gave us your personal feelings, the way you feel, and your turmoil in living here."

"Bishop Mangini, just one more thing I need to say. If business continues to grow like it has, I will be in the position to contribute a lot more money to build your new stone church!"

"That is wonderful, I don't know how to thank you. I'm completely caught without words, Mr. Notary. But I will say, with your new priest, Father Luca sitting right here, and my support, we will fill all those voids. Our community will be able to talk with God."

"Maybe tomorrow, if you have time, Mr. Notary, we can take a ride out to the property and take a look at it. We can start working on the project after this Sunday's service. There's really no need to put this off for another week or so," says Bishop Mangini as he smiles and nods to Father Luca.

"I'm busy tomorrow afternoon, but I can be here at around 10:00 a.m. for a couples of hours," says Mr. Notary. That would fit into our agenda as well. Meet us here, and I'll take my carriage," replies Bishop Mangini.

CHAPTER 8

Mr. Notary arrives at the mercantile the next morning on horseback. He's tying up his horse to a hitching post as a buggy arrives, driven by Christopher with Bishop Mangini and Father Luca sitting in the back There's a fabric canvass type of cover stretched over the top of the buggy, keeping the men out of the sun.

"Good morning, Bishop Mangini and Father Luca, it's such a wonderful and a memorable day today," Mr. Notary addresses as he tips his hat.

"Yes, it is," replies both men as they smile broadly. Christopher gets down off the buggy and pulls out the step for Mr. Notary to step up on as he gets into the carriage with both men. As Mr. Notary sits down, he says, "Christopher, if you go straight out main street heading south, turning right on Oak, and a short distance down the road, and we will be there."

"Yes, sir," replies Christopher, as he makes a command to his horse. He flips his reins, and his horse and buggy start to move. A while later, they arrive at the lot. All three men get out and causally walks around in the bleak dirt field covered with tumble weeds and sage brush. Both Bishop Mangini and Father LePore wearing wide brim church hats to protect from the intense sun.

"There's not much to look at," says Mr. Notary as he scans the emptiness of the barren land.

"Yes, but I can imagine a church built right here in the middle of this lot," Bishop Mangini says as he focuses and shields his eyes from the sun's glare as he looks around. "Oh, Mr. Notary, in which direction will the front of the church be facing?"

"I was thinking there won't be any problem with the wagons and buggies on the street at its entrance. The front of the church is going to be right over here," Mr. Notary says as he walks to the spot in the direction of a small dirt road. "We will expand the road, and making a drop off point directly in front."

"Yes, I can see that," replies Bishop Mangini.

Mr. Notary says, "The church will look fantastic, especially to someone who hasn't seen one before. Now we have to remember, it is to be only a cost-effective, temporary church."

"You're absolutely right, Mr. Notary," says Father Luca.

"And remember, a house of worship can be any size or quality," Father Luca says, as he continues to look around.

"And looks should not matter," Bishop Mangini continues with an afterthought. "We all know that, but some parishioners may not see it that way."

"I agree," replies Mr. Notary.

"A house of worship can be anywhere and anything," says Father Luca as he bends down and gets a hand full of sand.

"I have a strong feeling that we have found the perfect spot for our first church," he says as he closely watches the sand slowly pour from his hand as it slightly scatters among the weeds in the lot. He stands very still as he's kind of mesmerized as he pours the sand, as Bishop Mangini notices his behavior, not saying a word as he observes.

+ + +

It's Sunday morning service. Father Luca standing on his apple crates finishes service with a prayer he read from his Bible and closes his Bible. Not saying a word, Father Luca looks out at all the faces and sees happiness, joy, and excitement, then says, "I have some wonderful news I want to share with you this morning. I would like to introduce to you a wonderful and thoughtful man. I'm sure you all know who I'm about to introduce, and that is Mr. Notary. Myself, Bishop Mangini, and Mr. Notary had a very important meeting this last week about the development of our community's first church. Please, Mr. Notary, please stand for a moment." The congregation gasp with surprise and delight.

"From the result of an intense constructive meeting, we have an important announcement we would like to tell you. With Mr. Notary's success in his business and his personal life, he wants to give back to our new and developing community. He has graciously donated a parcel of his own land and fund the money to build a simple inexpensive church that we can use temporary for a period of time, I hope, for us to pray in. Now the church is going to be a simple construction with a canvas style roof to keep the parishioners out of the sun and light rain. The walls and floor will be made of simple wood. When it's raining hard and it's cold, we will have our service here in the mercantile building." Father Luca pauses for a moment then he continues, "After thinking about this for some time, I have thought on how I can increase the attendance to the church, which will help our donations. If we get enough attendees, I will talk with Bishop Mangini about having a second service, one hour after our first service. It's a thought we can explore. The donation plate that is passed around each week needs more money to build our church, the simple new one and the stone-made church of the near future. I propose that our church gives out free wine to all attendees, they must come to the service first, and get their drinks at the fun events after the service."

There were several gasps that came from a couple older women parishioners sitting in the front row.

Father Luca pauses for a moment then continues, "Ethan, will set up half a dozen tables to play cards and to meet new friends. If we give a glass of wine to every person"—he pauses and smiles—"maybe not children. I believe people who want to taste the grapes of God who hasn't come to our church will come again. And during this period of time, we and everyone sitting here and any people who want to come to our church start collecting money. Talk with business owners about securing donations to build a much larger and beautiful stone church that will be here for you, your children, and their grandchildren and their grandchildren. There is no time frame for collecting money. The sooner we can get enough money, the sooner we can start construction. After service today, here in this building, we are going to have our first meeting on planning the construction of our temporary church."

Ethan stands up and announces, "Please see me on where we are going to sit, it depends on how many volunteers are going to be here."

51

+ + +

Half an hour later, at the planning meeting for the new church, Ethan talks briefly to the group about there not having a lengthily meeting today because of the lack of information to tell the committee. All he needs is a list of volunteers who want to help at this time. The committee will have a weekly meeting after every Sunday service to get an update on the progress and different projects they can work on. Then he turns the meeting over to Mr. Notary, who talks about his decision of donating the land and funding the inexpensive church.

In the back of the crowded meeting sat about half dozen women and one man who did not like the idea of building a cheap church. This group of people must have heard about the plans of building a church but didn't live in the neighborhood. None of the volunteers in the meeting knew who they were, or where they are from. This protesting group were dead set against using any donations to build an embarrassing, cheap-looking church, and in their minds, they will not have anything to do with any such insane idea.

One woman of the group said, "I will not be part of this stupid group, and I with my money will join the Rocco family, who are going to build their own permanent church on the other side of town." She and the man sitting beside her, with the other women of their group, got up and stormed out of the meeting.

After a while, Mr. Notary became a bit frustrated with some of the other volunteers and their strange questions, but handled their complaints professionally with the constant interruptions, and the meeting closed early.

+ + +

During the next week, Father Luca and Mr. Notary had several meetings with a business acquaintance of Mr. Notary, who's name was Timothy Duncan, a building architect.

As Father Luca and Mr. Notary were reviewing some papers they were going to give Mr. Duncan in Father Luca's office, Mr. Notary says, "Father, you need to have help, like an aid, someone who can help with all these meeting, deadlines, filing papers, and all miscellaneous things that deals with the church. You know like finding and filing papers we have right here in front of us, and running errands, and with the church's weekly services. And in the near future, many more activities I can't think of at this time."

"You are right," Father Luca says. "I really need a full-time clerk since we are having church services and planning a new church. And I can't neglect my parishioners seeking the guidance of God. Yes, I need to think about your suggestion, I'm surprised I didn't think about it before."

+ + +

After a couple days reviewing the papers and sketches from Father Luca and Mr. Notary of what they think might look good, Mr. Duncan completes his rendition of the church and plans to show the drawings to both men at Father Luca's office this week. The next day standing at the open door of Father Luca's office, Father Luca and Mr. Notary are talking.

"Hello," Mr. Duncan says as he walks into the cramped office.

"Hello, hello," replies Mr. Notary.

"Come in," says Father Luca as both men stand up.

"Men, I think I got what you want," Mr. Duncan says as all three men begin clearing everything off the small desk in the room. Mr. Duncan, with a long roll of papers tucked under his arm, begins spreading them out on the table as both men hold down the corners as they begin looking at the plans.

Mr. Duncan begins, "Now the top paper is the general overview of the church. It's looking down at the church from the top, with windows in the walls, and again floors identified with arrows and measurements. Page 2 has plans of the entryway doors into the church, and the third copy is up at the altar, where Father Luca has a small room behind the altar and a back door. I have shown in details of how we will hang the canvas in the ceiling. The type of fixtures and the wooden overlaps to cover them up."

"Amazing, it looks beautiful, and you said this is going to be a simple built church," Father Luca says as he stares at the prints with bright eyes.

"I really don't know what to say, Mr. Duncan, you created an unbelievable church on paper. I can hardly wait until we start construction."

"We can start this in a couple of weeks," Mr. Duncan says as he looks over at Mr. Notary, who gives a nod with his head.

"Next week is fine," says Mr. Notary. "The money is in the bank."

Father Luca says, "We need to have a meeting soon with Bishop Mangini to show him your prints. I'm sure he will love them. I'm so excited, I just can't wait until Sunday service to tell the congregation."

✦ ✦ ✦

The next day, Father Luca is standing at the large dining table with Bishop Mangini at his villa looking at the future church's prints. Mr. Duncan, with the help from Father Luca and Mr. Notary, helps spreads out the print of the new church on Bishop Mangini's large dining table.

"This is the rendition of our inexpensive church drafted by architect Mr. Duncan this last week," says Father Luca.

"The church looks wonderful, maybe not like some of the grand churches I have seen in my travels. But under the conditions we have here, in this section of Denver, it is spectacular in all ways," praises Bishop Mangini as he adjusts his spectacles after taking several up close looks at the print. "You definitely have my approval. I'm a little curious, I'm not good in reading building prints. Where is the podium going to be? You're drawing seems to have it here." where's his finger is at. "Yes, Bishop Mangini, we got it here in this spot." Mr. Notary points in a new direction. We decided to have it off center to the width of the front of the church. The sitting will not be a full front row because of where the organ is going to be located."

"Oh, I see," says Bishop Mangini.

CHAPTER 9

The next Sunday at the mercantile, sun shining brightly, a slight breeze kicks up some annoying dust creating a small dirt devil dancing in the dirt street. Inside the building, Father Luca is standing on his rickety apple crates in front of his congregation, finishing up the morning service, Ethan standing close by to catch him in case he loses his balance and falls. For the last several days, there has been a buzz being spread around town that Father Luca will be giving a very special announcement about the new church at the end of this service. The large crowded room is packed with no standing room left in the building, the overflow crowd onto the wooden sidewalk in front of the building. Everyone wants to hear what Father Luca has to say about the possibility of a new church in town. Something a bit peculiar also happening today, as people who have never been to a Sunday service are showing up, showing interest in the news about a new church being built in the town with a newly arrived Italian preacher.

Father Luca finishes up the Sunday service as he says, "Amen." Standing there on his apple crate looking around at all the faces of the parishioners, most of them he recognizes, he notices a few new faces.

"Ladies and gentlemen, I have great news for you today," Father Luca begins. "I would like to welcome the many new faces to our temporary church today. It gives me the most pleasurable moment in a very long time. I would like to introduce two very important men who came into my life these last several months. These two men asked for nothing, and they gave plenty. They have volunteered many hours of their own time and has donated an enormous amount of money for our future church for this town. Now it gives me great pleasure to introduce them. I believe almost everyone in town knows both of them, Mr. Notary and Mr. Duncan, please both stand up." Everyone in the building applauds for a long time.

"I would like Mr. Notary to come up her and talk a little about his vision of the new church." Mr. Notary comes to the front of the room, and as being a short man, Ethan helps him up on the apple crates and stands close by just in case he needs assistance as he speaks.

"Ladies and gentlemen, it gives me great honor to give to the town. I think almost everyone in this room knows me, my parents and now my family have been in this part of the town long before most of you or your families came here. And I have seen it grow, I worked most of my live in the real estate business, and I have done well. Now we, the townspeople, need a church to pray in." Mr. Notary looks over at Father Luca and smiles. "Now we have a priest for our new church, Father Luca." Everyone claps their hands. "And it would not have happened if Mr. Duncan, our architect, donated a lot of time and drew the plans for the church, free of charge.

And his holiness Bishop Mangini for his support and wisdom." Everyone claps and continues to clap for several minutes.

"Now we will need everyone to come out and work on the church when construction begins. After everything has been approved and bought, we will start construction. We will notify everyone at the Sunday service one week before the work begins." He looks over at Father Luca, who gives a nod of approval.

"On that day, everyone, come to church in your working clothes. The women will bring pot luck and set up long tables for a wonderful lunch. All the men, bring your working tools. After service today, we will have a meeting right here in the mercantile and talk about everything that needs to be done and start a list of volunteers. I will have a copy of the proposed print of the church after service today, if you want to get an idea what it will look like.

"Thank you," he says as Ethan helps him down from the apple crates. The room fills up with volunteers and people with interests. In the corner of the room, the same group of people who protested about the building of a cheap church that they did not like are gathered.

One of the protesting women talking with another was saying, "Building a church without a wooden roof, cheap, cheap. Every Sunday, you see the money plates being passed around in the church with plenty of money in them, and they say they can't afford a roof, where is all that money going."

+ + +

Several days later, in a popular salon on the seedy side of town, a young girl around the age of ten, wearing a dirty shirt and pants, hair tied up in a dirty scarf, enters the smelly, noisy salon with nauseous smell of cigar smoke.

The man behind the bar counter yells at the girl, "Your late, the floors are filthy, get to work."

About a dozen men standing at the bar drinking, a couple of them showing signs of wealth, are dressed in suits wearing bowler hats, the rest are in old working clothes. They are drinking and smoking cigars and cigarettes, spitting chewing tobacco into spittoons located on the floor beside the bar.

The young girl goes into the backroom and returns with a large broom and a dustpan and begins to sweep up the garbage scattered all over the floor, with many cigar and cigarette butts ground into the floor, scattered everywhere. She then goes to the back room again and fills from the water tap a large wood pale of water with a block of lye soap in it. Leaving the pale in the back so the lye dissolves, she takes out three clean spittoons that she had cleaned earlier and starts picking up the filthy ones. As she works, she has to move around the men who won't move out of her way. As she's bending over, or crawling on her hands and knees to place one of the clean spittoons on the floor, one of the well-dressed men not looking spits his chaw at where he thinks the spittoon should be. Most of the spitters don't look, they just spit, and about half of their spit hits its target, the rest hits the floor or the base of the bar. As she was placing the spittoon in its place, his chaw hits her in the middle of her back as she lets out a gasp.

When he realized what he had done, he yells at her so he won't be embarrassed, "What the hell are you doing, girl, stay out of my way!"

Not saying a word for the fear of losing her job, the young girl keeping her head down goes back into the back room and removes her shirt. Using the bar of lye soap and water, she quickly washes out the revolting slimy chaw from her shirt, wringing it as best as she can, putting it back on. Not taking too much time, she picks up her bucket of water and a large scrub brush and goes back out into the room and start scrubbing the floor. She crawls around the feet of the drinkers as she scrubs the smelly thick slime of spit and chewing tobacco chewed into a chaw covering the floor, the worst part is where the spittoons are located close to the customers' feet.

That day, Father Luca wearing his wide brim hat to protect from the sun, is taking a longer-than-usual walk around the neighborhood meeting and greeting people. He's telling them about the church services at the mercantile and the preparation of building their future church, and he mentions the donations would be a blessing. As he's enjoying the nice walk, he breathes in the crisp fresh air, the sun shining brightly.

As he's walking, he's thinking how lucky he is. The decision he made back in Trenton, New Jersey, to become a priest and move to Denver, Colorado. He now has many friends, and he doesn't have to sell property in California to make a living. He makes good money now. Oh how blessed he is on that decision.

Today he's walking over in the seedy part of town, where there's many taverns and salons. As he strolls nonchalantly thinking about his new church, he passes the entrance to a salon. Out of the corner of his eye, he see's something disgusting in the salon, he stops to take a closer look.

There on the salon's filthy wood-planked floor, he thought he sees a young boy scrubbing the floor, but after looking closer, he realizes that the person scrubbing the floor is a young girl, a very young girl. Observing closer, he sees the young girl wearing an old filthy shirt and pants with old worn-out shoes, her face and hands filthy. Her dirty hair tied into a head scarf, as some loose strings hang into her face and into the bucket as well. Sitting beside the girl is a large wooden bucket of water, as she keeps dipping her bush to remove the crud from the floor. Standing close to the salon's entrance, he watches her scrub, and stop every so often to pick chunks of crud out of the scrub brush with her bare, hands trying not to get wooden splinters from the rough plank floor. After watching for a few minutes, he whispers to himself in disgust, "I never saw this when I drank my beers in Trenton. Absolutely appalling, she should be in school. I wonder does she have a family or is she an orphan."

As Father Luca starts to walk away slowly shaking his head, not wanting to create a disturbance with the owner of the salon, a man walks by heading into the salon, and Father Luca recognizes him. "Good morning, Tom," he says as the man stops. I noticed you were not at the service last Sunday."

"I'm sorry, Father, my wife is ill with a fever, and my neighbor was helping me with my horse. You see, Mr. Burns, the veterinarian, gave me some tonic that I had to get into my horse's throat, and she wouldn't cooperate. My poor horse, she fought me for hours, I think she gave up from exhaustion. It wasn't a pretty sight."

"I hope your mare gets better. Give your wife, Mary, my regards, and I hope she'll feel better soon."

"Yes, I will. Doc Murphy was out to our house and gave her some medicine, and she's feeling much better."

"I will be seeing you and your family at next week's service? I have a wonderful sermon planned, and I'm sure your family will enjoy."

"I will, Father, I will be there," the man says as he goes into the salon.

Father Luca finishes his walk, disappointed in what he had seen, heads to the mercantile building and his office, and sits down at his desk.

Talking to himself, he says, "Definitely, I need some help. I'll put up a notice on the bulletin board, here at the front of the mercantile."

He gets out his pencil and paper and begins to write.

1. Need a female office worker who can write and work odd office jobs
2. Need a male wrangler who can lift heavy items and drive a buggy

See Father Luca inside the mercantile

Father Luca, using a tact, secures the small piece of paper to the withered bulletin board at the entrance to the building. As he straightens up, two women pass by on their way into the mercantile building to buy a few things. Very politely, Father Luca greets the ladies, "Good morning, ladies," as they pass, and they reciprocate with "good morning" as they continue into the building.

Pausing for a moment, he looks back at the board at some of the notes posted. The board displayed all types of notices from people in or out of the area, all with a need. Some notices have been on the board for a long time, barely legible as they are faded with sun and time.

As he looked at the notices, he begins to reminiscence back not that long ago when Bishop Mangini was in need for a priest and ran an ad in a New Jersey newspaper. With the help from God, a copy found its way into the small salon where he and his buddy Nolan drank beers.

"I am very, very lucky," Father Luca says to himself as he walks away from the bulletin board.

"God bless that day," he says louder, feeling in good spirits.

CHAPTER 10

It's late Friday night, there's two old houses on a side road in the old rundown section of town. One of them houses a salon named Macaron; the other house attached is a house of ill repute. The outside of the attached house looks uninhabited, windows shuttered, doors locked.

The only way to enter was through the connecting front door to the salon. There's a back door that exits into the alley, for customers only leaving the property.

Inside the salon, several oil lights are mounted to the walls, adjusted low, keeping visibility limited. Several young single women sitting at tables talking with possible male customers, the women encourage the men to drink beer, or whiskey, as they talk business. Sitting at the front of the salon at the end of the bar, seated on a stool a young girl about twelve years old sitting with an older man drinking his mug of beer, as she's propositioning him for the night.

The bartender, carrying a round metal tray, makes his way around the tables getting drink orders from the men. He returns back to the bar with several used beer mugs and bottles, asking the older man at the counter with the young girl as he passes by,

"Sir, do you need another drink?"

The older man glances up at the bartender and says, "Yes, I'll have another, keep it a draft," the guy replies. Bar tender pulls the beer handle on the tap, fills a mug, and takes it to the customer.

"Put it on your tab?" bartender asks. "Sure."

At the opposite end of the bar counter, there's two richly dressed men with their nice fitted suits on and their bowler hats, standing and talking loudly as they watch the women of the evening pass by. Their appearance seems to resemble that of a couple male rosters strutting in front of the female hens in the chicken yard. The two men, drinking wishy shooters from shot glasses and smoking big cigars. Every so often, they spit their chewing tobacco chaw at the spittoons located on the floor near where they are standing. They are beginning to feel tipsy and obnoxious.

One of the men spots a lady of the evening entering the salon, walking past them as she's heading to a table. "Good evening, madam," the man says as he tips his bowler.

"Good evening to you as well," she says as she smiles at him and continues walking. The other man nudges him in the ribs and says, "Now that would be a nice catch for the evening."

"Yeah, you're right." He watches her walk to her table. They both turn back around to the bar and continue to talking business and drinking and smoking.

Then one of the men tells the other, "Tom, when are you going to move those fifteen horses? It's been two weeks now."

"Yeah, I know, Andy, we haven't built the corral yet."

"Damn, you promised me the yard was going to be done by now."

"Yeah, Andy, I know, but the shipment of wood hasn't come into town yet, and I have another issue about the right of way to get the horses coming from the North into the corrals."

"Well, let me know as soon as the shipment comes in. I've got another shipment of horses coming in several weeks, and I need the extra space. You know, Tom, I have to charge you extra for housing and feeding them horses because they are yours."

"Yes, I know it's costing me money. I'll try another source, maybe they have what I need."

Sitting at the bar, the young girl tells the older man dressed in working clothes in his fifties, "You will love me tonight. I'm cheap and young with a lot of experience. You can save money," she softly whispers into the older man's ear. Slowly she starts rubbing the man's arm lying on the counter. The old guy is looking at his beer thinking, as he takes another swig from his mug of beer. He's beginning to appear hot as he pulls out a big handkerchief out of his pocket and wipe his face and neck, then stuffs it back into his pocket as he takes another swig of beer. Using the other hand, he pushes it deep into his front pocket of his old work pants and pulls out a wad of dollar bills. Slowly taking a long look at his wad of money, concentrating, then he pushes it back into his pants and nods his head yes. "Yeah, honey, let's go," the old guy nervously says. "

You're going to make it worth my money, ain't you?" "Yes, honey," she replies.

Another customer walks into the salon, making his way up to the big oak bar. "Draft beer," he says in a deep voice to the bartender.

"Gotcha," replies the bartender, pulling the beer tap and filling a mug. "That will be two bits," he says as he sits it down in front of the man.

Customer drops a few coins on the counter as the bartender scoops them up and rings the sale on the cash register. The customer takes a long drink from the mug and turns around, leaning his back against the bar as he glances out across the room looking at the girls sitting at their tables. He turns his head back to the bartender. "It's a little slow tonight."

Bartender replies, "It's not too bad, will pick up later."

The young prostitute sitting with the older man begins to get impatient as she clears her throat as she looks at the bartender to get his attention.

"Hello, hello," she says.

The bartender at the other end of the long counter slowly cleaning glasses responds with a nod of his head, reaches under the counter, and gets a room key, laying it in front of the girl and says, "Number 2."

The old man finishes his drink, then pulls out his wad of bills again, holding them in his hand as the young girl pulls several bills from the wad and hands them to the bartender to pay the bar tab and a tip for the bartender.

She swoops up the key, hooks her arm under the old man's arm, and gets off her stool. As the old man's feet lands on the floor, he takes a moment to establish himself, probably he is feeling the alcohol from his drinks, as they both slowly exit out the side door that enters into the prostitution house. The bartender walks over to the register and rings up a sale.

A younger man and a woman enter into the salon through the front door, and the young man motions with his hand to the bartender for service and sits at a table in the dark corner of the salon. The bartender heads over to them and asks, "What will it be tonight?"

✦ ✦ ✦

The next day, back to the other side of town, Father Luca is doing paperwork in his office at the mercantile building, piles of papers scattered all over his desk. An unexpected couple of knocks came from the door, slowly the door opens, and Bishop Mangini walks in. "Good morning, Father Luca," he says as he smiles. "I hope I'm not disturbing you."

Father Luca, caught completely off guard, trying to say something, jumps up from his desk, knocking some papers to the floor.

"Absolutely not, good morning, Bishop Mangini, a very unexpected visit." He begins picking up his papers trying to clean off a chair for Bishop Mangini to sit on.

"Everything is fine, don't fuss with that. I'm perfectly conformable," says Bishop Mangini. "I was in the neighborhood and thought I would catch you here in your office. First of all, I just wanted to congratulate you on your tremendous accomplishment with the new church. I would never have dreamed in my wildest dreams that we would be having our own new church in just a short time from now."

"Thank you very much," replies Father Luca, looking slightly embarrassed from the praised comment.

"There is something important that I need to talk with you about," says Bishop Mangini.

"Oh, I hope it's not bad news," says Father Luca as he suddenly gets a hard knot in his stomach, thinking his cover was blown, as he tries to continue to smile. This is the first time that Bishop Mangini had addressed a question in a tone of urgency to Father Luca.

"No, no. I received a very pleasant letter from his Holiness Pope Leo XIII in the Vatican. I brought the letter to show you the seal of the Pope. Here, take a look, you've probably have never seen the Pope's seal before." He hands the letter to Father Luca.

"Beautiful," says Luca, who didn't want to hold the letter very long because he didn't feel worthiness to touch it as he didn't know what to say. He quickly hands it back to the bishop, after a brief look at the seal, and didn't read the letter.

Bishop Mangini notices his nervousness, to hold the letter, or to read it but didn't say anything.

In the letter, His Holiness explains to Bishop Mangini that Mother Cabrini wanted to go to China and teach, but his Holiness thinks she would be more beneficial to the church by working there in Denver, Colorado. Bishop Mangini says, "I believe his Holiness is excited about Mother Cabrini coming to Denver. She is extremely interested in our crises with so many homeless and orphan children. We are in dire need, and her energy would be more than welcome. But it all depends on the transportation of getting her here. With the ocean travel from Italy and the long rough journey across the United States." Bishop Mangini pauses for a moment as he seemed to be thinking about something else to say, then he continues.

"I'm not sure if his Holiness knows that we now have a new young priest here and that's you, Father Luca."

Father Luca is trying to smile as he still has that knot in his stomach as he's trying to figure out if the Pope has a master list of Italian priests in the world. Then a flashback pops into his mind. *The real Father Luca still has his church in Trenton New Jersey, how could he be in Denver, Colorado, and New Jersey at the same time?* Suddenly, Bishop Mangini's voice comes clear in Father Luca's ear again. "Well, Father Luca, sometime in the near future, I think we will be having a Mother Cabrini here in Denver."

"That would be wonderful," says Father Luca, with a sigh of relief that Bishop Mangini didn't mention anything about him or his background in the church. Feeling much better now, Father Luca says, "Yes, I know, Bishop Mangini. The travel across the United States can be extremely difficult, as you know, when you came across way back in the middle '80s.

"Yes, praise the Lord, it was tough, back then sometime I thought it was impossible. But it's getting a little easier now that the railroad is coming out west. It sure beats riding in a wagon for weeks at a time. And with the increase in population, our needs will also be needed with more in demand."Father Luca, I need you to write a compelling letter to Mother Cabrini with the sincerity of your parish, and you whom she will work with. Here is her address." Bishop Mangini hands him the address.

✦ ✦ ✦

That evening, Father Luca starts to draft up a letter to Mother Cabrini, which Bishop Mangini had ask him to write. He sits under the illuminating light from the kerosene lantern sitting on his table. He has the paper lying on the desk in front of him, and his pen and ink ready, but his thoughts are not in writing the letter. He feels an uneasiness and nervousness about writing the letter. He wishes to distance himself from her contact, as she may figure out by his inexperience and knowledge of being a priest if she asks questions. He will have to avoid Mother Cabrini once she has arrived here. Then he starts drinking a glass of wine to ease his nerves, as he begins to feel better putting the letter together in his mind. After some time and an empty glass, he has built up his nerve and yells out, "Yes, I'm ready." He begins to write.

Dear Mother Cabrini,

My name is Father Mariano Luca, I recently arrived here in North Denver, Colorado, United States of America. Bishop Mangini and I were delighted to have read a letter from His Holiness Pope Leo XIII, that you will be coming here. With the expansion of the railroad coming out west, there is an increase of accidents and deaths of its workers, working in hazardous conditions tunneling through miles of massive rocky mountains, resulting in many orphan children. We are in a desperate need for expert assistance with orphan children. Many railroad workers came to this town with their families, and due to many job accidents, the man of the family gets killed. With this problem, the families cannot take care of themselves, and we get orphans, or children that left their homes, and deserted children. We don't have a house of worship. We're using a mercantile building for services. Bishop Mangini and I have put together a building plan with an investor to build a simple church, which should be completed in about six months. We're moving in a direction of progress with the help of God. We are looking forward to your arrival. I pray that your trip will be a pleasant trip.

Truly,
Father Mariano Luca

CHAPTER 11

Father Luca steps out of his carriage as Christopher stands beside him to assist. It's a bit cumbersome for Father Luca getting used to wearing the robe priests wear as he exists the carriage.

"Thank you, Christopher," Father Luca says as he steps up onto the wooden side walk in front of the mercantile building. He starts to walk toward the building's front door, when a young woman stands up from a wooden chair she was sitting in front of the building. It appears she has been waiting for the father.

Christopher gets back into his carriage and drives away.

"Father Luca," she says

"Yes, my young lady," he says as he nods his head in respect, which he has learned to do. He pauses for a moment, taking a longer look at her, and says, "You look familiar, have we met?"

"Yes, Father, we sat together on the train coming from New York, and I got off in Chicago. You told me where you were going, and my job as a school teacher didn't pan out, so I thought maybe the Wild West was ready for me. So, here I am. Yesterday, I noticed a wanted ad posted for a secretary, and I hope the position is still open."

"Yes, the positioned is still open. Now you said your name was…" He was trying to remember her name."I'm sorry, Father, my name is Adela Finnly. I might want to remind you that you had written my name into your journal at that time."

"Yes, yes, I remember now. How wonderful, Adela, I'm on my way to my office here in the mercantile building. Would you join me, and we can fill out a few papers."

As they both walk a short distance to the front door, Father Luca opens the door and lets Adela enters first. They can hear Ethan and his employees working in another part of the building.

"Adela, as you have noticed, I don't have a church here in town."

"Yes, Father, I have noticed. I've been in town a couple days now, walking around, getting a look at it. I was by here yesterday, and it seemed I had missed you. So I figured I would meet you the first thing today."

"That was a wonderful idea," Father Luca says as he's thinking to himself. She seems to really want the job, and she's really cute.

They come to the door to his office, which looks like a back of the building storeroom door.

Father Luca opens the door as Adela enters. "My, this is a small room," she says.

I will be making some changes to the furnishings and get you a desk and chair."

Pausing for a moment, Father Luca, feeling a little uneasy by being in a position of hiring a person, which he has never done for employment, says, "I was wondering can you start to work today? It's not much of a notice, but I'm getting behind on a lot of paperwork. I'm working with several businessmen in town, and we are in the process of working together on some of the paperwork to build a church right here in town."

"That's a wonderful idea," Adela replies.

"Yes, I can start to work right this minute if you like."

Suddenly a knock at the door, Father Luca looked a little surprised. "Wonder who can that be?"

Adela gets up, takes a couple steps, and opens the door.

"Can I help you, sir?"

"Sure, ma'am," says an older man with partly graying hair, looking physically in shape. "Ma'am, I'm answering your ad for an odds and end man and who can manage horses and drive a carriage."

"One moment please, someone will be with you in a minute." She slightly closes the door.

"Father Luca, there is a man here looking for a job you had posted, for an odds and end worker and can manage horses."

"Thank you, Adela. Yes, I posted an ad for an all-purpose male worker." Father Luca paused for a moment, then says, "Do you think he would be a good worker?"

"Oh, he looks like he has good manners, looks like he can be a hard worker, and something about him I like. Sure I would hire him."

"Fine, then this is your first assignment of your new job. You hire him and have him fill out the same paperwork that I will have you fill out when you finish with him. After everything is complete, I will take you and him out to the stable and show where our horse and carriage are kept, and we have a somewhat place of a storage place for other things for the church."

Adela, goes back to the door and opens it. "Sir, what is your name?"

"Yes, my name is Thomas Kerry."

"Fine, Thomas, you have been hired. I need you to fill out a couple papers."

Thomas opens the door farther, with a surprised look, he says, "Ma'am, where do you want me to stand?"

"Oh, I'm sorry, Thomas. This is Father Luca, whom you will be working for."

"Oh, excuse me, Father Luca, I didn't mean to interrupt into your office."

"No, no, Thomas. I heard you tell your name to my secretary. She told me you can be a good worker for us."

"Yes, sir, I mean Father Luca. I'm a good, reliable worker, and I can do hard work and work with horses."

"That's good. Adela can help you with the papers. When can you go to work?" "Is tomorrow too soon?" replies Thomas.

"Tomorrow would be perfect. Be here around 8:30 a.m.," Father Luca says as he's thumbing through several papers on top of his desk.

"Thomas, come with me and I will find a place where you can fill out the papers." Adela goes out of the little room and finds a counter in the mercantile building.

Just as they are several feet away sitting at the counter in the building, Father Luca comes walking by sort of in a hurry. "I've got to talk with Ethan for a couple of minutes. He's the owner of this building."

Father Luca walking around in the building listening for voices, and he hears Ethan talking and heads in that direction.

"Ethan, how are you this morning?"

"I'm doing wonderful, it's such a beautiful day, Father."

"Ethan, while I was thinking about it, this morning, I had hired two new employees. One is a pretty girl named Adela Finnly, and the other a nice man in his fifties named Thomas Kerry. He will do odd and end work, and he works well with horses. When we are all together one of these days when it's not busy, I'll personally introduce them to you. I just wanted you to be aware of their presence in the building if I'm not around. I hope they will be around for a long time."

"Father, that is a wonderful thing. That will eliminate a lot of extra work you have been doing. Even if you're are young, stress can build up in your system and explode sometime. And I have to talk with you about some changes to our furniture in the office. I will talk with you later. I've got to go, Father."

+ + +

Several days later, Doctor Murphy, an older man with gray hair, the only area doctor, is holding a medical bag standing in front of the undertakers' small building, talking with Andrew (Andy) Hawkins, the local undertaker.

"Andy, we are going to need several more coffins by this weekend. There was a bad avalanche at the gorge, three poor souls died."

"Yeah, Doc, I heard about it. It's sad. The railroads need to protect those workers a lot better. Those rocks fall so easy. Every time they blast, the ground shakes and the rocks start to fall. Someone almost always gets hurt. When they blast those tunnels, it's so unpredictable. Sometimes tunnels collapse and many lives are lost, sometime they won't find the dead, so sad."

"Yeah, Andy, one of the workers that got killed today was a big Scotsman, standing at six feet, eight inches. He was a big man. I had to get a new operating table because the other one was too short. He was barely alive when they brought him in, but I couldn't save him, injuries were so severe. He had a wife and two young children. They were living over on the west side. I think he was one of the shift bosses. I was told he was a popular man on the job."

Father Luca, the new priest, hasn't experienced the funeral train yet. Not sure what the family is going to do.

"Doc, you said the man was six feet, eight inches tall?" Andy asked as he's making a few notes in his working pocket notebook.

"Yeah, he is a tall man," replies Doc.

"Doc, I'm gonna have to get into town today. I think I've run out of long boards. After having long boards for a while, it's a waste of money because there was no call for them, so I've been cutting them in half. But today, I need the long boards. So now I have to go and buy long boards again."

Doc stands briefly, looking into the distance not saying anything, then says, "Three men with broken bones, and two with severe headaches going to need bed rest, and three to bury."

"Hey, Doc, this next week, we may have to add another car to the cemetery train."

"Yeah," replies Doc. "It's starting to look that way. I need to talk with the railroad and find out what time frame we are looking at. I guess it depends how many mourners will be coming. I'll stop by and talk with Father Luca and see what he thinks. As being new to the town, it's probably going to be a big surprise to him. The big guy had a lot of friends and workers who liked him.

I heard the railroad will be hiring this next week. Maybe they might not hire here. I have a hunch they will bring them from another work site that's not busy."

"Andy, you know about Father Luca? He has hired some additional help."

"I heard something like that, but I'm not up-to-date."

"Doc," Andy says in an excited voice, "Father Luca hired a young cute woman named Adela Finnly, new in town, for secretary and work at the church, and a real nice guy named Thomas, didn't get his last name, good with heavy lifting and taking care of the church's horses. He really deserves the extra workers, especially as he's trying to get a church into town, going to be doing all these funerals and church services without a church and an adequate office. That place Ethan gave him was an old small tool room."

"Andy, you know if Father Luca has performed any wedding since he's been here?"

"You know, Doc, I really don't know."

Andy says, "I've got to make notes in my book or I will completely forget," as he's busy writing as he flips another page.

"Just found another note, I've got to get with Enrique and Louis to have at least three, maybe four, graves dug right away. You know it's been real hot up on the mesa lately, and may take some extra time, especially working at night, and that God-forsaken land they have to dig in. Sometime it's like trying to dig in stone. And that is if the weather is cooperating."

"Yeah I know, Andy, it's a shame. Yeah, know two of those poor souls were members of the new congregation that Father Luca is putting together with the new church."

"Yeah, I saw the list, so sad. Andy, I've got to get over to Marc Gegger's house, his wife, Winnie, is going to give birth in a week or so. Let me know if you run into any problems in making the coffins."

"I will do, Doc."

CHAPTER 12

Father Luca is sitting at his desk, helping Adela with some papers, when Thomas walks in. "Excuse me, Father, there is something with a possibility of urgency that happened, and I need to talk with you about it now."

"What is the problem, Thomas?" Father Luca replies with a surprised look and hint of fear that Thomas has found out about his past. Lately, every time someone addresses Father Luca with something of an urgency, he quickly feels the fear that his past has caught up with him. Heat and perspiration forms quickly on his forehead.

"Father, have you heard about the deadly avalanche at the railroad work site yesterday?" Thomas asks. "I don't believe I have," replies Father Luca.

"Three of the workers were killed, one of the killed was a big very likable supervisor. Since you are new here in town, I feel I need to explain to you how we bury the dead here."

"Oh god," Father Luca says with an urgency of surprise as he gets a nervous flashback.

"I haven't done a burial before," he quickly thinks. "I don't remember if I have any information to conduct one."

Thomas continues as Father Luca blankly looks on at him for a couple seconds. "Sometime ago, when the railroad started to put down their tracks through this part of the country, this part of town was small, but they worked out an arrangement to conduct funerals for the railroad and the town at our cemetery called Mt. Olivet. Their agreement was the railroad would furnish the transportation as a courtesy. I believe the railroad depended a lot on the town for a place to get food for their workers, water, and a place close enough where their workers can go to relax on their time off, have drinks, and meet women. Some of the important workers even brought their families here, and they started a school and wanted a church, but that hasn't happened until Father Luca has arrived. I don't know the reason why the cemetery is located where it is, way up on the dry mesa. But it's there and that's where the dead is buried, at Mt. Olivet. The railroad built a track into downtown, and the other end of the track ends at the cemetery up on the mesa.

"That seems very nice of the railroad," Father Luca replies.

"Yeah, now I will fill in the unusual details. The railroad needs a two-day request notice for the train to take the mourners with their coffins to and from the gravesite, but under certain circumstance that can be waivered.

There's three cars and a caboose attached to the train. The cars don't have sides, only a roof, because the train uses the cars to haul large objects. Now with no sides on the cars makes it easier to load on and off the coffins in from the side as they can be kept close to the deceased family. The caboose is used only by the railroad to carry their men in and small amount of supplies, and is off limits to anyone else. It has a stove to keep its workers warm during the winter. During the winter, when there is a funeral, and it's raining or snowing, the mourners need to bring blankets and heavy clothing because it's cold, wet, and miserable. During the summer time, it gets very hot, strong winds with blowing sand. The mourners need to bring their own water and food, at all times. Sometimes there could be several funerals at different locations in the cemetery on the same trip, which will mean an all-day, and part of the night, trip. Also, if there are many mourners, that will slow down the funeral service process.

"Oh, Father, there's one thing I forgot to tell you, there" one portable outhouse on the first car, and there's always a line at it. Father, I know all this because I went on a funeral for my aunt several years ago. We had no priest and only said our own prayers goodbye to her."

"How sad," replies Father Luca. "I will do my best to make a funeral a good and memorable experience."

"There's a station stop halfway to the cemetery a couple of hours out of town, where the train stops and the mourners can use the three outhouses located beside the station house. At the station house, there is no water or food for the passengers and no facility of staying overnight. Everything at the station is for railroad workers only. The railroad workers riding in the caboose unload their equipment and supplies into waiting wagons, then they head out to the work camps some miles away. Believe me, certain times of the year, the train trip will be very time-consuming and miserable.

"The train will be here this afternoon. The town didn't request the train this time, what I understand is because one of their favorite bosses, a big, popular Scotsman, got killed and the railroad company are helping the town, and many of the railroad workers will be pallbearers and mourners. I understand they will be sending some money to the church for your service of conducting the funeral. We need to go to the station today to get familiar with where you and the church team will be seated and the car the mourners of each deceased family will be riding in.

Thomas stops for a moment as he's thinking about something, then he continues, "Father, I'll be getting with Doc and Andy, the undertaker, to make sure everything will be ready in two days."

"Thomas, I truly appreciate all the information you gave me. I wasn't aware of all the details of performing a funeral here," says Father Luca as he begins to pile his papers into several stacks on his desk.

"Adela and I need to start getting things together fast."

"Adela, Father Luca," Thomas says as he's looking at both them, "if either one of you think of anything I have forgotten, please let me know."Adela, you will need to get with each family to help with their needs in the short time we have before burial."

"Father, and also you Adela," says Thomas, "I hope what I'm going to say will help for a little warning before we board the train. Remember, I'm talking with experience with my own family. When the train arrives at the cemetery, getting the deceased coffin off the train to the gravesite could be a couple hundred feet through very rough, uneven ground. This part of the cemetery has not been kept. During the summer, which is the time now, it may be very difficult. I have seen where some people have used something like a two-wheel cart, but in rough ground, the coffins are hard to keep on the cart and are heavy and very difficult to pull through rough ground. Using pallbearers is sort of good, but again some to those men have never experienced this hard labor and trip and fall down, or get overheated and can't finish their duty. I heard there was a problem with carrying the coffin this one time, and they used a rope and dragged it to the burial site. Then one other time, I was told that a coffin was dropped, and it broke open, and they had to get some nails and hammer it back together, which delayed the service for several hours. Just be prepared for a surprise."

"Thank you very much for all that information. I will be ready, I hope there are no surprises," answers Father Luca. "Adela, if you can pass that information onto the mourners, that will be a blessing to them if there is time."

Then Thomas asks Adela, "Can we get together? There's a few things I need to go over with you."

"Yes, Thomas, right after we finish here. Father, are you done?" Adela asks.

"Yes, I am," replies Father Luca.

Thomas tells Adela, "To get in contact with the families of the deceased, the man working in the train station here in town can give you the information. Sometimes he may have their address, or he may have to contact the working camp in the mountains, which may take time. It all depends on everything that's happening at that time."

✦ ✦ ✦

Several hours later, Father Luca had Thomas drop him off for a one-hour visit at the bishop's library at his villa, Father Luca frantically looking through manuscripts and books, on how to conduct a funeral. Bishop Mangini was not home. After a short time, he found what he was looking for and feels comfortable with its knowledge as he reads it over several times then making a few notes where he will post it into his Bible later just to be sure he understands.

Later that afternoon, Thomas has the church's buggy and its horse tied in front of the mercantile building. Father Luca exits the building with Adela following, carrying a satchel with papers as they approach the side of the buggy. Thomas has put a foot stool out so they can step up into the buggy.

Father Luca says, "Here, Adela, let me assist you," and smiles as he holds her hand as she gets into the buggy. Thomas assists Father Luca into the buggy and picks up the stool and gets into the driver's seat. Thomas, driving the buggy professionally as Father Luca and Adela sitting in the back as they head to the train station. Thomas parks the buggy next door to the station's office and joins them, as they begin walking around the station, looking at where the loading of passengers and the coffins is conducted.

Father Luca meets and introduce himself, Adela, and Thomas to the station master.

The station master gives Father Luca and Adela the train schedule and the instructions for arriving grieving mourners and how and where they can load their coffins.

The station master tells Father Luca, "The station will have a few porters on those special days who can assist with the coffins."

The station master stresses, "It is very important that the church staff arrives early because of the problem of parking, getting seats on the train, and everyone is not thinking and do stupid things."

✦ ✦ ✦

After saying goodbye to the station master, Father Luca and Adela get into their buggy and start heading back to the mercantile building, with Thomas driving.

Thomas is guiding the buggy down the dirt road, giving Father Luca and Adela a look of the town that they may have not seen while walking. Thomas talking over his shoulder tells Father Luca and Adela, "I will give you a nice tour of the town. We are passing a Chinese laundry that washes clothes. It has been here for many years. I think the family came here in the first place to work on the railroad. After doing that hard work of laying railroad tracks, they decided doing the town's laundry was more profitable, and not as hard and dangerous work."

Adela watches, as they pass by the laundry, a Chinese woman in the backyard of her family business, an old one-story building with no fenced yard as she's speaking loudly to several teenage Chinese boys as they appear to be washing clothes. They have two large wooden barrels with several wooden crates around each barrel to stand on, one large barrel filled with water and soap suds overflowing its sides. One of the boys is standing on one of the boxes scrubbing clothes on a large washboard and covered in suds. He uses a long pole with a hock on its end to hock the clothes that's floating around in the water. The other boy is rinsing the clothes in the other tub, hanging them on several clotheslines, one end attached to the back of the building and the other to a large pole imbedded into the ground.

Thomas, speaking over his shoulder again, says, "I can understand a little Chinese. The woman is telling the boys they are working too slow, and they need to pick up the sped and quit talking."Their business is looking better every week with more people moving here."

Thomas drives past a couple empty lots then several large parcels of land looking like many vegetable gardens planted together, and Thomas calls out again over his shoulder, "This is where you buy all of your fresh vegetables."

Then he makes a right. As they travel down several blocks, he says, "This is the only hotel we have in our part of town. Many businessmen stay here. Mostly visiting railroad bosses.

There's a large gold mine about forty miles from here, and some of the managers come into town to celebrate their wealth. Now we are passing a few homes and a grocery store on your right."

"And here we are, the mercantile building," says Thomas.

"Thank you very much for such a lovely tour of our town," says Adela.

"Thomas, that was an interesting tour. You shown me parts of town I had no idea were here. Thank you," says Father Luca.

"Adela," Father Luca says, "please write up a note and put it on the message board before leaving tonight. State that, 'The ground breaking on the new church will go on as planned.

Father Luca will be conducting funeral services at Mt. Olivet cemetery for all three men in two days. The train will be leaving sharp at 6:30 a.m., please don't be late. We will not be waiting for anyone. We anticipate there might be many mourners than planned because of a boss man railroad worker was killed and had a lot of friends. Thank you.' Put your name at the bottom as my assistant." Father Luca smiles broadly at Adela.

Thomas has put the foot stool down for them to step on as they exit the buggy.

+ + +

That evening, a group of about thirty people from the Rocco family, a prominent group in town, begin to congregate in the center of town, several holding burning torches, all chanting, "Down with the cheap church, and down with people who want it."

The leader of the group, Mr. Ordagal, standing in the middle of the group, shouting, "We the people of this town don't want a cheaply made church in our town. The church will be cheaply made and have a canvas roof. How ridiculous can this be, and it's going to be built with our donations that we give every week. We need to organize and run these swindlers out of town!"

The group gives a big cheer and continues to chant. After a few minutes, the group gets louder, making a lot of noise as a few townspeople gather around to watch, wondering what is going on.

About half an hour later, not getting very many onlookers, Mr. Ordagal, the leader of the group, decides to protest another night and disbands the group.

+ + +

The next day, Adela is busily trying to make contact with the families of the deceased. She has Thomas deliver the notes to the families there in town, telling them the church is there to help them. She gives them a list of things they need to do before getting on the cemetery train.

CHAPTER 13

It's 4:00 p.m., the bright sun starting to settle into the horizon. A single male driver in his late thirties named Enrique pulls his one-horse wagon up in front a small house with a white picket fence on the outskirts of town. He ties his horse to the fence and walks to the front door and knocks.

Louis, also in his thirties, comes to the front door, opening the screen. "Come on in, Enrique," he says loudly as they briefly give each other a friendship hug.

"Hey, Angie, Enrique is here."

Angie, who's Louis's wife, comes into the room carrying a pot of coffee and a stack of sandwiches and fried chicken on a plate.

"Hi, Enrique, here, I got you something to eat. You'll need the energy," Angie says.

Louis briefly leaves the room and comes back into the room carrying a coat and sits down at the table, as both men start to eat.

As the men are eating, Enrique says, "We have a big job tonight. We have to dig three graves.

Two of the graves are close together, but the other one has to be larger than the others and is on the other side of the cemetery. A popular railroad supervisor was killed in a rock avalanche and was a very big man. I was told he was six feet, eight inches. I think that's on the newer part of the cemetery."

Louis nods his head and continues to eat. Then he says with a mouth full of food. "You've got the location?"

"Yeah, will have to do some measuring to get it exact. I brought extra kerosene just in case it takes longer than planned."

Louis mumbles as he's eating, "Yeah, I'm bringing an extra pair of leather gloves. Do you know which grave they are going to do the services first?"

"I don't know, we now have a new young priest in town, and I haven't talked with him. I think he would most likely start with the first two and do the single one last that's on the other side of the cemetery. Thinking about it, I think the popular railroads boss will be the third grave. Unless they want to have his funeral first and do the others on their way back. I guess we want to get them all done before they get there."

"Oh, thinking about it, I hope you got all three grave markers done?"

"Yup, they're lying on the front porch, ready to be loaded," says Louis."Once the services are finished at the first two grave sites, as the train is firing up building steam, the engineer will blow to sharp tapes from its whistle, letting us know they are on the way.

It will take some time for the mourners to get aboard. Almost always at funerals, there are slow-moving mourners, taking a long time to get back to the train and then get settled in before the train will move. We'll have time to clear up everything and make it presentable and move out of the area."

After eating for a while, as they're almost finished, Enrique says, "If the dirt gets too rough, we may have to finish up in the morning, or maybe an extra day! Yeah, that's right, I just hope the wind won't be bad."

"Angie," says Louis, "you have some extra chicken, the possibility of staying an extra night might happen, just depends how rough the ground will be?"

"Yes, guys, I do have some extra chicken and a few sandwiches, and I also made a bowl of spaghetti, gives a lot of energy, if you want it." She gets up and goes back into the kitchen."Your right," mumbles Enrique through a mouthful of food. "Remember last year, we ran into, I think the ground was solid rock. I used two pairs of gloves just digging one grave. And it took us a lot more hours to dig, then just a standard-size grave."

"Enrique, how is your horse doing, you remember she was having some problem digesting her food last week?"

"Yeah, I got the doc out there, and he looked her over and he gave her some medicine. He told me she will be fine. I don't know what he gave her, but she is fine now."

Angie comes walking into the room with two baskets of sandwiches, chicken wrapped in paper, and fruits, with several large bottles of water. Both men finish up their meals.

"I don't want you guys to leave right yet. I have something special tonight. I'll be right back." Angie goes into her kitchen and quickly returns with two plates of peach cobbler.

"Oh, good, good," says Enrique. "It's my favorite."

"I knew that, and I also enclosed another piece in your lunch," replies Angie.

"Angie, you make the best meal in town," says Enrique.

"Thank you, Enrique. You two, be careful and don't overwork yourself."

Both men go outside to the wagon. Enrique standing beside the wagon, he lights the kerosene lantern and hangs it on the pole attached to the wagon's side.

Louis hugs his wife, Angie, and slips on his coat. She tells them, "Louis, and you too, Enrique, be safe and watch out for the scorpions and snakes!"

"I will, honey," replies Louis.

Both men are up in the wagon seat. As Enrique has the rains in his hands, they disappear into the darkness, anticipating a long ride tonight.

Enrique says, "Hey, Louis, I threw in a couple extra shovels, picks, sledgehammer, pikes, and tarpaulins and feed for the horse. Oh, yeah, I also added a couple blankets just in case. I have the feeling we might spend an extra day out there."

"Enrique, that cushion idea sure feels much better."

"Yeah," replies Enrique "Did you bring the pint?"

✦ ✦ ✦

It's 5:30 a.m., still dark. Thomas has picked up Father Luca at Bishop Mangini Villa, and has arrived at the mercantile building. Adela has already arrived and is in the office organizing things that need to be brought to the funeral.

"Father, here is your case." She hands it to him. "I put everything you'll need, including your personal Bible and hymn book in it."

"Thank you, Adela," Father Luca says and gives her a big smile.

"Father, you and Adela must use a parasol to protect from the sun, I will have them for you. The sun blaze is bad up on the mesa." "Thank you, Thomas. That's a great idea."

Thomas has lit the kerosene lantern and attached it to the pole of the buggy and loaded everything they will need. He has put the foot stool on the ground for Father Luca and Adela to step on to get into the buggy. Father Luca has dismissed Thomas of allowing him to assist Adela getting into and out of the buggy. Father Luca deliberately stands beside the stool instead of getting in before Adela so he can hold her hand to assist her getting into the buggy, then he follows. Thomas has noticed what Father Luca is doing with the assistance with Adela, and he stands aside and let Father Luca help Adela.

Thomas, sitting in the driver seat, gives a flick with of the reins and the horse heads down the road toward the train station. They have arrived early to the station, just like what the station master advised them to do to avoid the rush of mourners and wagons unloading the coffins onto the train. They notice one wagon has already arrived, and with the assistance of the station porters, using a dozen men, struggled to get the oversized coffin out of the wagon and into one of the cars. Getting a coffin into one of the train cars, if you have the right amount of helpers, is not too hard since there is no sides to the cars, but an extra big coffin becomes a major job.

Thomas tells Father Luca and Adela, "You must go and secure a seat, but not in the front of the first car. That is where the outhouse is located and will get a foul smell soon. I will secure the buggy. I have a friend who will take care of it while we are gone and come and pick us up on our return."

As Father Luca and Adela head to the second car, they see the train engineer walking around the train cars and the engine, looking at the undercharge of the cars, making sure everything is working and in order.

They could hear the loud roar of the coal burning in the engine as the fireman continues shoveling more coal into the fire, and the steam begins to build up.

After they get to their seats, they can see the traffic jam beside the station as many buggies, wagons, and horses all arrive at the station at the same time. Some of the buggies and wagons have lanterns, and others don't, which can become a problem in the dark.

As Father Luca sits there watching everyone moving about the car, he notices further to the end of the train where the caboose is attached. Four men are loading boxes of food from a wagon into the caboose. One of the men carries about a dozen, armload of trees limbs, tied into bundles cut in two-foot lengths. Father Luca assumes to himself, "Must be firewood."

One of the workers, a young man, walks over to the wagon driver and begins to talk, then the driver suddenly brings both of her arms up around the young worker's neck and gives him a big kiss that lasts for a minute.

Another worker calls out, "Leonard, let's go. Tell her you love her, and you'll see her next time," the young man rushes over to the caboose and goes in. Watching the passengers, Father Luca notices there's not much talking as the mourners move about the train; a few children are crying and their parents are trying to keep them quit. Most of the mourners are carrying armloads of coats, bags, and boxes of food and water for the long trip.

There is a large place at the front, and at the back end of each car where the seats have been removed so the coffins can be placed.

Father Luca pauses for a moment when he sees a grieving woman who must be the wife of one of the men that got killed, crying deeply as she's lying on top of the coffin while her family are trying to get her to sit down before the train starts to move. Father Luca, as he watches, begins to gets a pain in his stomach, thinking to himself as he quietly says, "How in the world did I get myself here? Please, God, help me."

Father Luca sees Thomas as he boards the train car, calling out his name, "Thomas, we are over here."

Thomas waves his hand with recognition and comes over and sits beside Adela.

"Adela," says Father Luca, "I'm going to give a little spiritual guidance to the men moving that coffin on this car," as he can see a handful of men struggling to lift a heavy coffin from a wagon up onto the back end of the train car.

Walking to the back of the car, Father Luca can see the men needing extra help pulling the coffin onto the deck of the car. Moving in beside the men, Father Luca reaches down and grabs on to a part of a hand grip on the side of the coffin and begins to pull with the other men, pulling as hard as he can.

"Pull, men, you almost got it!" Father Luca says loudly as he's grunting with the men while they pulled the coffin aboard. Father Luca stands there, taking several deep breaths to compose himself from the hard work.

Suddenly an older man has appeared in front of him, looking straight at him. "Thank you, God," he said.

"We were running out of energy, and you came along and became our savor."

"Strength comes in many ways, but not always in physical strength," Father Luca tells the older man.

"You're absolutely right, Father. I haven't been to one of your services yet, but I will be coming to your next service. I almost gave up on having a priest in our town, but now you will be seeing a lot of me at your services. I heard you have your service in the mercantile building?"

"Yes, the service for the time is held Sundays at 9:00 a.m. I'm planning other services but haven't come up with a time. I need to have another meeting with Ethan, who is the owner of the mercantile building."

Father Luca starts to walk around the congested car, meeting mourners, when suddenly he thinks, *Where did that come from of what I just said. What is happening to me? Is the Lord starting to talk to me?* Suddenly the train conductor begins to walk through the cars. "Everyone, please listen up," he announces. We are heading for a long train ride, you must get aboard, and find yourself a seat, get comfortable, and we will be leaving in ten minutes."

Father Luca walks to the next crowed car as he introduces himself, meeting more desperate mourners. Many are in pain, not knowing what will happen to their families and themselves. The railroad worker who got killed was the person who brought home the money to live on, buy food, cloths, pay rent, what are they going to do. Father Luca patiently tries to comfort their grievances and tells them God and the church is there to help them.

A loud train whistle cuts through the quiet town as the train begins to move. Some passengers still have not been able to find a seat they are comfortable with, and a few are still standing, not hanging on to anything, and they stumble, even falling over each other, as the train makes several jerks than moves forward down the tracks.

Father Luca works his way back to his seat where Adela and Thomas are sitting. He sits down beside Adela and whispers in her ear, "I think this is going to be a very long and difficult trip."

He takes and holds her hand in his lap, as they both try to get a little sleep. She snuggles up beside him and lays her head on his shoulder.

CHAPTER 14

It has been several hours since the train has left town, the sun has already come up over the horizon. The train is climbing a long, slow climb to get to the top of the first lower level to the mesa, as it zigzags across the land. Trees are sparse out here, many tumbleweeds cover the landscape. The ground has leveled out for a while, before it will climb another step incline to the mesa. Most of the passengers are still asleep, as the train begins to slow down for the stop at the halfway station. In the distance, one can see the tall water tank with its long hocked neck pipe used to water the train, hanging out in the air ready to be used. There's a line of smoke, slowly drifting out of the metal pipe smokestack on the lonely wooden building. Its wooden front porch and overhang protect several older men sitting in their wooden rocking chairs, watching as the train arrives. A small barn and a corral with half dozen horses fenced in, four wagons lined up in the back of the building. All the equipment has been staged by the railroad workers in the building.

The train engineer has guided the large water pipe into the opening on the engine and started the flow of water into the steamer.

Next to the small station building sits three outhouses built specifically for the passengers of the cemetery train and for the railroad workers.

As soon as the train had stopped, most of the women have immediately exited the train and are lining up in front of the outhouses. Hardly any men are in line as they have relieved themselves on the other side of the train on the tracks.

One of the younger women standing in line who's never been on a cemetery train asks the woman standing beside her, "Where are all these nice-looking men going, and what are they doing?"

The other woman looks a bit surprised by the woman's comment. "Oh, they work for the railroad and are heading to the gorge, where they're digging a train tunnel through the rugged mountains. They stay out here in the mountains at camps for weeks, even months at a time."

The other woman responds, "Oh, they look tough and rugged. Do they ever come to town for a visit?"

"I suppose they do," responds the woman. "And yes, it's hard work and extremely dangerous, and the pay is low but it's a job," she says to the wondering woman.

Father Luca, coming out of a slumber, tells Adela, "Let's get in line at the outhouses before the lines get too long." They both get off the train and head toward the three outhouses.

Several roughed, sun-tanned railroad workers come out of the building as they began to hook up the horses to the wagons, and several men begin coming out of the caboose bringing all the supplies and equipment they put into the caboose several hours earlier in town. Using a hand cart, one man moves the stacks of full burlap bags containing potatoes, carrots, turnips, coffee, and several boxes of beef jerky.

One of the men at the station asks a worker from the train, "Alex, is the train coming back soon after the funerals?"

"I don't think so," replies Alex.

"They have three funerals today. With this hot weather coming, it's going to take a lot longer. If we don't run into any problems, it most likely be late. We also have a new priest, and this is his first funeral up here on the mesa. Don't know how that will turn out."

"Yeah, I hope everything works out OK."

The train engineer walks past the men, carrying a mail bag, and goes into the building to deliver to the manager.

Many of the passengers are mingling around the front porch mostly in the shade as they are stretching their legs, and some passengers choose just to stay on the train. There has been a large pot of coffee put out on the table on the porch of the station for passengers, and several men are having a drink.

All four wagons are now beside the caboose as the railroad workers unload the food supplies and equipment into them. Two of the wagons has canvas cover over their tops for the protection of the food and supplies.

Father Luca tells Adela, "Look, it appears the railroad workers are loading up in their wagons and are heading to their work site."

"It looks very hard work and a hard life," she says, watching the wagons cross the train tracks as they head out across the rough landscape, heading down a well-used road into the distant mountains.

+ + +

One hour later, the conductor walks around the compound, walking past the outhouses, making sure no one is left behind as he calls out, "All aboard, the train is leaving in ten minutes, all aboard." Passengers begin to get back aboard the train, a few of them has been staying in the station house drinking some water.

Ten minutes has passed. The train blows its loud whistle and begins to slowly move. After several violent jerks, the cars momentarily shake as the train starts moving.

"We are leaving," announces the conductor as he hops onto the last train car.

Suddenly, the passengers hear a woman scream from the outhouse area. "Help me, don't leave me!" She's trying to run out of the outhouse as she's putting on her clothes.

Father Luca looks up from his seat and says, "Good God, we're leaving someone," as everyone stands up as they look at the woman running.

Thomas, sitting not too far from the side of the car, moves over to the edge and hangs out from the car, gripping one of the rooftop supports as he yells to the woman, "Run faster, the train will not stop!" his arm outstretched toward the woman as the train begins to pick up speed.

"You must run like hell!" Thomas yells again as the woman nears the car. Another man has gotten up close to Thomas with his hand stretched out as well.

Father Luca suddenly says, "Oh God, I pray for thee," as he grasps the cross hanging around his neck. Just then the woman suddenly gets a big burst of energy and moved closer to the side of the car. Her legs are pumping like pistons, as her hat blows off, her face showing pain. If they don't get her now, she will be left behind. Thomas leans even further out, as the other man hanging on to his shirt so he won't fall. Thomas stretched out as far as he can go without falling out himself and yells, "Throw yourself now!" Thomas grabs the woman by her wrist and yanks her into the car. They literally yanked her from the ground, into the car without dragging her.

Thomas, the other man, and the woman collapsed on the floor with exhaustion, not moving for several minutes to get their breaths back. Father Luca has gotten up and came over to where they were lying and assisting them to help if he can and praising the men for the great deed they had done.

+ + +

Sometime later the train has come to the second steep incline and begins to travel slower. The temperature is beginning to get hot, as the strong wind begins to whip up gusts of blowing sand, as a few tumbleweeds roll past the train.

Father Luca lifts up his collar and pulls his frock up, blocking the wind from Adela's face as she lays her head against his chest, as she grips his hand. He snuggles his face into her long black hair, protecting from the dust. He smiles as he strokes her hair as they begin to show affection for each other.

The train has reached the top of the mesa with its low rocky brown hills, dotted with patches of sage brush. The train has picked up speed; some passengers looking out in the distance see a quivering mirage of a lake as they think they have reached the cemetery. About an hour later, the train starts to slow down, then one of the train crew approaches Father Luca. "Father, would you come with me up to the engine cab and meet the train engineer? He hasn't driven this section of the track, and he wants to make sure we stop at the right location."

"Yes, that's a good idea, let me get my associate and we will follow you."

Thomas has already stood up when he saw the worker talking with Father Luca.

"Father Luca, I'm right behind you," Thomas says as they both follow the worker through the next car and up to the engine, where they meet the train engineer.

"Father, we are approaching the cemetery, and I need your approval for the two graves' location. I'm looking at the cemetery map and was told the site should be here in about ten minutes."

Father Luca says, "There should be two graves about one hundred feet apart beside each other about two hundred feet from the tracks on the right side of the train. A good sign of their location would be two high piles of freshly shoveled dirt beside the grave."

"That's good, we will keep an eye out. On other trips to the cemetery, we have noticed, there must have been grave robbers out here, where they dug up a lot of graves. There were many piles of dirt all over the cemetery," says one of the engineers.

Several minutes passed as the train moves along the relatively flat land when one of the engineers spots the two freshly dug graves. "There they are." He points in their direction as the train begins to slow down then coming to a stop.

Thomas goes to the car where the first coffin is to be buried and tells the family they can start moving the deceased to the grave site. "You can have a procession with the coffin at the front. It's your choosing, Father Luca, and Adela will follow."

The pallbearers began to move their crudely made wheel barrel type of rig, to carry the coffin, placing it beside the train car in the rough and uneven terrain. The wind was relatively calm earlier in the day but has increased its velocity, blowing as it's stirring up clouds of dust with sand in the air. After some time struggling, the men got the coffin out of the car and onto the rig.

They are now attempting to pull the rig through the soft dirt, rocks, gnarled twisted bushes, and deadwood with bad results. The cart tipped over after they traveled twenty feet, and the coffin crashed to the ground.

Everyone stopped in fear, as one of the men pulling the rig asked out loud, "Did it break?"

"No, it's OK," says a man who's on his knees looking closely at the bottom edge of the coffin.

"Let's get it back on the chart," another man speaks up. All the men squinting their eyes from the blowing sand bend down hooking their fingers into the handles and lift it up and place it back on the cart. One of the men barks loudly, "God it's hot out here, let's take a brief break!"

Waiting for a few minutes to get their strength back, and they start again. After pulling the chart through the miserable obstacle, going about five more feet, the coffin slips and falls the second time. One of the men says, "Men, what do you think, maybe we should carry it. If Anthony falls one more time, he could break open and we will be in serious trouble, and we still have over a hundred feet to go."

Another man speaks up, "I have an idea, let's leave Anthony right here. He's not going anywhere, and we go back to the train for a rest and cool off. Otherwise, I don't think Anthony will make it to the grave site." All the men agree as they head back to the car, for a rest and cool off, as the casket sits out in the hot roughed blowing sand for an hour.

Thomas says to Father Luca, "I think the hot weather is going to set us back by several hours."

Father Luca, nodding his head, says, "I was thinking, when they have to bring the big man to the grave site, there could be serious problems. We may have to wait until sundown when it's cooler, and hopefully the wind might lighten up."

Half an hour later, seven men come out from the shade of the train car to where the coffin with Anthony in it. They all have taken off the coats, rolled up their long white sleeves. The men got on both sides. As they lift the coffin up to their shoulders, one of the men is too short to carry, so the seventh man fills in his spot. They begin to walk, but as one of the men stumbles on a twisted root poking out of the ground and falls down, everyone struggles to keep the coffin from falling.

Stopping, the man that stumbled gets back into his position, and they proceed to the grave site shoveling their feet to walk. At the grave site, the men are very hot now and could not bend and lower the coffin to the ground. They all fell to their knees, one man smashing his face on the lid of the coffin and bloodies his nose as the coffin hit flat on the hard ground.

"Thomas had brought several heavy ropes to lower the coffin into the ground."

Finally, the men got the coffin into the grave.

Father Luca, Adela, and Thomas make their way trudging through the rough terrain to the gravel site. Father Luca is holding a parasol that is almost being torn apart from the wind for himself and Adela, with Thomas walking behind, choosing not to use the parasol because of the violent wind, to help with anything that's needed.

Father Luca conducts the funeral as gusts of sand swirl up among the mourners, many covering their faces with scarfs. Adela struggles to hold the parasol keeping it close over her and Father Luca's head. As he reads the underlined passages from his Bible, he stops several times to wipe the sand from his face and the pages of his Bible.

The mourners for the second and third funeral stay aboard the car in the shade, and out of the wind. At the end of the service, Father Luca says, "Does anyone want to cast a hand full of earth into the grave to say goodbye?"

Several people step forward getting a handful of dirt and cast into the grave as they say their goodbyes, and they begin to trudge back to the train trying to protect their faces from the wind. After the completion of the service, Father Luca, Adela, and Thomas head back to the shade of the train cars, stepping over dead twisted limbs protruding out the ground, to cool off, before they conduct the next funeral.

CHAPTER 15

Father Luca and Thomas is standing in the shade of the train car roof as Thomas says, "Father, I could go and do the service for you. You and Adela stay here in the shade. Show me the pages in the Bible, and I don't think anyone will object to me giving the service in this tremendous heat, and this miserable wind."

"Thank you, Thomas, for your offer, but a priest needs to do this burial for God. The grieving people would not understand if I sent you out there to represent me, and God. I asked Adela, if she didn't want to go to the grave site, she insisted that she support me and will be by my side at the site."

Father Luca, with his wide brim hat on, stands beside Adela in the car as they both drink a couple cups of water. They look out at the next grave site with a glazed expression, the faces blushed from the heat.

They have noticed a man and woman mourners have just came slowly walking back from the first grave site and the man can barely hold the woman up from collapsing, as she's sobbing uncontrollably.

Thomas has gotten with the next family to proceed with their pallbearers in moving the coffin to the grave site. They had made arrangements to borrow the same rig the first funeral pallbearers used to get their coffin to the grave site. Again, the men in white shirts, rolled-up sleeves, struggle getting the coffin onto the rig and start moving the rig through the rough terrain.

At this funeral there are at least fifteen men to help move the coffin to the grave site. They decide to use a different way to move the coffin. They hook a rope to the front of the configured rig, and several men pull like mules as the others keep the coffin from falling off and push from behind. The wind constantly sandblasts the men as they finally got the coffin to the site with no major problems. While waiting for Father Luca to arrive, the men with their backs to the strong wind take out their handkerchiefs wiping the faces and eyes, some tie their handkerchiefs across their faces.

Father Luca approaches the site holding down his wide brim hat, with Adela beside him struggling with their parasol and Thomas following. Father Luca begins the service as he reads new passages from his Bible as Adela, with a scarf pulled over her face, struggles to hold a parasol over both of them. Shortly after the beginning of the service, the parasol Adela is holding collapses and she drops it to the ground. While reading the passages, Father Luca keeps one hand over the page in the Bible because the wind and sand keep blowing it. Thomas has brought the ropes used to help lower the coffin into the grave. There were not many mourners at this funeral because of the intense heat and the sandblasting wind. As Father Luca says his short service, still many could not stand the wind and the heat and began to leave before the service was over.

One man says out loud, "I don't want to be disrespectful, Father, but it's too damn hot, and my wife is going to pass out. We must go back to the train."

After the service, almost everyone that stayed got a handful of dirt to cast in on the coffin, and they say their goodbyes. All the mourners trudge back to the train, tired from the constant blast from the wind and sand, and they drink some water after getting back to the car, which wasn't that much of a relief. A few of the women pour a little water into their handkerchiefs and are cleaning their faces and eyes.

The train engineer sees Father Luca coming back to the train and has the fireman start shoveling coal into the burner to start building steam as it makes a loud roar. A short time later, everyone has settled down in their seats covered up from the wind, and they prepare for the continuation to a new location to the other side of the cemetery as the sun continues to blaze down. The train fireman now has the steam built up and taps the train whistle a couple times.

The two taps of the whistle have signaled the grave diggers at the third site that the train is on its way to their location.

Louis says to Enrique, "Did you hear the whistle?"

"Yeah, we need to move out of the area," say Enrique.

"In a couple minutes, I just need several hard hits with the shovel and I'll have the grave marker in place." Both men begin to gather up their tools, picks, racks, pikes, shovels, and brooms, putting them in the back of their wagon.

As Louis stands beside a pile of shoveled dirt from the grave, Enrique asks, "Take the rake and smooth up the dirt pile a bit to make it look nice."

After removing a few gnarled dead roots out of the ground where the mourners would be standing, Enrique removes the canvas makeshift shade they have set up for their horse to keep her out of the sun, then he begins to harnesses her up. Putting all loose equipment still on the ground into the wagon, then he drives the wagon a couple hundred feet away from the grave site and parks it. Then he begins to unhook the harness on the horse again, as he begins to erect the makeshift shade again for the horse. After making the grave site presentable for the funeral, both men climb under the shade, sharing it with their horse until the funeral is over and the sun goes down.

Occasionally after funerals, a few of the mourners to show their appreciation would walk over to the men hunkered under the shade and drop off several coins for their hard work.

The conductor walks through all three cars, announcing, "All passengers, we will be leaving for the next funeral in about ten minutes. Everyone all aboard and get a seat." The train fireman shovels more coal into the furnish. As the steam builds up, the engineer taps his whistle again, and the train begins to move. Adela is leaning her head against Father Luca's chest as they sit, trying to stay cool.

Sometime later, the train arrives on the other side of the enormous cemetery at the third grave site. One of the engineers comment to the other one, "You see the red pole next to the track a couple hundred feet from here on the right?"

"Yeah."

"Look at the track as it approaches that pole."

"Yeah, I don't see the tracks. What happened to the tracks?"

"Well, you won't because that is the end of the tracks here in the cemetery. Later, with the expansion of the town and more funerals, they'll add more tracks to fit the size of the cemetery. The train will go all the way back to town in reverse."

There are at least fifty men who want to be pallbearers, many are big, rough-looking, strong guys. After seeing what the first two funerals had endured, they decide they will carry the large coffin on their shoulders from the train to the grave site. They don't want to have problems like the first two funerals getting the coffin to the grave site.

Since the big man was Scottish, they brought along a bagpiper to play as they carry the big man to his resting place. The pallbearers will wait until the bagpiper makes his way to the grave then they will lift their friend to their shoulders. The bagpiper started to play as he marched alone out toward the grave site; wind is sandblasting him as he held his head high and didn't miss a note. Stopping, he turns and stands at the head of the grave. With a lot of grunting and a few low voices swearing, sixteen men got the large coffin out of the car and on their shoulders. Many other men wanted to be part of the group carrying the coffin but couldn't because there wasn't enough room. The other strong men march to the bagpipe music with pride behind the coffin. A few stumbled but did not fall out. All the pallbearers wore white shirts, sleeves rolled up with their heads raised high. They did not appear to show they were tiring as the strong wind sandblasted their faces as they marched to the grave site. Fifty mourners followed the fifteen pallbearers, men, women, and children. Many of the mourners from the previous two funerals followed behind. There is an enormous amount of respect for the big boss man, and everyone wants to show their respect and say goodbye to such a well-respected man. The weather has not changed; it's still blazing hot, with very strong gusts of wind and sand blowing into everyone's eyes.

Father Luca and Thomas head toward the grave site, as they shovel through the sand behind the mourners, using their scarves to protect their faces.

Father Luca had said to Adela before leaving the train, "I think it would be wise, Adela, that you stay in the shade on the train this time. I'm concerned about your health. You're very hot and tired from the sandblasting wind, just like most of the mourners. The weather is not a bother to the railroad workers who are accustomed to this hot and windy conditions."

"Thank you, Father," Adela says as she sits down on the bench. She pauses for a moment as she squeezes his hand and says quietly,

"Mariano, you be careful."

Father Luca, holding down his wide brim hat and his scarf across his face, and Thomas also wearing a wide brim hat trudge across the rough terrain a couple hundred feet to the dug grave. The reason for not having any graves dug within two hundred feet of the track was decided years ago when the train track was laid, with the possibility of expansion of the tracks, which never happened.

Father Luca begins the funeral, but he's beginning to feel the strain from the heat and the strong sandy wind. He's using a few new passages from his Bible because of the severity of the wind and heat. Father Luca let a few pallbearers make some personal comments, but they were hard to hear because of the blowing wind. Several women came forward and laid a few flowers on the coffin using a few rocks to keep them from blowing away, and other women began crying.

The pallbearers have both ends of the ropes and lower their friend down into the ground. Everyone at the service gets a handful of dirt and get in line to toss into the grave, saying they're goodbyes. Father Luca slowly walks with Thomas back to the train, happy that all three services are over, but saddened for the death of the big man who lost everything. As Father Luca gets into the train car, he removes his scarf from his face but keeps it around his neck for the occasionally savior cross winds, and turns to Thomas and grips his shoulder telling him,

"Thanks so much for your help. I would never had done it without your help"

Thomas replies, "Father, you are an amazing priest and man. You did it all, the very first time and you did it well, and thank you too and God."

A woman standing in line at the smelly toilet in the first car makes a comment to the woman standing beside her, the senseless woman pauses as she looks out across the bleak landscape and asks, "Where does the train turn around? I noticed there are no more tracks ahead of us. Were they covered by the blowing sand? Will the driver of the train be able to see the tracks if they are covered? I hope this is only temporary, I didn't bring any sleeping clothes."

The other woman didn't want to get into a lengthy conversation, and she slowly shakes her head and tells the woman, "The train does not turn around, it backs up all the way back to town."

"If what you mean everyone will be going home backward, is that dangerous?" she says with a strange look on her face as she turns around and walks away.

Once the sun has dropped over the horizon and the temperature begins to cool down, both Enrique and Jeremy will fill in the graves. Lighting up their kerosene lanterns, they harness up their horse and load all the equipment and drive to the other two grave sites. They will fill in both grave sites tonight, then head home, getting there hopefully before sunrise. They know they had done a good deed for themselves and for the town.

+ + +

Conductor begins to walk around the train, "We will be leaving in twenty minutes. Have time to go to the restroom and get settled in before we depart for a long drive home. Once we leave the mesa, the temperature will get cooler."

Father Luca tells Adela, "I'm going to walk around the cars and to talk with some parishioners who are troubled. I won't be gone long."

Sometime later, as the train moves along the tracks heading for home, Father Luca and Adela snuggle together, trying to get comfortable, not aware of a man and woman sitting next aisle over from them, who were part of the protest in town about the building of the cheap church.

The protesters ideas of building a cheap church with their donations was defiantly a dislike as they stared at them with hate in their eyes.

+ + +

Several hours later, the train arrives at the halfway station. It's dark and quiet, and an older man is sitting in a rocking chair on the front porch smoking a pipe watching for the train.

The engineer walks past the man on the porch, telling him, "Good evening," as he passes by as he enters the building. Several minutes later, the engineer comes back out and starts to get the water for the train from the water tank. Climbing up the ladder on the tank, he releases the water valve and guides the spout into the train's water opening and pulls the rope, and the water comes gushing into the train. A few half sleepy passengers woke up and are using the outhouses beside the station house. A couple of railroad workers come out of the building and begin moving equipment from a wagon they brought up to the caboose. When finished, they return the wagon back to the corral and got into the caboose. A couple more minutes pass, and three more workers come out of the building and get into the caboose. The workers appear they will be spending the night in town.

One hour later, the conductor standing at the end of the train beside the caboose calls out, "All aboard." He waves a lantern letting the train engineer know everyone is aboard, and he hops onto the car and the train begins to move toward town.

CHAPTER 16

Several hours later, Father Luca and Adela are awakened by a couple jerks of the cars and the hissing from the steam coming from the brakes as the train makes its final stop at the train station in town.

The conductor walks through the cars waking anyone who hasn't woken up. "We have arrived home, it's the end of the line. Thank you and good night."

Passengers begin milling around trying to find all their belongings, bundling things up and start getting off the train. Many buggies, wagons, and horses are moving around in the darkness, some with lanterns on and some moving through the darkness, trying to get out of the area.

"Well, Adela, the funerals are done, and we are home. Thomas is out in the street looking for our buggy."

"Thank you, Mariano, for your help and support. It was a very exhausting experience," Adela says to Father Luca as she briefly holds one of his hands.

Thomas comes up to where Father Luca and Adela are standing. "Father, I found my friend, and he has our buggy parked very close by."

"Here, let me help you." Thomas picks up the blankets and their bags. "If you will follow me, it's a bit dark out there."

✦ ✦ ✦

Back at the cemetery, Louis is talking with Enrique as they are standing beside their wagon with its lighted kerosene lantern on. "All the tools are in the wagon, the horse got its water, the graves are filled, and a little food left to eat on our way home."

"Yeah, it was a hard one this time, three graves in one trip."

"It always puzzles me, why there was such a distance between the graves?"

"Yeah, I'll explain it to you on our way home. Well, let's get going. It's a long ride home."

+ + +

Back in town, Thomas, driving the buggy with his buddy sitting beside him, stops and lets Adela off at her house. Father Luca hops out of the buggy and puts the wooden step down for Adela and walks her to her door, pausing for a moment as they both look at each other. Suddenly Adela puts both arms around him and hugs him, putting her head on his chest. Then Father Luca brings both his arms around Adela as the both stand there for a few minutes.

Then they step back from each other as Father Luca bids, "Good night, Adela," and gets back into the buggy.

"Father," Thomas says as they're heading to his house, "I'm going to let you off at your house. I will go back to the mercantile and unload the equipment and will see you in the morning."

"Wonderful, Thomas. Don't stay up too late tonight, get some good rest."

"Thank you, Father. I will."

+ + +

The next day at the grounds of the new future church, workmen are unloading lumber of different lengths from several large wagons, and several men are digging trenches of the outline of the church. A couple of surveyors with their poles and tripod equipment are measuring as they drive a few stakes in the ground.

A well-dressed man and woman driving by in their buggy stop and ask one of the workers, "What is happening here?" "Sir, we are delivering the first load of lumber for the construction of the new church." A few men are mixing some concrete in a wheelbarrow as they're pouring part of the front part of the church's foundation.

+ + +

Church service at the mercantile the next day is quite different than the usual Sunday service. All the parishioners, male and female, are dressed in their work clothes, eager for the service to be over so they can start work on their new church. All working tools are stored at the entrance to the building and not brought into the service. Women will be going back home after service to finish making the festival meals they have been preparing and have them back in time for lunch and dinner. While the women are gone to get their meals, a group of volunteers are setting up a dozen long tables with chairs to eat on.

An hour after service, Father Luca, Mr. Notary and his associate, and several experienced workers are standing in the middle of the proposed church with a large table made from several saw horses and a dozen two-by-four lumber used as a table. Mr. Duncan has arrived, he's the architect who drew up the blueprints, answering questions. The men have several blueprints stretched out across the boards as they are talking and pointing in different directions.

"Father, the hangers for the fabric will be hung on these hooks." One of the workers points to a box of brackets on the table, as workmen with building experience are busily instructing people with no building experience on how to do simple projects.

"These brackets," the workman continues, "will be hung in these locations." He points to the locations on the blueprint as several workers are looking on.

Looking up, Mr. Notary sees two wagons of railroad workers arriving. "Ah more professional workers have arrived." He walks over and greets them and introduces a couple of workers who can help with any questions and what they can help to work on.

"Oh, Father, these are the framers that will be building that part of the structure," says Mr. Notary.

"Nice," replies Father Luca, getting a bit confused with the designed locations of the brackets.

"The canvas will be arriving in a couple of days, coming in by train," says Mr. Notary as he's checking his notes. I'll have two wagons there at the train station to pick up the canvas and bring it out here. The construction is moving along very well."

"Oh, and I might add, the weather is going to be beautiful," Mr. Notary says to Father Luca as he's interrupted by a workman asking a question about the blueprint.

"Sunday's the only day of the week when the entire town will be working on the church. The rest of the week, professional workmen will be working every day on the church until its completion.

Hopefully the church will be completed by next Sunday. The townspeople have their own jobs they must work at during the week, except Sunday, when everyone can come together, with a festival atmosphere."

+ + +

As the volunteer workers finish their Sunday dinner at the church's work site, Father Luca makes an announcement. "Everybody, it gives me great pride and pleasure to announce to all our dedicated workers, construction is going very fast and with a little bit of God's help, our new church will be completed and a festival to celebrate its opening next Sunday. All women, if you will get with Adela, she has the list of all the ladies' names to coordinate with her what meals to bring so we won't have too many duplicate meals. And if you can't get with her, contact Mrs. Silverwood. She can give you the answer you are wondering about."

+ + +

The following week, the builders are working from sunrise to sundown trying to meet the deadline with plans to finish building the new church by Sunday. Thursday, three days before Sunday church service, workers have stretched out and installed the fabric canvas roof. The floor and walls have been installed. Now they are installing the seating benches and doors. The windows will be cut into the walls and installed at a later date because of time of availability and price.

It is Sunday, the big day has arrived. The entire town must be there, including all the children in and around town. Everyone's excited as they arrive at the new church, almost everyone dressed in their festival clothing, with plenty of parking for the wagons, buggies, and horses.

Some parishioners and guests can't afford nice or maybe clean clothes, so they wear their old clothes. Father Luca is standing at the front door of the church greeting the regular parishioners and welcoming the new parishioners to the new church. As the parishioners enter the church, they gaze with amazement looking around at its the interior, smiling at what they see. The beautiful seating color coordinating with the simple wooden walls and floor, and the drab-looking tapestry hanging from the ceiling with a curve look stretched from corner to corner.

Father Luca stands behind the simple-made lectern positioned several feet up into the air in the front corner of the church, and he begins the service, "It's wonderful, our very own church.

Standing up here, I sort of miss Ethan standing beside me, in case I fall." Several parishioners chuckle at his joke.

Father Luca's plan to get more worshipers to come to the service was to give a glass of free wine to all parishioners after the service. Father Luca, trying to get more single men to come to the service, gives the complimentary wine to each individual after service at their meet and greet. Instructions were if you don't come to the service, you won't get any wine. The tables for the big celebrations of the new church has already been sit up, covered with bright festival colored fabric. Strings of handmade ornaments has been stretched out over the area where the dancing and eating will take place.

The sermon was well-thought-out by Father Luca. He took extra care picking the right things to say with the building of the new church, which will bring new people and families to the town. He talks about the burial of the three railroad workers up on the mesa at Mt. Olivet and how they and the families will be missed. Giving this sermon today is to be the most important day to him, Antonio Ferretti, or who is now Father Marino Luca. It had to be good. All the parishioners sit on long benches with plenty of additional room. Father Luca introduces Bishop Mangini, who speaks for a couple minutes and gives great praise to Father Luca for accomplishing one of his dreams in having a real church built in their town. After reading from some underlined phrases from his Bible and several prayers, Father Luca closes his Bible.

Finishing up his sermon joyfully, he similes, as he looked out over the full congregation seated in the church when he notices a young man standing in the back of the church that he sort of recognized, but he wasn't sure who he was. The man disappeared after the service was over.

As Father Luca is bidding farewell to the parishioners while standing at the exit of the church, he suddenly remembers the mysterious man, who he was. It was "Nolan," as he blurted out his name. Yes, Nolan, whom he worked with back in New Jersey. Both were selling useless parcels of land out in the Wild West.

Thinking to himself, *Why would Nolan be here in Denver, Colorado? Does he want something? By him being here, will my cover be blown?*

Father Luca begins walking among the parishioners, showing a little stress as he's trying to locate Nolan. Everyone's busy preparing for the festival as his mind is a thousand miles away.

"Father, your sermon was fantastic," a voice says, and he responds not realizing what he said or who he or she was. Then another voice he recognizes complements him, snapping him out of his trance. It was Adela.

"Father, what a wonderful and meaningful sermon. It warmed my heart," she says.

Coming out of his trance, he responds, "Thank you, Adela, I felt good." He holds her hand for a few moments as he looks warmly at her.

Walking with Adela through the large crowd of parishioners, Father Luca starting to celebrate the festival has helped him come out of the depression briefly. He's been thinking that he made a mistake of someone who looks like Nolan. After a while, he dismisses the idea that Nolan is there in Denver.

A roaming mariachi band has started playing music, and they walk around the grounds playing wonderful Mexican music, then they try playing a few Spanish songs. Several piñatas are hanging from tall poles as a few blindfolded children are trying to hit and break them with long sticks, spreading nice sweet candies all over the ground. Several men in the empty part of the lot are putting into place a dozen high-flying rockets and sparklers for the big fireworks show scheduled later during the festival. The women volunteers are continuing to put more of the festival food on the tables, like barbecued chicken, cooked potatoes, gravy, corn on the cobs, cooked cabbage, and on the end of the table a large ball of spaghetti with meatballs and corn bread and many other dishes out on the tables.

A young boy walks up to Father Luca and asks, "Father, when will the fireworks start."

"Yes, my son, I believe it will begin after dinner."

"Thank you," replies the boy as he runs off to tell his friends.

All the festival participants are seated, some of them are done eating, as they are now drinking and talking with other people. A young teenage boy is showing off his talent. He's doing rope-twirling tricks as he jumps in and out of the rope, getting applause from some people watching.

Father Luca, sitting with Adela as they have finished eating, are sipping a glass of wine, and Thomas joins them.

"Wonderful time, Father," Thomas says.

"Everyone is having one of the best festivals they have ever had. The service was a true blessing."

"Thank you, Thomas."

+ + +

On the edge of the area of where the festival is taking place, about six members of the Rocco Society are standing together, making derogatory comments about the festival for the new, ridiculous, ugly church with a fabric canvas roof that was built using their weekly donations.

One of the male members says, "What are they partying for? The church is an embarrassment to the neighborhood with that stupid-looking roof of fabric instead of a normal wooden roof. When it rains or the wind is blowing, you can't use the church."

A woman speaks up, "Yeah, where did all that money that was collected every Sunday go? certainly not to the church."

+ + +

Dinner is finished, and everyone is preparing for the fireworks. All the children are sitting at the tables, when suddenly a loud burst of the first rockets explode high in the sky with beautiful colors flying across the sky.

Then another rocket is fired, then other rockets are fired and the sky is filled temporarily with beautiful colors. People are awing with pleasure. Then several flashes of bright twirlers, sparks flying everywhere as sparks are bouncing on the ground and others fill the skies while the children scream with joy. Everyone is mesmerized with the short moment of pleasure. Then as quickly as the show began, it's quickly over. The party is over. Yes, the festival is over, and some families begin to leave and some of the adults begin to drink and dance to a guitar player. Suddenly a terrifying thing happens.

CHAPTER 17

A s the festival winds down, most of the partiers are listening to a guitar player and drinking wine and beer and a few are dancing, when suddenly someone screams, "Fire!" For a moment, everyone is in shock and disbelief what is happening. The fabric canvas roof of the church explodes into a ball of flames as it burns wildly. Quickly everyone who is sober or not jumps up from where they are sitting and races toward the fire, grabbing table cloths, their coats, boards from the dining tables, anything they can grab, trying to beat down the flames. For a moment, Father Luca stands with total shock on his face staring at the blaze. Out of impulse, he grabs the cross hanging around his neck on a cord saying what he thinks is a quick prayer, "Oh God, help us." Then he grabs the table cloth from his table and races toward the fire. Adela is right behind him. They both quickly move in beside several other people all swinging at the flames with what they could find, trying to fight the fire. Their efforts quickly became in vain as the flames tore through the cloth roof and the wooden structure, as they could not bring the fire under control. The heat so intense, the flames high, Father Luca holds one arm up in front of his face, shielding from the flames and heat. He swings the table cloth into the flames to no avail. Suddenly he feels a strange thing happening to him, something is pulling him back from the flames. What is happening? As he uncontrollable stumbles back from the flames, he then realizes two men had grabbed him and pulled him back from out of the flames, saving his life. There is no water, no hoses, or anything to fight the fire. A few people who lived close by raced home to get something to fight the fire, like wet blankets, a few buckets of water, but returned too late. The fire quickly consumed the entire church, only a few smoldering timbers were standing as they returned.

An exhausted Father Luca, with Adela standing by his side, hanging from their hands burnt blackened table cloths, are staring at the skeleton charred remains of their church. His black hair singed, his face red from the intense heat, his clothes covered with soot and smoke. Adela, crying, hangs onto Father Luca's shoulder, dressed in her nice festiveness dress blackened from flames and smoke. Bishop Mangini, exhausted, coughing, trying to get his breath, lying on the ground covered in black soot.

Father Luca mumbles, "How quickly the church burned," as he continues to stare at the burnt church, then he notices the bishop on the ground, turning as he rushes over to help him.

"Bishop Mangini, you all right?" Father Luca says, deeply concerned if he's hurt as he squats down beside him, helping him up into a sitting position.

"Father Luca, don't fret with me, I will be OK. See about the others," says the bishop, appearing dazed.

Adela comes to the bishop's side and offers him a cup of wine. "Bishop Mangini, this is all I could find,"

"Thank you, Adela." He takes a sip from the cup.

Other firefighters stumble around the church ruins, in shock. They can't believe what happened, talking with each other in disbelief how fast the church had burned.

✦ ✦ ✦

The next several days, the townspeople are talking about what happened about the church's fire and why it could not be saved. The church's followers could not bear the pain of seeing the charred remains of their church and had to remove it as soon as possible. In several salons, and also the mercantile building where groups of people would congregate, the big conversations and debates were, why did the church burn so fast, did someone start the fire, why would anyone want to burn down a church, and the festival fireworks had stopped almost two hours before the fire started. One day, Father Luca with several bandages on his face and one hand wrapped in a gauze is sitting in his little office doing paperwork. Two older ladies walking by the mercantile building decide to make a visit to Father Luca's office to talk with him about the loss of the church. The ladies were upset about the only church they ever had in town, having only one service in it and then it burns down. What is happening?

The older lady tells Father Luca, "It took forever to get a priest in town. I, that is we, hope you, Father Luca, will stay in town. It disturbs me that you got burned in the fire. I hope it won't hurt your handsome looks."

Feeling slightly embarrassed from the woman's comment, he replies, "Ladies, I assure you, I will stay in this wonderful town for a long time," with a big smile as he pats one of the women's hand with his bandaged hand as they leave his office.

+ + +

Several days later, Ethan, the owner of the mercantile, came into Father Luca's office.

"Father, do you have a moment? One of my employees had mentioned something to me about the church's fire, and I think you might be interested in what he knows."

"Hello, Ethan, sure. I'm always interested in things people want to talk about. Is this your employee?" he says to Ethan, as he looks at the young boy. "Yes, this is Marvin. Marvin, this is our new priest. His name is Father Luca."

"Nice to meet you, Marvin. What sort of work do you do for Ethan?"

"Well, sir, Father Luca, I mostly sweep the floors and try to keep the mice out of the building."

"That sounds like it could be a hard job at times."

"Yes, I mean, Father Luca, yes, it's hard sometimes."

"Wonderful, now you want to tell me something about the fire at the church."

"Yes, it was the day after the fire, and a friend of mine who works at the stables told me he saw something strange that night. He saw about five or six people that were not partying at the festival, standing in a group by the corner of the stables watching the fireworks, and they did not see him. He had to go and calm the nervous horses down because of the rockets and fireworks. He couldn't see their faces. My friend thought they were watching the fireworks but thought it was wrong why they were not at the festivities like everyone else. He heard them talk about the disrespectful church that was built, and why the townspeople were celebrating its first service. One of the men seem upset about the completion of the church, said to the other people with him that someone ought to burn it down. He had to go again to calm the horses down, and when he returned, they were gone."

"Interesting, Marvin, I'll pass the information on," says Father Luca as he bids goodbye to the boy as he leaves with Ethan.

"Thank you for that information," Father Luca says to Marvin and waves goodbye to Ethan as they both leave his office.

Shortly after Ethan and Marvin left Father Luca's office, Mr. Notary knocks at his open door.

"Hello, Father. Oh, I hope you didn't get burned bad," Mr. Notary comments as he's looking at his bandages.

"Not too bad, a couple firefighters got burned kind of bad but not life-threatening. They will have scars, but they will live to be very old men. Thank God."

"Yes, thank God, they are alive. Father, I have been giving some serious thinking about what I'm going to tell you with a heavy heart feeling. I am my family's third generation living here in Denver. I have four children, three boys and one girl. Two of the boys are in college in New York, and I have a wonderful wife and we are happy. I made plenty of money in the early days when people paid a lot of money for things and equipment. When the miners and the railroad first came here, they paid big money for everything. I sold a lot of land and made a fortune. Now I want to give back to this small town and help it grow into something big and prosperous and leave a good legacy for me and my family."

"Mr. Notary, I appreciate what you want to do, but I can't accept your generosity. You will be giving too much."

"Father, I knew you we're going to say that, but I have more money than I can spend."

"Yes, Mr. Notary, but I have received many inquiries from people who want to donate. You gave your heart to us when you help build the first church."

"Father, let the people donate to the church. We want to build a stone church that will last for centuries. Put their money into the stone church. I will come forward with the money now, and we will have a new church in months instead of years. It won't be a spectacular church, but it will be a grand church, a beautiful place of worship. I might add it will not have a cloth roof. I've already got the blueprints made, compliments from Mr. Duncan, our friendly architect, and all I need is yours and Bishop Mangini's approval. The construction can start within two weeks."

"You drive a very strong deal. Let's have a meeting with Bishop Mangini, and he can review the blueprints. OK, Mr. Notary."

✦ ✦ ✦

The next night, it's early evening at one of the railroad camps in the hills outside of Denver. The workers finished work for the day, and they are getting ready to eat chow. The cook has several large pots of food cooking on the fires, with a large rump of beef cooking on the grill.

Rory, a big muscular man with plenty of bulging muscles wearing a large western hat, a railroad supervisor, is talking with five of the workers. "Boys, I have to tell ya, you did an excellent job in blasting that damn boulder out of tunnel 3 today. We didn't have that much of a problem in removing the rock, and there was no collapsing of the tunnel. So I have decided that since we aren't working tomorrow, I'm going to treat you five to a celebration for an all you want beer, at a salon in town. After you have eaten and everything is cleaned up, meet me here, and we'll load up into the wagon and go into town."

The men are whooping and hollering as they danced and jumped all over the place with excitement. After the men eagerly finished their chow, they hurry to clean up everything and are waiting by the wagon for Rory. Some of the other workers that aren't going were jealous of the five workers. Rory walks over to the wagon and lights the kerosene lantern hanging in a pole on the side of the wagon as the men pile into the back end.

He gets up into the driver seat and says over his shoulder, "Are you all in?" and their answer was, "Yup."

"Giddyap." The one-horse wagon moves out of camp heading to town.

+ + +

Same night on the other side of town in the seedy red-light district in town, a bartender named Tub is standing behind the long bar, cleaning glasses in Murphy's Salon. Several women are sitting alone at a table, and in walks two big tough-looking men, dressed in three pieces pin-striped suits, wearing derbies, the short man fancying a long twisted black mustache.

"Hey, barkeep, two drafts," the shorter one calls to the bartender as they look around the salon.

Tub brings the beer over and starts to tell them the price, and the short guy flashes a couple bills in his direction. "Keep the change," he says.

"Thank you," replies Tub.

After drinking their beers for a while, the little guy calls, "Hey barkeep, come over here. Got something to say."

Tub comes over as he's polishing a bar glass with a towel. "What will it be?" "No, no, I've got something to tell ya. Me and my buddy here are down from Chicago, and we will be your protection. You see, you need protection from the police and any unruly people that may cause you to lose business. We will eliminate any people who protest about your fine house here for your women," he says as he looks over at the table with several women sitting and smiles at them.

"We will bring in women from out of town to beef up your profit, with a split of the profit for our superb service." As the short man is barking out his rules, the big guy says nothing but casually opens up his coat, exposing a large handgun hanging from his underarm holster.

"Now," as the short guy continues, "we will build a nice house for your women not too far from the railroad camp and of course with a substantial down from you."

He stops for a moment and asks Tub, "Do you have any problems with the neighbors, customers, or even the police?"

Before Tub could answer, the short guy cut's him off.

"All you have to do is give us a monthly payment for our services and protection. We require an advance payment tonight, then we can talk about the price later."

Looking flustered and nervous, the bartender responds with a shaky voice, "Thanks, thank you for your important information. But before I can make any decisions, I must talk with my partner, who is not here right now, and I'm not sure when he'll be back."

"Mr. Bartender, maybe you didn't understand what I just said." The little man's face begins to turn red, and his voice becomes deep in tone.

"We require a payment now, tonight."

Both men pause for a minute as they stare at the bartender, trying the intimidation look, the bartender begins to sweat. Just then a business type customer comes into the salon standing at the bar and orders a beer, breaking the intimidation stares from the tough guys.

"Com'n right up," Tub nervously calls out. After pulling the beer mug, the bartender brings the drink to the costumer and notices the two men are gone.

Releasing a sigh of relief, he see's something dark on the bar counter where the two men were drinking their beers. Thinking they may have left something, and will return to pick it up, he walks down to pick it up.

"Holly shit," he spurts out, stopping, not believing his eyes.

After composing himself, he takes another step to get a closer look to make sure it's what he thought it is. Laying in the middle of the bar counter is a large black hairy rat with his head recently ripped off, blood oozing from his body, forming a pool on the counter. The customer standing at the bar glances over at the rat and almost upchucks, holding his hand over his mouth, rushes out the salon and throws up in the street. The bartender frozen for a moment, not knowing what to do, then he heads into the back room and reappears in a couple of minutes with a shovel and a bottle of lye and several rags. He scoops up the rat with the shovel and walks out the front door and throws it out into the street. Taking the rags, he starts mopping up the oozing liquid that came out of the rat and pours the disinfectant on the counter and uses another rag to clean the area up. He takes all the cleaning material back into the back room and comes back out to the bar. He's ready for business.

CHAPTER 18

Its early evening, Rory has been traveling for a couple of hours on a rough dirt road driving his wagon from his campsite in the mountains as he pulls up in front of the salon in town, his wagon filled with five railroad workers eager to celebrate and drink beer. He gets down from the wagon, walks around, turns off the kerosene lamp, and ties up the horse to the hitching post as the men scramble out of the wagon and rush into the salon. One of the men mumbles, "Thanks boss man," Rory's nickname the workers call him.

Rory walks in and up to the bar, telling the bartender, "Give these guys all the beer they want, and it's all on me."

"Gotcha," replies the bartender as he starts filling mugs, with two mugs per person. The workers heads to the back of the room carrying their beer, taking over several tables, and begin to drink.

Sometime later at the salon, as the men are celebrating and drinking plenty of mugs of beer, keeping the bartender busy going back and forth from their tables, Rory leans with his back to the bar having several beers himself, watching the men get shit-faced.

Half an hour later, a tough-looking guy named Merle, a railroad worker, comes to the entrance of the salon. Standing at the door, he looks around, then walks over to Rory.

"I decided to come for my free beers," he says. Rory causally looks at the tough guy. "You weren't invited."

"Hell, I don't need an invitation. Riding in the back end of that damn wagon, it's too goddamn hard on my ass, so I rode a horse."

"The horse is not yours. It's a company horse for business only."

"I was given the horse, Ask Charlie when you get back."

"Sorry, Charlie is sitting over there in the corner getting drunk with his friends. The free beer is over, and you missed it."

Both men stand, staring at each other for a moment. Merle with his fist clenched knows if he got into a fight with the boss man, he will lose his job and most likely lose the fight. He hits his fist hard on the counter. "Yeah, I'll order a beer and you can pay for it."

"It's your choice," replies Rory.

"Hey, barkeep, give me a free beer."

The bartender looks at Rory as he shakes his head no and starts to walk away. Suddenly, Merle pushes his finger into Rory's gut to make a point. Rory grabs Merle's wrist, twisting and whirls him around with his belly facing the bar using his other hand and puts Merle's face down on the bar as Merle's face showing pain. Briefly talking through clinched teeth, Merle apologizes to Rory as he calms down. Rory agrees and gives Merle one free beer as Merle moves down to the other end of the bar.

Sometime later, as business picks up in the salon, about a dozen customers arrives drinking and eating food. The bartender is very busy now, when a young boy about the age of ten arrives and begins cleaning tables using a wooden tray, piling mugs, bottles, and plates into the tray. The boy, just little taller than the tables, moves around through the crowd, carrying everything into the backroom.

In the backroom, there's a large two basin washtubs with a water hose. The boy gets up on a wooden box besides the tubs and starts washing the plates, glasses, and eating utensils using the hose to rinse them off. The boy takes the used glasses with any liquid in them and pours their contents into one glass on his counter. Almost all of the glasses are from drinking beers, a few are wine. Most of the glasses with whiskey, gin, and vodkas have a little residue left in them.

Once his glass gets filled, he drinks it. If any food or food scraps are left on the customer plates, he cleans them off into a pale he has beside the tubs. This food will be his only meal, it's the way he survives. The salon owner knows this; it's his benefit for working there.

Several hours later, the boss man announces it's time to go, "Let's load up, were heading back to camp, the party is over."

As the men start to stumble out to the wagon, the boss man pays the bartender the bill.

"Thanks, Rory, our place is always open to yeah." The bartender rings up the sale on the cash register.

Rory walks outside as he's checking and adjusting the horse's rigging, lights the kerosene lantern, and hangs it on the pole attached to the wagon. The drunk workmen with difficulty make their way outside to the wagon. Two of them are holding each other up as they weave through the tables stumbling on several chairs as they work their way outside. One of the men is wobbling, barely standing as he's peeing on the wagon wheel talking to himself. Another drunk is hanging on the end of the wagon on his belly, as he keeps trying to lift his leg to the edge of the wagon, then he tries the other leg and that won't work either. He's trying to get his legs into the wagon as he mumbles, "They won't go up into the wagon, what can I do?" "Here, Carlo, let me help you into the wagon," the boss man says, using one hand, grasps him by the butt of his pants and lifts him up into the wagon. "Is that better?" Rory, not sure if everyone is in the wagon as they are laying all over each other and it's dark out there, walks back into the salon to take another look. "Hey, Rory, did you forget someone?" says the bartender jokingly.

"Just making sure they're all out there, until next time," he says, tipping his hat as he goes back out to the wagon. Rory takes a brief look at the drunks lying in a pile in the back of the wagon.

He gets up in the seat and calls back over his shoulder, "Is everyone here?" He doesn't hear a reply. "Hey," he yells, "I said is everyone here?"

He gets a couple muffled replies, "Yeah, we're," and that is all. The big man picks up the reins and calls out to the horse, "Giddyap," as the wagon heads down the street going back to camp.

It's late now, the old wagon, its worn wheels squeaky as it rumbles along the rough trail, seems like it hit every pothole there is. A time down the road, Rory starts to get a little tired eyes. He reaches into his shirt pocket and pulls out a small harmonica and begins to play some music and throws in a few lines to one of his old songs he used to sing when he needed company.

After being on the trail for an hour or so, it takes longer traveling at night. Chester, sitting at the end of the wagon, begins to get sick. Gripping a rope that's tied to the wagon's side, with one hand, he manages to hang out over the end of the wagon and begins to throw up. He is sick to his stomach. He's making all sorts of ugly noises, coughing, throwing up, gagging, and making horrible sounds like he's gurgling in his vomit.

The drunk sitting beside Chester yells, "Shut up, you're making me sick."Chester continues to upchuck. The complaining drunk gives Chester a hard elbow blow to his back, knocking him out of the wagon. Chester hits hard on the dirt, not making a sound.

+ + +

Sometime later, Rory arrives at the railroad camp site. He gets down from the wagon, turns out the kerosene lamp, and walks around to the end of the wagon. "Everyone, wake up, we're back at the camp. Go and get some sleep," he says. The drunk men begin to stir around as he helps them out of the end of the wagon.

"Hey, wait a minute," the boss man says. "There's only four in the wagon. We are short one guy. I counted everyone before we left the salon." Rory looks at one of the men. "Did you see anyone fall out of the wagon?"

"I don't know, I was sleeping."

Not being able to see well in the dark, Rory gets up close and looks each man in their faces and realizes Chester is missing.

Rory, standing in the dark as the drunks start stumbling toward their tents to go to sleep, mumbles to himself, "Damn, Chester is out there, and I don't know where he is. Got to go back and find him now, hope he is alive."

Quickly he begins to start looking through the tents for someone who's not drunk, who can go with him to look for Chester. Rory finds a horse wrangler who is sober in one of the tents, and they head back down the trail where he had come up earlier that evening from town.

Rory, wearing his western hat, and the wrangler are both riding slowly down the trail heading back to town.

"We may have to go all the way back to town. I don't have any idea of when he fell out of the wagon. If he's walking, I hope he stays close to the trail," says Rory.

After riding for a while, Rory says in a tired voice, "After all that beer they drank, I can't visualize him walking at all, he's probably passed out somewhere. I don't know where."

"It will be hard to see him if he gets off the trail, with these clumps of bushes and small ravines since the moon is not out tonight," the wrangler says in a questionable tone.

"Yeah," replies Rory.

"Slow down, I think he's over, no, go on. It's just a shadow."

Rory quietly says, "Yeah, these shadows can really trick you."

Sometime later, Rory says, "There he is, on my side. Right on the edge of the trail." Rory quietly lets out.

Stopping the wagon, both men get down and walk over to retrieve Chester. Rory pulls off one of his leather gloves and puts his fingers on the side of Chester's neck, feeling for a pulse. "Yeah, he's alive, got a pulse."

Putting his glove back on, he tells the wrangler, "You grab his feet, I'll get his shoulders." They pick up Chester, carrying him to the back of the wagon, and put him into the back.

"He might have hit his head when he fell out, or maybe broke his neck," the wrangler mentions.

"Yeah, I want the doc to check him out in the morning. There's not much we can do for him tonight, what's left of it." He looks out at the horizon and sees the morning glow in the sky as morning's right around the corner. Both men get back into the wagon and head for camp.

✦ ✦ ✦

This is not part of the novel *Usurper*, which you have been reading. As the Author of this novel I wanted to write a small snippet of history about a circumstance that correlates with this story of a drunk man, and another drunk man who was a famous author you are about to read, falling out of a moving vehicle and is retrieved hours later. Ernest Hemingway, a famous American author who won a Nobel Prize in literature in 1954, was traveling around in Africa writing his novels. Him and his friends were staying in an African village somewhere out in the wild parts of Africa, possibly near or in the country of Kenya. Ernest's friend was driving a jeep, and they went to another village to meet other friends and have dinner and drinks. Mr. Hemingway was a very heavy drinker. His friend took the shortcut, not using a road, going out through an area with wild animals such as lions, leopards, hyenas, elephants, and other wild animals that are looking for food. In those days, wild animals were more prevalent, and Africa was still wild in most parts.

After the dinner was over, Ernest and his friend were totally drunk, They helped each other to get into their jeep and headed back to their camp miles away. As Ernest's friend drove the jeep, he was weaving everywhere, and Ernest falls out of the jeep somewhere on their way back. The jeep did not have doors, so there was nothing to keep him in. After taking a long time to get back to camp, upon arriving, their friends came out to help Ernest and his friend when they noticed Ernest was not in the vehicle. After a quick search of the vehicle, they were shocked that he was not in the jeep. It was hard for his friends to accept the fact that the driver did not know that Ernest had fallen out, a man sitting right next to him in the front seat had fallen out of his vehicle as he drove back to the camp. For a few moments, Ernest's friends theorized there could be foul play. After some arguing and finger-pointing, the friends at the camp got into several vehicles and drove with their high lights tracking back to the other camp made by the wheel tracks on the ground. Everyone was very concerned that Ernest could be eaten or mauled by some wild animals. They found him several hours later, passed out laying in the wild bush. People had speculated the reason no animals ate him was, he horribly stunk from alcohol.

CHAPTER 19

A couple weeks after the horrible fire, Father Luca before the Sunday service, sits in his office at the mercantile building. He's struggling to write an explanation to tell the parishioners of why the burning of the church. He keeps writing over and over again; he needs to say something that has logic, but nothing was making any sense. There needs to be compassion and forgiveness and where does he start. He keeps looking through all the notes he had written, and his Bible with underlined prayers and things that were said in other church services while he was in New Jersey. As he sits, his mind keeps coming up with blanks; he needs to say something. Adela comes into the office and sees he's getting frustrated. "You look very tense, Mariano. Is there something I can help you with?"

"Adela," he begins, then he stops, he's frustrated, and seems to him there is no other way out, and decides he will tell her the truth about himself.

Stopping himself again, he begins to think, *Can I really tell her that? A lie that I have kept from everyone in town, Father Mariano Luca is not my real name. It's Antonio Ferretti, a man with nothing from Trenton, New Jersey. I'm not a real priest. I hadn't had any teaching or training to be a priest. I stole a priests name, I stole his church's stationery to write my lie on, and mail it to Bishop Mangini here in Denver. I'm just a guy from New Jersey, my hometown. I made a very bad mistake, lying and using everyone to get what I wanted. My journey has come to an end.*

Back home, when I got this cozy idea about becoming a priest to make a lot of money, oh how blind I was. I remember my close friend, Nolan, telling me back home, if I get caught and my identity is revealed, the townspeople will be very angry and may kill me, or put me in prison, or shame me and run me out of town.

"Mariano," Adela says, not knowing that she has just saved his live from total self-destruction.

"Are you trying to write something about the burning of the church? I can see all this notes you have all over your desk."

"Yes, Adela, it's hard. I have no words to say, nothing appears on my paper."

Adela begins, "I can understand, it's hard to explain something that was so bizarre. Who has the answers? The only person who has the answer is the one who's done it. Speak with your heart, and it will sound right. Relax, you have given beautiful sermons before. I'm sure you will have a wonderful sermon."

Listening carefully to what Adela is telling him, Father Luca has decided to change his mind. He won't tell her about his past. Her encouragement and her convincing talk, brought him back. Yes, he can do it, he gets his confidence back and begins to write the words that he has been seeking.

✦ ✦ ✦

It's Monday afternoon, the day is almost over as Father Luca and Adela put away the paperwork they've been working on as they prepare to go home.

Father Luca tells Adela, "When we finish tonight, I need you to stay for a while. I got something very important to show you." She looks a bit suspicious at him, wondering what he is planning. He has never acted this way before.

After Adela has put her papers away, she's having a conversation with a female clerk closing out her register around the corner in the building. Father Luca is still in the office working on something.

Sister Stella, who periodically helps with the extra work in the office, is somewhere in the building or maybe she has gone home. The clerk puts the money in the safe and tells Adela good night after a brief talk and leaves the building, turning off the lights before leaving the building.

Adela turns around and walks back to her office to see what Father Luca wants to show her.

She abruptly stops at the door, not saying a word, with an astonished look on her face. "What's happening?" She gasps. The office looks very different since she was in there twenty minutes ago. The tables and chairs have been rearranged and there is a lighted candle in the middle of the table. Getting her eyes adjusted to the candle light, she can now see better. Father Luca had moved his desk over against the wall and put a dark red velvet fabric over the end table, where their lamp had been and replaced it with a tall candle, moving it to the middle of the room. He had moved the two chairs on the opposite side of the table.

She see's Father Luca smiling, standing beside the table. He asks, "Adela, will you sit at the table on the right side," as he motions in that direction. Stunned, she slowly moves to the chair, not taking her eyes off Father Luca, and sits down. She's trying to figure out what is he's thinking, what is happening, and why is he so serious? She notices there's a Bible and a red rose on the other side of the table and a beautiful head scarf neatly folded lying on her side of the table.

Father Luca sits down smiling, never moving his eyes off her, looking at her for a few moments as he sits down, not moving or saying anything as his smile turns serious.

"Adela, I have something I need to say to you, and it won't wait." Pausing for moment, like he is thinking of something, then he says, "I love you very much, and I have always loved you ever since we met on the train heading to Chicago, some time ago."

The candle in the middle of the table, burning brightly, flickers ever so often. He then lays his right hand on the Bible, then he asks her to put the lovely head scarf on her head. He patiently waits as she puts on the head scarf, as the candle between them flickers several times almost going out from a draft coming from under the door. Father Luca hands Adela the red rose.

Their eyes are locked on each other, their faces are sober. Adela slowly puts her hand on his and follows with the other hand holding the rose. He puts his other hand on hers as the both squeeze each other.

He softly says, "Adela, I love you very much." She smiles with tears beginning to form in her eyes.

Then Father Luca begins as he slightly chokes on his words. "Do you, Adela Finnly, take Mariano Luca to be your husband?" Adela, dazed and surprised, as she struggles to speak, then she finally, in a soft voice, says, "I do."

He continues, "Do you, Mariano Luca, take Adela Finnly to be your beautiful loving wife?" Then he quietly says, "I do."

Then he brings out a wedding band from his frock and slips it onto her finger as tears begin coming down her face.

Father Luca, in a stern and quiet voice, says, "Under the watchful eyes of our God, I, Father Mariano Luca, of Denver, Colorado, in the United States of America pronounce both Adela and Mariano husband and wife. We may now kiss."

Father Luca carefully moves the candle over to the side of table. He slowly leans over the table being careful of the flame, and Adela leans over as well. They both kiss, holding the kiss for a long time.

After they kissed, they sat there looking at each other for a while, not saying a word, then with sad faces, they both reach over and slowly started to slide the wedding band off from Adela's finger. Halfway down her finger, they both stop. Father Luca in a sad voice says, "Dear, I love you very much, but this is the only way we will ever be together."

She starts weeping. "I know it has to happen. I love you so much. For the sake of our lives and God, we cannot reveal our marriage."

"Yes, it saddens me very much. Marriage is strictly forbidden for a priest in the church and society."

Slowly they both remove the wedding band as she puts it into her handbag. "I will keep it here for the rest of our lives."

As the candle flickers, it shows a shadow of Sister Stella that helps out in the church operations, standing, not moving beside the filing cabinet in the corner next to the door with a shocked look on her face as she quickly disappears.

+ + +

About a week later, Bishop Mangini comes by the mercantile building in his carriage with Christopher driving to pick up Father Luca and head to the train station to greet and bring Sister Cabrini to the bishop's compound, the train arriving around 2:00 p.m.

As the bishop's carriage arrives at the mercantile building, Father Luca is waiting out in front of the building with Adela talking about some business issues. Father Luca tells goodbye to Adela, gets aboard the carriage as Bishop Mangini waves to Adela. "Good morning, Adela," he says as she waves back.

Bishop Mangini's driver, Christopher, decides to bring the large carriage so they will be able to accommodate all of Sister Cabrini's luggage. Their ride takes them through different parts of town as they talked about what Sister Cabrini can do for the children. After arriving at the station, they are told by the station manager the train is going to be late, maybe half an hour to an hour, so they decided to wait in their carriage in the shade of their carriage cover.

As they sat, Father Luca is thinking that he is going to meet a holy sister who knew the Pope from the Vatican personally. She will have traveled over thousands of miles, sailed across the Atlantic Ocean, and traveled halfway across the United States just to be here in Denver, Colorado. It will be an honor to be riding with her in the bishop's carriage, and that he will be working with her and the bishop in projects especially with the children. But he must be vigilant and stay his distance, hoping she will not notice his inexperience as a priest.

As they sat waiting for the train, the bishop, feeling a bit sleepy, relaxes and falls asleep. Sometime later, the noise from the trains steaming, being released as the train arrives, wakes the bishop up. Sitting up, he looks around, it appears he is trying to wake up, and says to Father Luca, "Well, it's time, I hope she is on the train." Both men get out of the carriage and walks over to the passenger and unloading dock.

Before her trip to come to Denver, Sister Cabrini had planned to go and work in China, but her mission was reworked by Pope Leo XIII at the Vatican. He told the bright and very intelligent Sister, "Not to the East, but to the West," so she came to work in Denver, Colorado, with the many children that needed help.

As Sister Cabrini got out of the train and recognized Bishop Mats and Father Luca, she starts to walk over to them. As she walked toward them, the petite young woman seemed to radiate with a sense of holiness. Bishop Matz did all the introductions, and Christopher started to pick up all the baggage she had brought and started to pile them into the carriage.

After Christopher loaded all of Sister Cabrini's luggage into the carriage, they all were off to Bishop Mats compound, where she will live. Sister Cabrini is very excited to have finished her trip and is very tired from the long, grueling trip and needed some time to recuperate. As they rode in the carriage, she briefly talked about her travels and her ideas of what she will be working toward, especially with the children of the town. Father Luca, knowing to himself that he was a fake, had trouble looking at Sister Cabrini in her eyes, thinking that she could see through him and his lies. He politely talked briefly to her, asking a few simple questions and just hoped she would not ask him about working in New Jersey.

Bishop Mats explained a few things to Sister Cabrini about what was happening with the children in this part of Denver. There was an enormous amount of Italian, Irish, and Chinese immigrants in the area. Many adults could not make a living to support their family, and the children suffered. Going to school was not an option for some families, where the children had to work as well. There were parents who could not make it and left town, leaving their children behind to survive on their own. Children grew up fast and were working in gold mines, and many died building the railroads. As the children grew up, they were considered to be adults at the ages of ten to twelve years. Many worked in salons and even prostitution. There was no child labor in those days.

As they were riding in their carriage, Bishop Mangini and Father Luca planned to take Sister Cabrini for a tour of the town, showing her where everything was, but then they realized she was very exhausted from her trip, and postponed the tour for another time.

After arriving at Bishop Mangini's beautiful compound, Sister Cabrini insisted that she needs take a nice warm bath and some beautiful rest time.

CHAPTER 20

Several days later on a gorgeous sunny day, Thomas walks with Adela as they go shopping at the outdoor produce lot several blocks away from her house. Thomas had nothing to do today and volunteered to help Adela carry home her groceries. She's made plans to cook a special dinner that evening and decided to pick up some special meat and greens. She also felt the office needed to be spruced up and planned to pick up a bouquet of flowers at the flower stand on the way back home.

As they walked along the dirt road, they talked about their idea of what their town is going to be like in several years.

As they talked, Adela brought up the subject. "Do you think that Father Luca would be able to get financing or a developer would be interested in building the new stone church?"

"I did hear that Mr. Notary was interested in talking with Father Luca about another church. He might have another investor who is interested. He was over at the bank talking with the manager, Mr. Youngblood, last week, and that's all I know," says Thomas.

"It would be wonderful if we got a nice big stone church built, right here in this part of town," Adela says as she's looking up into a tree where a bird is chirping.

"Yes, that's also my dream, and I hope I will be part of it when it happens," says Thomas.

As they walk, they got closer to several large vegetable lots, as they see many tomato plants, several long rows of carrots, beside several rows of broccoli, turnips, radishes, cauliflower, green beans strung up on stretched wires, and a lot of cucumbers winding along the edge of the garden. They see a man and a woman hunched over, working in one of the parcels. They are busy working hard pulling weeds and harvesting a few plants. As Adela and Thomas got closer, they could see the two people working in the yard are older Italian farmers in their sixties. As they got closer, both farmers stand up and greet them.

"Good morning," the farmers say.

"Hello," Thomas and Adela replies.

"We want to buy some vegetables this morning."

"That's wonderful," replies the woman as she stretches her back. She starts walking up to the front of the garden where there's a small stand and picks up a knife and a small hand shovel.

"Tell me, what would you like, and I will get it for you. Do you have something I can put them into?"

"Oh, yes," replies Adela as she hands the woman a cloth bag that she brought.

"I would like one head of broccoli, half a dozen carrots, a small head of lettuce, and a red pepper."

"Yes, is that all you wish to have?"

"Yes, that would be all."

As the older woman went out into the garden looking for the items, Adela is standing there watching the older man working in the garden.

Not long after, the older woman returns and Adela asks, "Ma'am, I was wondering how do you make business, not very many people come by here."

The older Italian woman replies, "Oh, we don't sell much here. Twice a week, we hook up our horse and wagon and take all the vegetable downtown and sell almost everything we take."

As they were talking, the older woman looks at Adela like she was thinking of something, then says to her, "I think I saw you at church at the mercantile building a couple weeks ago. That was the first time me and my husband went to church here. There hasn't been a church here, ever, and we have to start planning if it's going to be every week."

"Oh yes, the church service is going to be Sunday. Oh, Father Luca, he's a very personable and charming priest. When you see him next week, introduce yourself to him. He's a wonderful man, and I hope to see you there next week."

Adela pays the woman, and she and Thomas continues walking down the street looking for a meat store.

+ + +

Later that evening, as Adela prepares a scrumptious dinner at her small house several blocks away from the church, a knock comes from the front door, and she answers.

"Hello, hello, Mariano," she says as she greets her dinner guest.

"And a very good evening to you, my love," Mariano replies as he hands her a bottle of red wine and gives her a little kiss to her lips.

"I see you got my note," she says.

"Yes, a real nice surprise. Something smells real nice," he says as he's trying to open the bottle of wine.

"Time to eat," she says as she comes into the dining area carrying a large plate of meat.

"Here, I'll help you,"

"No, no, you stay seated. I'm the cook, I'm in charge here," she says as she giggles.

+ + +

As they're eating the wonderful dinner, Mariano suddenly notices that Adela is wearing the wedding band that they both removed when they got married.

"Adela, your ring looks beautiful," he says as he raises his glass of wine. "I want to make a secretive toast." She raises her glass of wine as well.

"I want to toast to the most beautiful woman I have ever met, and to my loving wife."

"Thank you very much, my lovely, handsome husband." They touch glasses and take a drink.

+ + +

Around a week later on the other side of town, Bishop Mangini and Father Luca arrived in their carriage at an empty dirt lot in the corner of town. Mr. Notary and Mr. Youngblood, the local bank manager, arrived in their carriage as well. The four men begin to walk around the large lot, looking at the open land talking about building the long-awaited stone church for the area.

Then Father Luca and Mr. Youngblood, a well-dressed big man wearing a black stove top hat, were talking about how many parishioners come to the services at the mercantile.

"So you are telling me, Father Luca, there are about fifty, possibly more parishioners that come to your service every Sunday, and new parishioners are coming every Sunday. That sounds good. I should be coming to your service soon."As they talk and walk around the large vacant lot, Mr. Youngblood is smoking a large cigar as they dodge large clump of weeds and walk around numerous dried-out tumbleweeds. Every so often, Mr. Youngblood turns his head and spits some of the cigar juice onto the ground.

Mr. Notary mentions, "This parcel of land is considerably larger than the parcel that was used to build the wooden church that had mysteriously burned down last year."

"Yes, that's right," says Father Luca. "Adela and I where both there battling the blaze with nothing except our tablecloths. We had nothing to fight the fire with. There was no water available. I could not believe what was happening."

"That fire was horrible, it almost killed me as well!" mumbles Bishop Mangini as he continues to walk around looking at the ground. As the men walked around the land, having a few small talks, Bishop Mangini quietly walks around reminiscing the past. He looks at Father Luca and Mr. Notary. "It was maybe just a little over a year ago, that both of you and myself walked around in a smaller part of land on the other side of town talking about our new church."

"Yes, it was that long ago, or was it longer? So sad," Mr. Notary says as he playfully kicks a small rock lying on the ground.

"Mr. Notary, you know you don't have to put any more money into building of this new church."

"Nonsense, Bishop Mangini. I owe this new town a lot more than you realize. Sometime when I'm sitting alone thinking about the mistake I had made, I get this knot in my gut, and it won't go away for sometime. When I made the simple wooden church, I made some people in the area very upset and mad, which some people called it the cheap church. I have my suspensions on who and why the church was burned down, but I won't talk about that now. There has never been a church in this area, and I go and build a simple wooden church. What was I thinking? I can understand their feelings."

"No, no," replies Bishop Mangini. "You and all of us thought what we were doing was the right thing to do at that time because of our finances and some other trivial things. Things have changed now, so let's all plan together, and no regrets."

"OK, I need to focus on the new magnificent stone church. There's a lot of people here that had waited for a very long time for a church, and now I'm going to give them what they have been waiting for a very long time."

"You're right," replies Bishop Mangini.

"Well, Mr. Notary," says Youngblood, "tomorrow, stop by the bank, and we can talk about a few small essential things, and then we can get this going."

"That sounds wonderful, Mr. Youngblood. Say about ten in the morning."

"Agree."

All four men got back into their waiting buggies and head back into town.

+ + +

Several days later at the church service in the mercantile, almost everyone in town has shown up as they are crowded into the building, all trying to find a seat. Bishop Mangini has his preferred seat, sitting on the bags of potatoes off to one side. A few of the parents had put their children standing on the service counter next to the cash register. Father Luca comes out of his office and squeezes his way up to the front of the building, where his apple crate is at and gets assistance from Ethan to get up on it. "Let us bow our heads and pray," he says as he conducts the service, using the underlined pages out of his Bible.

As the service ends, Father Luca makes an announcement. "Mr. Notary, who everyone knows, would like to update you on the progress of the new stone church. Please, Mr. Notary, if you will come to the front so everyone can hear you."

The audience erupts into a long-lasting applause.

"Thank you, thank you," replies Mr. Notary.

"Yes, I have very good news about the construction of our new beautiful church. I got with the bank in town two days ago, and we signed the papers. Now comes the waiting period. I will keep you posted on when the construction is scheduled to begin. Hopefully it won't be too long, much of the material has to be shipped in by wagon or by train. I can tell you, after looking at the blueprints and talking with the designers, the church is going to be a wonderful, spectacular church with many details to its exterior and interior, made out of stone, and will last for hundreds of years."

+ + +

A couple days later on the other side of town, Doc Murphy, the town doctor, talks with Andy, the undertaker, as they are standing in front of the undertaker's building with several completed coffins standing on their ends leaning against the wall. Andy is telling Doc a strange story about what just happened this last week.

"Doc, there's this rancher, way on the south side of town, I don't think you know them. Well, anyway, the rancher suddenly dies, and his wife didn't have any cash to bury him. So she was going to have some of her workers dig a hole and bury him in their back country. I told her she can't do that. There is a law about that. She has to have someone look the body over and write a death certificate. You didn't hear about this guy dying, did you?"

"No, I don't know anything about a death out there." "Well, anyway, she's going to give me one of their cattle to pay for the proper burial. I can't accept a cow. I think that is way too much money to pay for a funeral. Besides, I don't know anything about cattle. Where am I going to keep him? Thinking about this, I think one cow is way too much of a payment for a burial, unless I add many extras, like maybe a special coffin, and dress him in fancy clothes. But that is too late now. The rancher is already in the ground. I don't know what I'm going to do."

"Hey, Andy, I'd like to stay and talk, but I've got to get back over to the Mac Greggers. The wife is having a few problems in preparing to have her delivery. Hopefully in a couple of days she'll have her delivery. Maybe by then, you can tell me what's your decision on how the woman rancher is going to pay you."

CHAPTER 21

nother nice and warm day, Bishop Mangini, with Mother Cabrini in his carriage, pulls up in front of Mr. and Mrs. Notary's house in their circle driveway. Christopher, the driver, gets down from his seat and puts out the foot stool for Mother Cabrini and Bishop Mangini to step on, and they get down from the carriage. Mother Cabrini comments to Bishop Mangini, "What a lovely house they have, looks just like the way you had described it."

Just at that moment, the front door opens, and out walks Mrs. Carmine Notary. "Hello, Mother Cabrini and Bishop Mangini. Isn't it a wonderful day for a ride?" She opens both of her arms out wide to greet both of them. As they approach the front door, she puts out her hand to assist Bishop Mangini as he steps over the threshold, as they enter her house.

"Mother Cabrini, how was your long trip from Rome? Must have been a grueling trip." Carmine asks."It definitely was grueling at times, but I enjoyed all the interesting people I met along the way. Yes, there were days when I said to myself, why, but then I deeply knew this is where I should be."

A Mexican housekeeper comes walking around the corner into the room where they were seating, carrying a tray with a hot teapot and cups and a few finger pastries for everyone.

"Ah, a nice cup of tea will help take that dryness out of our mouth after a ride in the carriage," Mrs. Notary says, and Mother Cabrini nods her head of approval.

Glancing around the room, Mother Cabrini compliments Carmine on her house. "You have a very lovely house."

"Thank you, Mother Cabrini. My husband has a wonderful gift in selecting just the right furnishings." Mrs. Notary helps with passing around the cups of tea.

Bishop Mangini looks at Carmine and says, "Someday, you should stop by for a visit and try Christopher's amazing tea. He uses flower petals."

"That sounds wonderful. I will have to try his tea one of these days," says Mrs. Notary.

Bishop Mangini addresses, "Carmine, I had suggested to Mother Cabrini about your suggestion of using part of your house as a school classroom to teach the orphan children."

Carmine looks at Mother Cabrini. "Oh yes," she says. "I have this nice large room at the back of my house that would be perfect for what you are looking for. There's a small toilet attached that can be used by the children. My husband had used this room for his office, very convenient with its own exit door to the outside."

"Sounds wonderful," Mother Cabrini says.

"I think you would love this room. Would you like to look at it right now?"

"Yes, that would be a nice," replies Mother Cabrini as both women put their cups down and stand up and start walking, Mother Cabrini following Mrs. Notary.

As they walk to the back of the house, Mrs. Notary suggests to Mother Cabrini, "I was thinking, instead of you staying on the other side of town at Bishop Mangini's bungalow at his villa, you can stay here. There is a small room that my husband had used for storage attached to the large room, you can use as a bedroom. A few things we can move around, and it will be a bedroom in no time."

"That sounds like a wonderful idea, but I must talk with Bishop Mangini. He had made all these plans and other things long before I arrived, and I really don't want to spoil any of his plans."

"Yes, I understand. Talk it over with Bishop Mangini, and let me know. You realize by staying here, you won't have to take a carriage ride to get here and go home every time you give a class." "I'll talk with Bishop Mangini and let you know."

+ + +

High in the mountains about forty miles from town, the railroad workers are in the process of drilling and blasting several tunnels through the hard granite rock. The railroad is bringing the train tracks west, splintering several lines in other directions. The railroad has a large mountain range it has to go through heading west to California.

Rory, a railroad supervisor, standing a couple hundred feet from the entrance of one of the tunnels that's being worked in, starts to review the safety procedure with several dynamiters, Jaree, Mizo, and Arturo.

Rory's giving the class as he says, "Prepping a blasting area is paramount in all conditions before the actual blast. Guys, now listen up, this is very important. After we have a blast, and before we start hauling out all the rocks and debris, I want you guys to be responsible in making sure the support beams both top and side are secured. After everything is cleared, do a once over, making sure everything is good. We don't want a tunnel to collapse. Some of those beams will loosen up from the shockwave and the movement of the ground. Once everything is on a go, then you start organizing your long fuse and start drilling your holes. You have a long way from the blasting site to the entrance of the tunnel. In the back of your mind, when cutting the fuse, always remember how far the entrance is from you. Now remember when you are cutting the fuse, don't short cut the fuse and the dynamite explodes while you are still in the tunnel because you can kiss your rear ass goodbye. At that time, it's all up to you and your team. I don't want any cave ins while you guys are drilling to place your charges.

"Hey, boss," says Jaree, "do we bring Arturo with us each time we go in? Normally we don't bring him when we light the charge."

"Yes, in the past, we didn't need him every time, but I got some flack last time from the higher ups. Now all three of you guys go in together every time. If you run into problems, three is a lot better than two. I want you guys to be our three-man team with experience. You remember last month, we had a cave-in in the other tunnel when those guys were drilling a hole in the soft part of the rock to place the dynamite charge. It must have been the vibration in the rocks, making the timber loose, and two men were killed. I don't want that to happened again. OK, I've got to get up to the tracks where they are bringing in the rail ties. There's some kind of problem. See ya later," Rory says as he leaves and gets on his horse and ride away."Let's get your sulfur torches," Jaree says to Mizo as they walk over to their wooden storage shed. "Grab a few of those picks and the sledgehammer.""How many sledgehammers?" Mizo asks.

"Two would be fine."

"OK, let's do it by the manual," says Jaree.

"Both you guys, get your hand picks and spikes, putting them into several backpacks."They close up the door and head toward the other building.

Jaree opens the door to a small metal building with dynamite printed on its door and walls. He picks up a shoulder satchel, picks up four sticks of dynamite, and picks up a roll with forty feet of fuse. Dividing them up, putting fuses in one side, and the dynamite on the other side. He then picks up the ignition striker, used to light the dynamite fuse, putting it into a small pouch on the outside of the bag.

"Let's go," says Jaree as they start walking toward the entrance of the tunnel.

✦ ✦ ✦

About an hour and a half passes, when suddenly male voices can be heard yelling from inside the tunnel entrance. "Blast in the tunnel, blast in the tunnel!" Three men came running out of the tunnel heading about one hundred feet toward a metal blast wall to hide behind from flying rocks and debris, located slightly off center to the tunnel entrance. A large piece of steel imbedded into the ground for workers, dynamiters, and observers to hide behind for their protection.

The men sprinted toward the steel wall, making a spectacular dive behind it as they crash together on the rocky ground. There they lay for a long minute waiting for the blast, when Mizo says, "Damn, I hope the fuse didn't go out."

"Yeah, I think everything was set correctly," says Arturo.

A couple seconds passes, suddenly an enormous loud roar belches out of the tunnel, ground shaking violently, feeling like the end of the world is happening. All around the edges of the work site, falling rocks can be heard coming from high places. A barrage of flying rocks bounces off the metal plate the men are shielding behind. "Holly shit!" yells Jaree."How many sticks did you use?" asks Mizo."I used four, just like what the manual called for."

A large black cloud of dust and powder smoke blew out of the tunnel hanging over the tunnel's entrances. The men slowly get up from the ground dusting themselves off, wiping their faces to remove the dust.

+ + +

Couple weeks later on a warm afternoon day, Doc Murphy is breathing heavy as he came walking up to the front of the mercantile building as Father Luca was out putting up a notice on the bulletin board.

"Hello, Father. I was hoping that I would find you, and here you are, thank goodness."

"Hi, Doc, I'm just putting up a notice for Mother Cabrini. She's going to have a meeting for all ladies interested in working with her to help the orphans and homeless children. She'll be working with Mrs. Notary, and they're going to set up a classroom at her wonderful house. She has this spectacular back room perfect for a classroom, used to be her husband's office when he was busy working in his earlier days. I think she may be living there instead of Bishop Mangini's villa."

"Yeah, I know," says Doc. "It would be too far to travel every time she has a class if she stayed at the bishop's villa."

"It's just going to be a ladies' gathering this Thursday here in the mercantile. I think she's looking for suggestions and ideas."

"Father, there's just one little thing I can think of. Who is going to gather up these children, and where are they going to stay? Some of those kids have full-time jobs, most likely being paid cheap pay. It's going to be a large task. I truly sympathize for Mother Cabrini in her efforts. Is Mrs. Notary going to house some of the children in her house?"

"I'm not sure. She's thinking about it, but we'll see what ideas Mother Cabrini has. She is the expert. I have seen some of those poor children working like slaves, Doc. These are the things Mother Cabrini is going to talk about at her meetings."

"Father, I almost forgot the reason I came over here, it's important."

"Doc, are you saying you didn't come over here to say hi and have a good conversation?"

"Mariano, you know what I mean."

"Yes, I know, Doc. What is so important on such a beautiful day, what's happening in your part of town?"

"Father, I was out at the Gardner's house yesterday. I think you know him. He owns the lumber company on the outskirts of town. If I'm correct, he is the man who donated a lot of the lumber to make our first church, the one that burned down."

"Oh, yeah, I remember him. That was some time ago, shortly after I had arrived here in town."

"It takes me hours to get to the Gardner's house, and that's when the weather is good. Poor Mr. Gardner is right on the edge of leaving this earth. I have been trying everything that I can't think of, and there is no hope. His health is deteriorating as we speak. His wife is extremely stressed out, and she don't know what she is going to do if he dies. She told me that I need to get with you, and you have to get out there and give him his last rites before he dies.

Now, like I said, I can't guarantee how long he is going to live. So I think you better get out there right now, or hell is going to happen if he dies before he gets his rites. I just know it."

"Doc, it's already in the afternoon."

"I know it, Father."

"You have to ride with me, I'll never find his house!"

"Father, when you are ready, stop by my office. I've got a couple things I need to do before we leave."

"Doc, can you find Thomas and get him to set up the buggy for a late-night trip? Have him meet me right here. I've also got some important things to do in my office before we leave."

"OK, Doc. I've got to go and get things moving."

Father Luca rushes into the mercantile building heading past the cash register, making a quick right turn, and enters into his church's office.

"Hi, Adela," he says as he rushes in and starts rummaging through his desk drawers looking for something.

"Mariano, can I help you? You look like you have lost something and are in a rush."

"Yes, I mean yes. I just talked with Doc, and he told me Mr. Gardner is deathly ill and may die any moment. Him and I are going out there to his house as soon as we get things organized.

Not sure what time we will be back. Doc told me it will be at least a couple of hours or more just to get there. He told me Gardner's wife wants me to give him his last rites before he passes."

Adela picks up Father Lucas's leather satchel that was sitting on the floor and hands it to him.

"Thank you, Adela, have you seen my old Bible?"

Adela looks around the small office, then asks, "Did you look in your satchel?"Father Luca takes a quick look into his satchel and sees his Bible and other things a priest will need in preforming last rites and other items. "Here it is," he says with a sigh of relief.

"Thank you very much." He gives her a quick kiss on her cheek as he starts heading toward the door.

"Mariano, take your blanket, it may get cold if you're out there too late."

Father Luca stops, walks over to the filing cabinet, and picks up the folded blanket lying on its top. He waves goodbye to Adela as he rushes out the door.

✝ ✝ ✝

Half an hour later, Thomas pulls up in front of Doc's office in the church's buggy, and Father Luca calls out to Doc.

"Hey, Doc, we're here. You ready?"

Doc Murphy comes rushing out of his office pulling on an old jacket, closing his door as he carries his doctor's bag.

"Father, you got here faster than I thought," he says as he climbs into the carriage.

"Father, I think it's going to be a long night."

As Thomas drives the buggy down the road, Doc's preparing to take a nap. Father Luca opens his satchel and pulls out his Bible and starts reading his old notes he had written back when he was living in New Jersey, about what a priest needs to know in the last rites. He comes to the page with last rites written on the top of the page and begins to read. As he's reading the instructions, he starts to get a little nervous, thinking that he will be giving the last rites to a dying man. He hasn't been that close to a man who is dying, and the man may even die when he is talking with him.

As he reads, he's thinking he must compose himself. He quietly says to himself, just follow the instructions that he had copied into the Bible and everything will be all right. The dying man's wife won't know if he makes a mistake. She is grief-stricken, tears flowing down her face, her vision impaired as relatives and friends sit with her, not paying any attention. Will anyone notice if he makes a mistake? "No," he mumbles.

After a few minutes he glances over at Doc as he's sound asleep.

"I need to do the same," he says as he puts the Bible back into his satchel. He moves around adjusting the pillow he's sitting on, gets a comfortable position as he spreads his blanket out over his legs, and closes his eyes as he falls asleep. Thomas skillfully drives the buggy as they head out into the countryside to Mr. Garner's house.

CHAPTER 22

Mother Cabrini stands in front of a group of about a dozen women sitting around in the mercantile building, listening to her talk about the need to take care and educate the children in the town.

"Ladies, I would like to introduce myself to the ones whom I have not met. My name is Mother Cabrini, and I was directed by Pope Leo XIII in the Vatican to come here to help with the homeless children, the orphans who lost their parents, not by their choosing, the children that ran away from an unpleasant home, the little ones who think they can survive on their own. We have to set up some form of training to educate the children, with adults' help. It seemed to me that I was kind of a trouble shooter for the Vatican, maybe because I love children.

"I think that in my life, I choose to help God, and didn't make the move to get married and have a family. I'm a normal hot-blooded woman, but I choose to help God. At times, I think I had missed not having children. Before I made my choice to work for God, yes, I did meet some wonderful, handsome, and educated men, but I felt that God needed me more. That is the reason why I am here to build a place where children can come and learn things and help educate the adult people who have not learned or don't want to learn. Not everybody is a learner. Some people don't have time to learn and must work for many hours a day and many days of a month until there life has run out of life. Bishop Mangini did a wonderful job in convincing the Vatican I should be sent to Denver, and he was the sole instrumental person in getting me here, and working with Father Luca, a charming and hard worker. I have some ideas I would like to share with you and work with the politicians here in developing laws that will protect your children right here in your town."

"Mother Cabrini," says a woman sitting in the audience.

"Please, go ahead," Mother Cabrini acknowledges her, "but first I need to explain. This is not a formal meeting. Anyone who wants to say something, go ahead and speak. All I ask, don't speak if someone else is speaking. Wait your turn."

"What I would like to say is, before we get more involved in our meeting, we probably need some men to come to our meeting. With just women trying to change anything, it will not work."

"Yes, I agree. But first, let's just have women talk about ideas that we could bring up when the men are present. If you can get a man to do something by your suggestion, he may think it was his idea in the first place."

Some of the woman laugh at Mother Cabrini's comment.

+ + +

The next afternoon, Doc Murphy is talking with Andy, the undertaker, in the back of Andy's building as he's making a casket, as Andy's cutting lumber with a hand saw.

"Andy, Father Luca and I was out at the Gardner's house yesterday, not getting home until late in the night."

"Why did you get back so late?"

"Well, I was getting ready to tell you if you would let me. I knew Mr. Gardner was a sick man for a long time. It didn't matter what I did for him. I tried all different kinds of medicine but suspected he didn't always take it. One time I arrived at his house and was tying up my horse, I saw a couple of the medicine pills I gave him lying on the dirt, so I confronted him about throwing away his medicine. Well, to make the story short, we got into a big heated argument.

"Even when that man looked like he had one leg in the grave, he sure could get fired up and argue until he almost passed out one time. I ask him, if he didn't threw them away, then who did. I felt he was getting tired of living. It just seemed like he was slowly dying.

"Well, I was out at his house a week ago, and he could hardly walk. He looked terrible, he didn't get out of bed the day before. His wife is going crazy not knowing what she's going to do if he dies. She insisted that I get Father Luca out there and give him his last rites before he dies. She wants to make sure he goes to heaven. So that's where we were last night, as Father Luca was giving him his rites, he died. We got there just in time. It was horrible, his wife just lost it. It took both of us a long time to calm her down before we came home."His wife wants you to make a nice-looking coffin, not one of those cheap looking ones. She's going to have a large funeral for her husband. You know, Andy, I'm really going to miss that foul."

"Doc, I'm making a slim line coffin for this other customer who was in here yesterday. His wife had died four days ago. He told me if I could make it a smaller slim line, I could save wood for another coffin. Yes, I will have Mr. Gardner's ready."

"Andy," says Doc.

"Father Luca told Thomas to get with the railroad and make an appointment for the cemetery train in three days. Remember the railroad requires a two-day notice to have the train. There shouldn't be any problems in having Mr. Gardner's casket done by that time, and it's supposed to be a nice one."

"Yeah, Doc, no problem," Andy replies.

+ + +

Two days later, Father Luca in his church office is having a meeting with Thomas, making sure everything has been taken care of for Mr. Gardner's funeral at the Olivet Cemetery.

"Father, I got with Enrique and Louis, the grave diggers. They left last night for the cemetery.

They have several private funerals that's not using the railroad. They are going in by wagon.

They are conducting their own funerals. So Enrique and Louis have a big job to do, so they have left a day earlier."

"A little extra money is always good," replies Father Luca.

Adela comes in the office. "Father, I'm having a problem with Mrs. Gardner. Thomas told me he went to see her to get the papers signed for the funeral, and she has sort of lost her mind. She doesn't know why she has to sign papers for her husband when he is alive. We have made a big mistake. Her husband is visiting some friends on the other side of town and will return in a couple of days."

Father Luca says, "I think Doc needs to go out and see her before the funeral. They may have some grown children, but I don't know where they live. Maybe Doc knows something. Thomas, can you talk to your volunteer group that you belong to, if they would be interested in carrying a coffin from the cemetery train, to the spot where we are going to intern Mr. Gardner? If we can't find any relatives of Mr. Gardner and his wife has lost her mind, we are going to need some help."

"Yes, I'll check and see who I can find. The weather up there is miserable right now. I might have some problems getting volunteers."

Father Luca and Thomas is sitting in their office thinking about a possible solution to the problem when Adela says, "Maybe you can bring some food for the volunteers on the train. Make it enough for two meals, that's about twelve meals."

"Yes, Father, that might work. These guys like to eat," says Thomas.

"Good, tell them about the food. Remember they have to have enough energy to help carry a heavy coffin a couple hundred feet in blazing heat, and maybe blowing sand."

"Father, you make it sound like we are going to be in the middle of the Sahara Desert."

"Thomas, you remember the last time when you and I were up there, I really thought we were in the desert."

"The old saying goes, the first time is the lasting time, and that was my first time up there."

+ + +

Very early the next morning before sunrise, Thomas has picked up Father Luca from his house, and they had driven to the mercantile. They both had agreed last night that Adela won't be needed for this funeral, with only one or maybe two funerals to perform. The severe weather is still hot up there, so it would be best Adela stays behind this time.

"Father," asks Thomas, "did you get your satchel with everything you'll need for Mr. Gardner?"

"I'm getting it right now, thanks for the reminder."

"Oh, Father, there are some of Gardner's friends coming to the funeral. There will be six men to be pallbearers, so I didn't have to get any of my friends to come. We won't have to make a large dinner. Most of Mr. Gardner's friends didn't know he was sick, and none of them knew he had died. He was not a social kind of guy."

Thomas carries a basket of food that Adela had prepared and puts it in the buggy.

"Adela made us some sandwiches and fried chicken and there's a surprise in there. It looks delicious. You are not supposed to take a look until we are on our way."

"That sounds tempting," says Father. "Got to keep the basket in a shady place on the train."

"Do you think we have forgotten anything?" says Father Luca as he's looking around.

Thomas says, "No, I think we have everything."

"You go ahead and get the buggy organize, and I will be out in a quick minute," says Father Luca as he sits down at his desk. He finds a paper and pen and sits there for a moment looking at the paper, thinking, then he begins to write.

"My Adela, everything is going to be fine today. Thomas is going to help me, so don't worry about me getting hurt. I'm sure we will enjoy the meal you made for us. Take care of the office, and I will miss you. As you know, I'm not sure when I will be back. Love, Mariano."

Father Luca gets up from his desk as he looks down at the letter and reads it again. He smiles, then heads toward the door. Stopping at the edge of the desk, he turns off the light and closes the door. He heads to the buggy where Thomas is waiting.

✦ ✦ ✦

A short time later, Thomas and Father Luca, arrives at the train station mildly surprised there wasn't a lot of wagons and buggies like the last funeral they had performed. It must have been the popular railroad supervisor who was buried that day, bringing many mourners and friends to pay their respects. He was a big handsome Irishman that made friends with every person he met. A lot of people were saddened that day.

As Father Luca and Thomas get settled in, they notice there isn't more than a couple dozen mourners who got aboard the cars. They could see two coffins in the car next to theirs, with the family huddled around them.

"Thomas, I'm going to walk around in the cars to console the grieving." Father Luca gets up and begins to walk through the cars talking with the mourners.

+ + +

Twenty minutes later, the conductor comes walking through the cars. "All aboard, we'll be leaving in five minutes," he announces. Hours later, the train stops at the halfway station, as the mourners dismount and line up at the three outhouses beside the station house. The railroads workers that were riding in the caboose car start to unload the supplies they brought from town, and were loading them into several wagons that were waiting at the station for the train. Since there were not that many mourners on the train, the waiting time was cut in half, and the train was ready to continue on to the Olivet Cemetery in an hour.

At the cemetery, the temperature was extremely hot, the pallbearers, dressed in white shirts consisted of older men, a few were younger ones, struggled to get their coffins to both graves.

The funeral procession made it with only one pallbearer, who could not make the full distance, and a replacement filled in. The wind is blowing as usual, with sand kicking up every few minutes as the wind burst got stronger. Father Luca, with a scarf wrapped around his face, performed well. He felt better this time because his confidence was building as he performed the funerals, as he secretly learned the profession.

+ + +

After both funerals are finished, everyone's aboard, and they're heading back to town. Father Luca, sitting beside Thomas, says, "Thomas, I was thinking, I haven't had much time to have a friendly talk with you about anything since we met."

Thomas glances at Father Luca, giving him sort of an odd look, "You're right," he replied. "I think we have been busy every minute since you hired me."

"I've been meaning to tell you how impressed I'm with your work. When I need something done, I don't have to worry if it's going to be finished. You're amazing."

"Thank you, Father. I have always believed, do a good job, and people will believe in you and become lifelong friends."

"That is very true," replies Father Luca. "Since I've been here, I'm beginning to feel more confident in what I do, and the warmness of the townspeople."

"Father, you're from New Jersey? Did you do well and deserved working there, which I'm sure you were rewarded by the church?"

Father Luca stopped for a moment as he's thinking how to answer that question without bringing up the church where he got his name, or selling land in California. Then Thomas ask another quick curiosity question, thinking that he may have asked the wrong question.

"Father, what brought you here to wild Denver? The comparison between the two cities are not close."

"Adela is a very lovely lady, wouldn't you say," Father Luca tries to deflect the questions."Yes, she's very much a wonderful lady. One of these days, I'm sure she is going to be a wonderful wife for some lucky guy," says Thomas.

"Yes, she's a wonderful woman," repeats Father Luca as he stares out into the dark distance, hoping Thomas won't bring up the subject again, and both men stop talking as they doze back to sleep.

Around an hour later, a loud voice calls out, "We are arriving in town, we are arriving in town." The conductor walks through the train, waking everyone up. A hard jerk is felt through the train as it comes to a stop, with a loud hissing sound as steam is being released.

"My friend should be here soon with the buggy. He lives not far from here and hears the train when it comes into town."

CHAPTER 23

One evening after the mercantile building had closed, all the employees gone home when Ethan, the mercantile owner's voice can be heard coming from the front of the building. "Father and Adela, I'm going home." As the door closes, he bids them good night.

Father Luca and Adela are working on some late paperwork that needed to be finished that day, so they planned to work until they got it done. After working for a while, Father Luca takes a long look at Adela sitting on the other side of the desk doing paperwork. He stops writing and gets up and walks around the desk to where she is seating. He puts both hands on her shoulders and slightly massages her shoulders. "How are you feeling? We have been so busy lately, we haven't had time to talk."

"Yes, we have been very busy. And we need to talk about our baby. I can feel the time will be coming soon."

She stops talking for a few minutes. "Mariano, are we going to have a problem if we have Doc deliver our child?"

Mariano stops massaging Adela's shoulders. "I don't know. I've been thinking about that for a while, and I didn't know how to ask him." Just as the words came out of Mariano's mouth, that deep secret came flooding back into his memory—he is not a real priest, and Mariano Luca is not his name. Quickly his mind focuses. *That idea would not be a sensible thing to bring up. The entire town who has trusted me would hate me, and most likely run me out of town, or maybe put me in jail. I'm not sure what Bishop Matz would do. And yes, what would Adela think of me, a big liar.* Adela says, "Let me talk with Doc. He might help us out and keep a secret. He is such a real nice man. We have been working together well, for some time. I think doctors have a kind of oath that they must obey to for patient's privacy. Yes, I remember, that oath is called the Hippocratic Oath, which protects him from revealing patient's secrets. "Maybe we can arrange a meeting at his home one of these nights, but it needs to be soon. Not many people are out at night where it won't be conspicuous with both of us going at the same time."

"Adela, I just got this idea," Mariano says. He has now focused on the way Adela is thinking. "Yeah, it sounds good, I think it might work. After the birth of our child, we can tell everyone that a poor family had the child, and they could not afford another child and were leaving town that night. They decided to leave the child with the church, who usually will find a family who wants a child. You can turn in the paperwork for adoption of the child with the support from the church.

"Mariano, I truly wished there was another way we could do this, but we can't take any chances of losing our little baby."

Thinking for a moment, she says, "Yes, that is a good idea. In our hearts, we know this is our beloved child, and we will cherish that thought for the rest of our lives. I think this is the right way to do this. I'm going to stop by Doc's office tomorrow and see what he thinks. It won't look suspicious for me to stop by a doctor's office by myself."

+ + +

The next afternoon, Adela walks into Doc Murphy's office.

"Hello, Doc," she says.

He's sitting in a comfortable chair, reading a book in the waiting area of his building. Looking up, he replies, "Hello, Adela, what a wonderful surprise of your visit. I was wondering when you were going to stop by."

"Oh, how presumptive you are," she says.

"Why would you say that?"

"Adela," he says as he lays down his book, "I've been a doctor long before you were born, and I like to think I know a lot of medical jargon gobbledygook and all that stuff. One of my specialties are delivering babies, if you know what I mean."

Looking surprised, she questioned the doctor, "How?"

"I have seen many pregnant women, and they all have their preference on how to live their life being pregnant. Some women's bellies stick way out, and they want everyone to know they are going to have a child. Other women prefer to wear bulky cloths, loose-fitting, some don't even look like they are pregnant. You prefer to keep it a secret, and it is a secret with me if you desire."

"Yes, I understand, Doc!"

"I have an oath, called the Hippocratic Oath, and all secrets are kept with me."

"I would prefer it being kept a secret," says Adela.

"Oh, would you like to tell me who is the father?"

"Doc, at this time, I think it's best if I don't tell you."

"That's fair, will he be here when you give birth?"

"Yes, he will be here. We love each other very much."

"Are you going to get married?"

Adela pauses for a moment, trying to figure out how to answer Doc.

"Doc, it's complicated."

"Adela, I'm not trying to pry into your life. You're a lovely young woman, with a lot of life to enjoy and see. Stay in touch, come and see me if you need any help, be sure to come in for a checkup soon."

"Thank you, Doc, I will."

✦ ✦ ✦

Later that week at the mercantile building, there's an area Ethan has placed four tables and chairs for men wanting to play cards. One day, Father Luca, not busy, walks by the tables.

One of the men asks, "Father, one of our players is to be here, and he is running late. We're hoping that maybe you can fill in until he gets here."

"Guys, I would love to, but I'm not familiar with the game." He was telling a lie, Father Luca knew how to play card games. Back when living in New Jersey, he and several friends used to play cards and drank beers on weekends. Now as a priest, he didn't want anyone thinking he was that type who regularly played cards.

"We are playing a real simple card game," the player says.

"Maybe we can show you how, and you can fill in until he arrives."

He briefly thinks about the offer. "The game wouldn't be long, there would be no harm in a friendly game." "OK," he replies, "just a few hands, and just for fun." Deep within his feelings, he has to be careful not to give away his past secret. After showing Father a quick way to play the game, they started to deal out the cards.

After playing about twenty minutes, deliberately making obvious mistakes, the card players' missing player shows up, giving Father Luca a chance to exit the game. A few of the players were relieved to see Father Luca leave the game out of frustration.

+ + +

A mile way at Mrs. Notary's big house, Mother Cabrini and one of the nuns, Sister Anna, from Bishop Mangini's villa have successfully converted one of the rooms into a classroom, using Mrs. Notary's furniture. All the children will be seated together on the long sofa for classroom chairs.

Two of her end tables will be used as working desks. There are four children, one boy eight years old and three girls, one was eleven, one was eight, and the other was ten years old. The housekeeper helped by getting the children bathed and found some clothes that kind of fitted them. The children were being taught to be nice children, and they don't have to be tough, like when they were living on the street. Once the children become accustomed to the environment and living quarters, one of the nuns will start to teach them English and arithmetic. Mother Cabrini has decided to live at Mrs. Notary's house for a time, to see if it fits into what she would prefer.

At the meeting with Mother Cabrini, the older nun, Sister Anna, told her about the idea of burnt sticks for pencils. Back when she was a child, a nun had shown the idea to her and the students in her class at school, so she feels she should pass it on to all students she teaches.

It's an idea to show the fortunate how lucky they are to have pencils, so they will use the burnt sticks for a while. They're great for drawing pictures and to write with.

A couple days before her class, the nun went out into the back country and found some burnt trees and bushes. Using her gloves, she broke off several small burnt branches, placing them in her basket.

After getting back home, she patiently broke off the small straight limbs that could be used like a pencil, about five or six inches long and about one-fourth inch in diameter.

In the classroom, Sister Anna shows the four children. "Now, children, watch me. I'll show you how to make a pencil." She guy in her basket and found four burnt sticks the right size, and put them in front of each child, and also a strip of cloth about five inches by one inch long.

She says, "To keep your fingers from getting nasty and black, take an old strip of cloth, wrapping it around a straight burnt stick, which can be used like a pencil."

After assisting the children in wrapping their sticks, she says, "Children, be careful in using the knife that you have in front of you. Slightly whittle the tip of the stick to a point. Now don't whittle too much, which will weaken the point and it may break off. You won't be able to draw. Don't make a mess, please do your work on the cloth cover on the desks." The nun had put another heavier cloth on the tables to collect the black shavings from the whittled charcoal pencils. The children are smiling and are having fun. As the children are making their pencils, Bishop Mangini stops by to see how the new classroom is working out.

"Hello, Mother Cabrini. How are all the little ones doing?"

"Hello, Bishop Mangini. They are doing wonderful. They catch on so quickly. Sister Anna is almost done showing the children how to make pencils."

"Making pencils?" says Bishop Mangini with a question to his voice.

"Yes, you want to take a look?"

"Sure."

"Amazing," says Bishop Mangini as he carefully watches the children whittle the burnt sticks.

"We are going to take a break soon so we can clean up the charcoal. Don't want to make a mess in this novel house that Mrs. Notary has donated. We are going to save these pencils and use them in our classroom as long as they last."

"That was really a wonderful idea," says Bishop Mangini.

"It was Sister Anna's idea. She always has these great ideas, good for the children. In a way, working with burnt sticks sort of bring science into the classroom."

"Your right. I'm sure she has other ideas that keeps the children's interest, and also educate them at the same time," says Bishop Mangini.

"Mother Cabrini, your living quarters are adequate here?"

"Yes, the quarters, are nice, although I do miss Christopher's cooking."

Bishop Mangini chuckles. "Yes, he's the best cook west of the Mississippi River. I guess I can stop by for something to eat occasionally."

"Bishop Mangini, I hope you will stay for a while. I'm going to use steam from boiling water on a window glass that creates condensation to write on. For a short period of time, you can use your finger to write in the condensation on windows. You can write words, arithmetic problems, even draw figures. By using boiling water to create condensation is an example of what can be done on a window during the winter time. I'm sure everyone has experienced at one time or another where you can't look out the window because of it being covered with a mist. This is done by having cold weather outside and warm weather inside that creates the mist on the window. I'm going to show the children where we are going to work our arithmetic problems, on when wintertime comes around.

"Yes, I think I will, sounds interesting. I remember very well, when I was young, drawing something on the mist in our house. Thinking about it, I would do it right now, drawing something crazy, even at my age now."

"Children, my name is Mother Cabrini, and I'm going to show you one way we can study until we can get school supplies. During the wintertime, has any of you tried to look out a window and you can't because there is frost on the glass?"

All four children put their hands up in the air.

"The only way to look out is wipe the frost away. Now this is summer time, so I'm going to use steam from boiling water to cover the window with a mist just as if it's wintertime."

Mother Cabrini moves a water kettle with boiling water in it. Guiding the spout close to the glass pane of the window, the glass steams up. She moves across the glass and steams the windows.

"Now we can write on the window. I want all of you to come up to the window and draw something on it using your fingers. Draw your favorite animals, or can you draw a picture of your mother?"

As the children were drawing things on the window, Bishop Mangini walks up to Mother Cabrini. "You have wonderful ideas for these children. I'm sure you are going to make this program into something big for this town. We need to build a school and have all children learning, does not matter who they are or where they're from. You're going to get, hopefully, all of the children around here and give something to them that they have never experienced.

"I like what you've done today, and I'm going to try hard to get some money to buy supplies for your class, and the possibility of adding more children to the class."

CHAPTER 24

Father Luca working late one night, which is not unusual for him, hears a knock from his closed door. Thinking it's probably Thomas, who want to talk about something, he says, "Come in." Maybe it's a habit from living in New Jersey, keeping your door closed at night, and sometimes locked for some reason, but he didn't tonight. Father Luca with his head down, reading papers, hears the door open and footsteps enter. Causally glancing up, his face suddenly transformed into a distorted shock.

"What the hell." He gasps as he's trying to catch his breath, he's totally in shock. As he's gasping, he's trying to talk. He begins waving his arms, moving his mouth with nothing coming out then, "Nolan," he finally spews out. He finally pushes the word out of his mouth. "Where did you come from?" He gasps again as he jumps up from his chair rushing around the desk to greet him.

"Antonio, Antonio, how in the hell are you. I can't believe it's really you," Nolan replies. "Nolan, I never thought I would ever see you again when I left."

Both men are giving each other big bear hugs, lasting for a couple of minutes. Father Luca, so excited, he locks the door, telling Nolan to sit down.

Nolan is sitting there with a big smile, looking at Antonio, "Tell me, what you have been doing, how is your life? I can tell, you have made it."

"All right, I'll tell you a little bit. I don't want to bore you."

"I'm sure your story will not bore me," replies Nolan.

"I'll try to keep my events in order. When I first got here, I thought for sure I had made a big mistake. But the townspeople came out and made me feel wonderful. Bishop Matz was a wonderful person, and he supported me on everything I done. This rich man in town, the bishop, and the town banker put the money together and made the town's first church. It was made with wood and a fabric roof to keep the price down."

"That's sort of odd making a church roof with fabric," says Nolan, looking serious.

"There was not enough money at that time," says Father Luca. "But let me tell you the horror story about that church. Someone, or a group, no one really knows, set it on fire, and it completely burned down on opening day."

"No! It burned down?" replies Nolan, looking shocked.

"Yes, it was such a sad day for everyone, at least no one was killed."

"Tell me, have you made it rich?" says Nolan, with a big smile. "Yes, but I can't tell you how much. I've made a lot more money, than I could ever have dreamed living in New Jersey."

"No way," says Nolan.

"I also have a girlfriend, but I can't talk about it, as you know priests can't have wives or girlfriends."

"Yes, I know, what a bad thing that could happen to you."

"Tell me, Nolan, how did you find me? I'm sure you had a hard time doing that."

"Oh, how could you imagine. When I first got here, I thought it was going to be impossible to find you, especially using your new name, Father Luca. With so many people not knowing you, I started to think that maybe I was using the wrong name, or I was in the wrong town and started to doubt my memory. Honestly, there's a lot of people that don't know you."

"I guess it takes a long time to be popular," replies Father Luca as he laughs.

"So I started to hang out at this salon on the other side of town. I met this guy who worked for the railroad, and we began to be buddies, I guess, because we both liked to drink beer. One day we were talking and drinking, I asked him if he knew where all the Italians lived, and he told me. Boy, I was a long way off from here. He also told me, be careful, it's a rough part of town. Well, I wasn't really looking for any trouble, so I didn't come over in this part of town for some time. Then one Friday night, as we were having a few brews, I had mentioned Father Luca for some reason, I don't remember about what, and someone gives me directions on how to get here, and here I am.

"Now, here's the interesting part in this puzzle. I didn't immediately come here. I had other things I was working on. I'll get to that in a minute. Finally, when I did come here, I got to your church service a little late, you call it the mercantile building, and had to sit on a bag of hard corn. When you came out from the back wearing your priest clothing, I think there where some horse bridles hanging in your way, and you had to push them aside to be able to get to the apple crates that was your stage. I couldn't believe it was you. My good old friend Antonio, a priest, it was unbelievable. And during your sermon, you sounded just like our priest back home. I couldn't come and talk with you at the time. You were a new person doing something you loved, and I couldn't interfere. I could tell that."

"Nolan, I'll tell you a little secret," Mariano said as he's smiling.

"The reason why my sermons and prayers sound so familiar is that before I left New Jersey, I copied and underlined all the sermons and prayers in my Bible at the church services in our town before leaving town. I brought them with me out here that's why they sounded just like back home." He chuckles. "Even to this day, I still use most of the same prayers here, and the parishioners got used to the same prayers. I use different sermons, though."

Nolan continues, "Now, I'll get to the other part of my story. This friend of mine tells me that while working in one of the tunnels for the railroad they are digging, he discovered gold in one of the walls and didn't tell anyone. So we made a handshake partnership to our gold mine. We can't stake a claim because it's on railroad land. Now let me warn you, be careful with the railroad. There are many tough and mean guys working in the railroad. If we can get into that tunnel and take out a big load, without them seeing us, we could make a bundle of money. So I was thinking, it appears you have a lot of money, and maybe you could help out a good old friend. We will bring you in as a partner and split the money. So maybe you might be able to loan me enough money to buy a horse and some equipment like a pick, shovel, and wheelbarrow."Now this is the best part, take a look at these stones I have." Nolan pours five pieces of rock containing bright shiny flakes in them out of a bag onto the top of Father Luca's desk.

Father Luca's face suddenly brightens up as he begins to look over the rocks.

"They look real nice," he says.

As Father Luca continues to look over the rocks, pointing out a few shiny spots with bright flakes, he says, "How much are they worth?" as he gets a couple in his hands. Nolan says, "We have to keep this a secret. We can't tell anyone, especially close friends."

Thinking for a few seconds, Father Luca says, "I would love to see where the gold is at. How far a ride is it from here?"

"It's a long ride from here, may take two or three hours by horse."

"I'll check my schedule. I'll need a couple of days to set up the trip, with two horses. We'll have to travel at night."

Nolan explains, "Sometimes the railroad will post a guard at the entrances to the tunnels, but not always."

"Just a moment," says Father Luca as he gets up and goes to the door and unlocks it and leaves. A few minutes later, he comes back into the office carrying four bottles of beer. "Here we are, a gift from Ethan, a few brews to celebrate our old friendship. I'll pay him tomorrow."Nolan, I have an idea," says Father Luca. "Leave your rocks with me, and I'm going to have Thomas go to an appraiser tomorrow and find out the quality of these rocks. See if there's enough gold in them to make our effort worthwhile."

"That sounds like a good idea. I'll come back in a couple of days, and we can start a plan."

Both men finished up their beers and started to call it a night when Nolan says, "Antonio, does your friend Ethan have a couple more brews? They sure tasted good."

"This is the first time I've had a nice cool beer for a long time, as it brings back good old memories. Nolan, you remember that night across the street from where we worked, we we're talking with those businessmen we used to see every time we got off work. They showed us the *Trenton Journal* newspaper, about that bishop out in Denver, Colorado, in desperation to get any Italian priests to come out west. Those guys told us that is the business we should be in, that's where the money is at. You didn't want to do it, and I did, and look at us. I'll be right back." Father Luca gets up from his chair and goes back out into the building, returning five minutes later with four more beers.

+ + +

The next morning, Thomas stops by the church's office to see if there is anything he needs to do before he goes to the other side of town on a short errand. Sticking his head into the office doorway, he says, "Hi, Father, is there anything that you need me to do in the next several hours while I'm in the area."

"Yes, Thomas, I do have a favor to ask of you." He glances around, making sure Adela is not around to hear what he's going to say.

"Thomas," he says as he's looking very tired, trying to nurse a hangover from all the beers him and Nolan drank last night.

"Are you sick?" says Thomas, looking serious at Father Luca, who slowly moves around in the office as he's trying to locate a bag of rocks he got from Nolan last night.

"No, Thomas, I didn't sleep well last night. I'll feel better later."

Thomas is not a fool, he can recognize a person with a hangover. He's done his share of drinking when he was a young wild guy.

"Thomas, I have a few rocks with hopefully some gold in them." He opens the bag and dumps a couple out on the desk.

"A friend of mine came into town last night, and we talked, and he asked if I could help him out with an appraisal on them."

"Sure, Father. It would be no problem."

"Oh, Thomas, could you not tell the appraiser where you got these from, you know, let's keep it a secret."

"Sure, Father, I can take care of it right now. I have something I need to do later when I get back."

+ + +

A short time later, Thomas walks into the mineral appraisers office, looking around as he sees an old man sitting in a chair behind the counter smoking his pipe. "It's quiet today," he says to the old man.

"What's ya got there, mister," the appraiser says as he gets up from his chair and walks over to the counter.

"I have these rocks, and I would like to get the gold in these rocks appraised."

"Before we go any farther," the man says, "the price for appraising these five rocks is on that chart on the wall, right there as you walk in."

Thomas takes a look. "All right, I'll take number 1."

"That's fine," says the appraiser. "Just fill out this paper here and sign the bottom." He hands it to Thomas.

"You pay me now," he says. "Be back in two hours and I'll have it for you."

Thomas pays the man and gets a receipt for the rocks.

+ + +

A couple hours later, Thomas comes back to the appraiser's office to get the rocks, and the appraisal value of the gold in the rocks he had left.

Thomas approaches the counter, and the old man sitting behind it looks up.

Getting up, the old man immediately asks, "Where, did you say you got theses rocks? Did you get them somewhere around here?" he asks with pushy tone to his voice."I didn't say, does the location of where the rocks came from have any bearing of their appraised value?" ask Thomas."No, I was just thinking where you got them from. Anyway, these rocks are worthless, and you can leave them with me. I will discard them for you. It's one of my services I offer to so many people, who find worthless rocks."

"You're telling me, these rocks are worthless?" says Thomas with a surprised look on his face.

"Yes, so many people with no expertise see these gold flakes scattered all through these rocks and think they have real gold, and they go wild. The name for these gold flakes are called fool's gold. I've had hundreds of people come in here, just like you, with fool's gold. I feel sad for these people, thinking they have found thousands of dollars of gold, which turns out to be worthless. Now, why don't you give me your rocks," says the old man as he starts picking up the rocks.

"Just a moment, just one moment, give me back my rocks!" says Thomas. "I'm going to keep them to look at my fool's gold."

"But, Mr. Thomas, it's real easy for me to get rid of them for you. I'll just put them in the container right here under the counter." The old man starts putting Thomas's rocks back under the counter.

"I said no, Mr. Appraiser, these are my rocks, and I'm going to leave with them right now."

"All right, all right, you don't have to get huffy about it," replies the old man. Thomas takes the two rocks out of the appraiser's hands and has the old guy give him the others he had already put under the counter, making sure they are the right ones with plenty of good flakes in them.

Thomas puts all five rocks back into the bag and leaves the office.

As Thomas leaves the appraisers office, he starts thinking, *Why was this old man so dead set on keeping the worthless rocks? Was he just trying to be nice and take them off my hands so I wouldn't throw them in his front yard out of disgust...unless.* "I don't think so," says Thomas to himself. "These rocks are not worthless, and he's playing me as a fool. Maybe these rocks are worth a lot of money!"

Thomas decides he will tell Father Luca about the odd old man at the appraiser's office tomorrow. He didn't want to antagonize his headache any further than what it is. Thomas said, "That headache Father had seemed to him was a classic case of a hangover. Wonder who Father Luca was drinking with last night."

✦ ✦ ✦

The next day, Thomas comes into Father Luca offices, and he's sitting at his desk working on papers. Adela is not in the office.

"Father, how is your headache today?" he asks as Father Luca looks up. "I'm much better today." He smiles. Thomas smiles back as both men meet eye to eye for a split second.

Father Luca could sense with that brief gaze into his eyes, Thomas knew about his drinking last night. Neither man said anything. Maybe the red eyes, the smell to one's breath, headache, never know.

Then Thomas says, "Father, I got the appraisal done on your rocks," as he sets the bag down on Father Luca's desk, and he takes a quick look into the bag then puts the bag into his satchel and snaps it closed.

"I experienced a really strange thing after the appraisal was done. Couple hours later, when I was to get the appraisal results, this old guy, the appraiser, told me the rocks I had were worthless. He said the gold flakes in the rocks is called fool's gold. The gold flakes are nice to look at and trick a lot of people into thinking they have a lot of money. Now when I insisted I wanted my rocks back, I almost had to pry the rocks out of his darn hands. I thought for a moment there was going to be an altercation, just to get my, or that is, your, rocks back from him."

"Hum, that does sound strange," says Father Luca as he picks up his satchel from the floor and dumps the rocks back out onto his desk and starts to handle them, looking closer at them.

"Where's Adela this morning, she's busy?" asks Thomas, as he looks around the office. "Oh, she's over at the stationery store looking at some new office supplies. Thomas, I got another favor to ask. Can you get with our stable boy and have him saddle up two horses tomorrow night? We're planning to leave late. My friend and I are going on a ride, and we won't be back until late that night. And please, don't talk about it with friends, I would appreciate it."

"Sure, Father, will get right on it," he says as he leaves. Thomas is wondering where Father Luca is going on a long horse ride, getting back late at night. Maybe he's going to someone's house for a prayer, or counseling someone. It's kind of strange, he didn't mention it earlier to him. It wouldn't be Doc he's going with, he doesn't ride a horse, it's too hard on his bones. Thomas continues to wonder. "Since he's been working at the church, this is the first time this has happened. It's odd that all this is happening right after he got that bag of rocks with those gold flakes in them. I wonder who is this new friend of his," he mumbles to himself as he heads toward the stable.

+ + +

The next night, its late, Father Luca decides to walk to the stables to meet Nolan instead of having Thomas drive him in the buggy. Father Luca, before leaving his house, has changed out of his priest clothes into wrangler pants, a hat, and a heavy jacket. Both friends got to the stables almost the exact time, 9:00 p.m. The stable boy greets both men with their horses all equipped ready to ride. There wasn't any lights in the stables, so the stable boy didn't notice Father Luca's clothing had changed. He put a saddle bag on Father Luca's horse filled with some food and a bottle of water for his trip.

"Antonio, you're ready for a long ride?" Nolan asks Father Luca. "I think so, haven't ridden a horse for this length of time, but I hope it won't all be in vain."

The moon's shining brightly as they ride the road heading toward the mountains, where the railroad is laying tracks through the extremely rough terrain, as Nolan is leading. They galloped for quite a while, and Father Luca comments as he looks out across the land, "Nolan, doesn't this land look beautiful under a full moon? There's nothing out here, it's quite different than New Jersey."

After another hour, Nolan says, "Let's stop for a few minutes."

✦ ✦ ✦

After resting their horses and themselves for a time, Nolan says, "Antonio, are you ready, we are getting close?"

"Sure, let's ago," replies Antonio as both men mount back on their horses and continue on toward the tunnel where the gold is at. As they get closer to their destination, they are now riding on a rough dirt road that seems to be used often. They are riding beside each other now. Nolan tells Antonio, "We want to avoid any workers or security tonight, especially this time of night. They have had a few problems of equipment missing mysteriously overnight. They have to protect their equipment from thieves." As they continue to ride, Nolan is familiarizing himself from the terrain. "Here, let's get off the trail here." He points off to the left. There's a usable path heading into a clump of trees.

Now surrounded by a few trees, Nolan tells Antonio, "Let's dismount here and hide our horses. My friend usually sleeps up close to the tunnel's entrance."

They put up several tents in this area for immediate supplies. He's in charge of that, and his security. The two men sneak up close to the vicinity of the tunnel's entrance, hiding behind several rocks. Scanning the area, they spot a security guard sitting in a chair at the entrance, who looks like he's almost asleep with a rifle across his lap. Both men wait there for a few minutes, trying to figure out how they are going to able to get into the tunnel.

Quietly, Nolan says, "It doesn't look good. This is new with the guard at the entrance. It would be impossible that he would let us into the tunnel. I can't see any other way. What do you think?" he says to Father Luca.

"Well, it's really late, we have no pass or permission to be here. I wouldn't want to challenge him. He could shoot us," says Father Luca.

"Thinking about it, I can't think of any way to get in that tunnel except being a worker. I don't know where my friend could be," says Nolan as he watches the guard half sleeping.

"There's also another problem," says Father Luca. "If we get past the guard and go in, what are we going to do when we are ready to leave? We just can't walk out. And it's all over if they catch us in the tunnel digging a hole in its wall looking for gold."

Father Luca says with a distant tone to his voice, "They are working during the day, and they have a guard at night time. How are you going to find your new buddy, or partner, of your gold mine?"

Both men look at each other and shake their heads. Nolan says, "Hey buddy, I thought I had a real good ringer."

"Yeah, I thought you had something going myself. Yesterday I had a strange result from our local appraiser. It sounds like there might be real gold in those rocks. Thomas, the man that works for me at church, told me he almost had to pry the rocks out of the appraiser's hands to get them back after he told him they were worthless. The appraiser insisted that Thomas leaves the rocks there so he can throw them away. It sounds very suspicious to me." Both men got back on their horses and headed back to town.

+ + +

Hours later, around 3:00 a.m., the two men riding back into town, Nolan tells his good friend Antonio, "Let's go to your house, I'll drop you off, and I'll take both horses back to the stable. I have my old horse there, and I will go home myself. We don't need the stable boy talking about our trip, and your change of clothes for the night ride.

"That sounds good. Stop by in a couple of days, and we can talk more about your gold," replies Father Luca, starting to look tired.

CHAPTER 25

The next morning, it's eight o'clock, the opening time for the church's office. Adela unlocks the office door and see's Ethan coming through the front door of the building, with a frown on his face. He turns his back to her as he opens the front door and she greets him, "Good morning, Ethan." He turns around and greets her in a grouchy manner. "And good morning to you too, Adela. I do hope it will be a lovely day today."

Ethan walks up to Adela. "Where is Father Luca, is he out and about doing something?"

"I don't know. He didn't tell me if he was going to be doing something this morning. Oh, I'm sure he'll be here shortly. He must have slept in."

"Well, have a nice day, got to get going, some deliveries coming in this morning, and I got to figure out what happened to a dozen beers that's missing out of the box."

"Problems, problems, problems," Adela says as she slightly shakes her head, goes into her office, and gets out a few papers, as she's thinking why Ethan is so grouchy this morning. She sits down and starts to review several files. Half an hour later, their nun that usually works for Father Luca a couple times a week comes into the office.

"Good morning, Adela," she says.

"Oh, good morning, Sister Stella. Will you be filing today?"

"Yes, Father Luca left a full file of papers he wants me to file."

"Sounds wonderful. I'll move to the other side of the desk to give you more room."

"Thank you, Adela."

✦ ✦ ✦

About an hour passes as both women work, and Father Luca hasn't come into the office yet.

"Sister," says Adela, "by any chance do you know when Father Luca will be coming in?"

"No, he didn't mention anything about coming in late."

"Strange, no one knows where he is," says Adela.

Then Sister Stella looks up from the filing drawer and says, "Adela, I was wondering, how are you feeling today. You're not tired, are you?"

"Oh, I feel fine, I'm not tired. Why do you ask?"

"I was just wondering. You seemed a little pinkish lately."

"Oh," replies Adela, sort of puzzled, wondering what that was all about. Her mind starts processing what she had said. *She's never asked that question before. I wonder if she knows about my pregnancy, but how would she know that? She couldn't possibly think that Father Luca is the father? Has she noticed the bulge that I've been carefully hiding?* Neither woman said anything after that, as they continued working.

✦ ✦ ✦

Father Luca lying in his bed suddenly opens one eye, his head buzzing and foggy as he mumbles, "Am I still alive. Oh, that bright light, where's that coming from?" as he throws one leg out of his bed.

Now his brain is starting to clear up, as he remembers, "Must have been too many beers last night with Nolan. It's been awhile since I've had a beer." Then he realizes the sun is up, and he's late for work. He climbs out of bed, gets dressed, grabs a couple plums to eat off the counter, runs his hands through his hair, puts on his hat, and exits his house.

✦ ✦ ✦

A little while later, Father Luca, walking down the road to the office, he had no way to contact Thomas to pick him up. Thomas was driving down the road in the church buggy when he saw Father Luca walking.

"Good morning, Father Luca," he says as he pulls up beside him. "Do you need a ride?" he says with a smile."Ah, you are a blessing this morning." He gets into the buggy.

As Thomas drives toward the office, he mentions, "Father, are you getting sick? You slept in this morning."

"No, Thomas, I'm not sick. I have something on my mind that's been bothering me. I didn't sleep well last night."

"Oh, Father, did you get back with your friend about those rocks with gold flakes I took over to the appraisers the other day?"

"No, he should be getting back with me in a couple days. He told me he had to leave town for a while, will be back soon, and we can talk about his gold mine then."

Thomas drops Father Luca off at the mercantile building and continues on his errands.

Father Luca came into the office. "Good morning, Adela, that is, what's left of it. I'm sorry I couldn't sleep last night, stayed up late. Thomas saw me walking and gave me a ride."Adela, looking at him with a concerned look, says, "You need to be careful, you had me very nervous today. I didn't know what was happening. I was going to have Thomas come and check on you when he got back from an errand."

"Hello, Sister Stella," Father Luca says as he noticed her filing the papers.

"Hello, Father Luca. I should be done in a little while," she replies.

"Don't worry, there's no rush."

"Oh, Father," says Adela, "Ethan was looking for you this morning when I opened the office. He didn't appear to be in a good mood this morning. He was mumbling something about missing beer bottles from his box."

"Thanks, I'll get with him after lunch," says Father Luca as begins to think, *I've got to get with Ethan soon and pay for those beers. Can't tell him I was drinking. I'll tell him I had two friends in my office last night, and they drank the beers. I've got to go and find him now and take care of the problem.*

+ + +

Fifteen minutes later, Father Luca finds Ethan on the other side of the building moving several bags of beans and corn. "Hey, Ethan, better watch your back with those bags. They look heavy."

"Oh, hi, Father, these bags are light. I must move a couple dozen every couple of days. I'm getting these ready for a pickup in an hour."

"Ethan, were you looking for me this morning?"

"Yeah, Father, I wanted to ask you if you saw someone taking a dozen beers out of my box last night. I saw you working late, and thought..."

"It was me Ethan. I'm really sorry about that. I was going to pay you this morning, but I had too much on my mind last night and couldn't go to sleep until early this morning. And that got me up late this morning. I had a couple unexpected friends over at the office, and they drank the beers. I want to pay you for them now."

"Father, get with me this afternoon, when I have some spare time and will talk.

I'm glad you came and told me, Father. I was getting nervous about the missing bottles and thought someone was stealing from me."

"How about three thirty?"

"Good, just look around for me. I'll be in here somewhere. I won't be going anywhere today."

+ + +

Father Luca comes back into his office. Sister Stella has finished filing the papers and has gone.

Father Luca says, "Adela, I just saw Ethan and everything is fine. There were some beers missing, and he thought maybe I might have seen someone take them."

"Mariano, something happened when Sister Stella was here doing your filing. She said to me, how was I feeling, and was I tired. This was the first time she has said anything like that to me since she's been coming here. I really didn't know what to say, it was such a surprise. Then I asked her why she asked me that, and she told me I looked a bit pinkish. I'm not sure what she meant or knows. She made me feel she knew about my pregnancy. I've tried very hard to hide my bulge, I've been wearing baggy dresses. I've been trying very hard. I find it a bit odd for someone like the sister who has never been married, with no children, know the symptoms of a woman who's pregnant." Adela begins to tear up. Father Luca comes around the desk and puts his arms around her and holds her for a few moments.

"Now, now, don't worry. She doesn't know anything. She hasn't seen you too often lately, maybe she's just making comments to start a conversation. Do you suppose when you bend down or may lift something, your posture changes?" says Father Luca, trying to find something right to say. "That's all I know. I'll leave that up to a woman's intuition."

"Mariano," Adela says, "yesterday, I stopped by and talked with Doc Murphy and made an appointment for a checkup tomorrow night after dinner. He reminded me to bring the baby's father with me."

✦ ✦ ✦

Late in the evening the next night, the streets are dark and quiet on the way to Adela's house. Hardly anyone on the street, except the party people in the salons getting drunk. Father Luca had hooked up the church's buggy and has driven to Adela's house, parking along its side. Adela is in the process of cooking dinner for both of them.

Coming up to Adela's front door, Father Luca opens the door and peeks his head inside and says, "Hello, Hello." As he hears something being fried in the kitchen, he pushes opens the door and walks in. In one hand, he has a small bouquet of flowers he had picked from her neighbor's yard, he starts quietly toward the kitchen planning to surprise her. Then he hears her voice, "I hear you, find something to put the flowers in, they're beautiful. Pour a glass of wine, and I will be out very soon with dinner."

After a while, as Father Luca sits sipping his glass of wine, flowers in a vase on the table, Adela's appears in the room carrying a large plate of meatloaf with baked potatoes and greens on the plate. "Wow, that looks good," Mariano says.

They both begin eating dinner, having a wonderful conversation, when she asks, "Mariano, have you given some thought about a name that you are going to call your child?"

He stops eating, not saying a word, as he looks at Adela for a moment. "I haven't thought about it." He looks kind of sheepish at her. "I don't know why."

Adela says, "Most parents usually have a name for their child. Tonight, Doc is going to tell me about when I will be delivering. I have a strong feeling that the child is going to be a boy. Maybe because the way he has been bouncing around in there."

"You mean he has been moving around, isn't it dangerous to you?"

"I don't think so, he's got a lot of padding in there." Mariano laughs strangely at her answer.

Adela asks, "What is your parents' name, maybe your father? Do you have any brothers, maybe an uncle?

If he's a boy, you can name him after one of them."

"Yeah," Mariano says as he's thinking and not eating.

After a few minutes, Adela says, "You should finish your dinner. We have an appointment with the Doc in a while. You still have time to come up with a name."

Mariano, looking at Adela smiling, says, "What if the child is a girl, have you thought of a name?"

"Yes, I have. I started to think about that, but just lately with so much movement in there, I'm convinced it's going to be a boy, and I'll leave that up to you for a name."

After finishing dinner and cleaning up the dishes, Father Luca and Adela get into the buggy and head toward Doc Murphy's house on the outskirts of town, parking in the back of the house. Doc was expecting them and left the back door open as they come through the house to the living room.

"Good evening, Father Luca and Adela," says Doc. "I just finished eating and have been cleaning this place up a little. Why don't you both sit down for a few minutes. I've got hot water boiling up for a cup of tea."

After having their tea and a small conversation, Doc says, "Father, I'll just start off like this. I have a Hippocratic Oath that I obey by. What happens here stays here, no need to worry about anything. My oath is similar to your oath, to God. What people tells you, it stays with you, so help you God. In all my years of being a doctor, and that is a lot of years, you would be shocked knowing what I know, what strange and mysterious things that have happened in this town and long before it was even a town."

"Yes," Doc says, as he takes a moment to think back in time, as his face turns expressionless.

Quickly, Doc's mind comes back to the present time.

"All right, Adela. I have a small room down the hall on your right. My patients that miss me at my office in town use that room on their visits here. Go and change into the gown that's hanging on the door. I'll be there in about ten minutes."

Both men talk about how Father Luca has done such a wonderful job in conducting the church services at the mercantile building, working closely with Ethan the owner.

Doc tells Father, "The business at the store increased by twofold since you have been in town."

"It's time," says Doc suddenly as he stands up looking at the old grandfather clock standing in the corner with its ticktocking.

"Father, you stay right here in the living room. I'm going to check Adela and see when you're going to be a father. Oh, Father, there's one more thing. Do you have a name picked out?"

"Well, Doc, we were talking about that on the way over here."

"What you're trying to say, you don't have a name."

"Well, yes, you're right, Doc."

"Here, Father." Doc hands him a pencil and piece of paper. "You can keep your mind occupied while we are gone. Make a list of girls and boys."

✦ ✦ ✦

Father Luca is starting to wonder why Doc or Adela has not come out of the room. It's been two hours and forty minutes as he looks at the grandfather clock in the corner. "I wonder what is taking so long," he mumbles.

Fifteen minutes passes, then Doc comes walking slowly out of the room. Hair all mused up, looking worn out, sweat on his forehead.

"Father," he says as he comes out into the front room, cleaning his glasses with the corner of his shirttail as it hangs out of his pants.

"Adela is amazing, she is such a strong woman," he begins, then stops as he's wiping the perspiration from his forehead with his handkerchief from his pocket.

"What is it?" says Father Luca, looking very concerned. "Is it bad?"

"Oh, no, no, Adela is fine. It was so unexpected. I never thought that she was so close of giving delivery. I took a look, oh my god! She is going to deliver now! It was long and hard work. The little guy put up such a strong fight, he didn't want to come out."

Doc stops and stares at Father Luca for a moment, then says with a big grin, "Father, you are a proud father of a fine looking baby boy, congratulations. You can go in and take a peek. It was very hard on Adela, but she pulled through. She is exhausted and sleeping. I've got the little boy in a basket next to her bed, and both are resting peacefully.

Try not to wake them." Doc mutters and collapses from exhaustion into his big stuff chair and closes his eyes.

Father Luca gets up from his chair and slowly walks down the short hallway to the room, trying to not make any noise. He opens the door, leaving the door open with a faint light shining in from the living room. He can barely see Adela sleeping and his baby boy in the basket next to her.

Slowly he walks up beside both beds, looking at Adela how peacefully she looks, then looks at his beautiful boy with a wonderful full head of black hair, when suddenly he mutters quietly, "He needs a name."

Leaving, he closes the door and heads back to the front room, picks up the paper, and starts to write down names. He writes and writes many names, but nothing was really ringing a bell.

Then suddenly the name Victor comes to Father Luca's mind. "Victor," he says again. "It's a strong name, might have been my great uncle's name, not sure. Wait, I think one of my uncles was a general in the civil war named Victor. Yeah, that would be a good name, to be named after a military general." As he's trying to think of another name, sleepiness takes over and he's asleep.

CHAPTER 26

Father Luca wakes up early the next morning, aching from sleeping in the chair the rest of the night. His head's plugged up when suddenly his sense catches a whiff of baking biscuits and coffee that awakens him. He slowly stands up, stretching his arms wide as he slightly loses his balance then recovers. As he keeps his balance, Doc walks into the room drinking a coffee.

"Morning, Mariano, it looks like you need a jolt of something."

"Yeah, got an extra cup?"

"Sure, come into the kitchen, I'll fix ya a cup. The biscuits should be done any time."

Father Luca is standing there watching Doc take the biscuits out of the hot oven, laying them out on the table too cool. He pours Father Luca a cup of coffee and hands it to him. "I think this will help."

"Excuse me, Doc, but how can you be up so early and have so much energy this morning? You collapsed last night from exhaustion and slept in your old chair. How?"

"Son, one of these days, I might reveal my secret, but right now, I'm concerned about Adela and your new boy, what is his name?"

"Doc, it's Victor."

"Wonderful, my son, I'm mean Father Luca. Now I have to finish the gravy. Just a little more milk and it's done. Do you like beef chips and gravy over hot biscuits? I have that melon over there on the table. Can you slice it? The knife is lying beside it."

"It's been a while since I had biscuits and gravy, but I'm sure I'm going to like them. I'll get right on that melon slicing."

Doc puts one biscuit and gravy and a few slices of melon on a plate, and put them on a tray, adding a cup of hot tea.

"Here," he hands Mariano the tray. "Go and see if Adela is hungry. She might be, or she might not, never know until you try. Go ahead, and go and check. If she's asleep, leave the tray on the end table beside the bed. We'll check on her a little later."

Father Luca quietly opens the door and enters the room. Victor and Adela are both sleeping, and he leaves the tray on the end table beside Adela's bed and leaves.

As both men sitting at the dinner table eating their biscuits and gravy and melon, Doc says, "Father, I was thinking about the situation you are in, with the birth of your child. For the health of Adela and Victor, I think it would be a good idea to have both of them stay here in my back room for about three or four days. Late at night, you can stop by for a visit, but not too long. You don't want to create any suspicion. You can tell Ethan at the mercantile building, Adela is sick with some kind of sore throat, *strep* would be a good word to use, it's highly contagious, and she is being cared for here at Doc's place. She stays here for three days then come back to work." Then after Adela returns to work a couple days later, you spread the word that someone left a newborn child at the door of the church's office with a note to you, Father Luca, telling you to find the child a home because they cannot take care of the child and are leaving town. Tell everyone you are going to take the child to the doctor to make sure the child is in good health.

"I'll do my part and give the child a full looking over, making sure he is in good health. I will recommend that Adela take care of the child, and later she can apply to adopt the child, giving Victor his name. I will swear to this, that it's the truth."

"Doc, I don't know what to say. We are indebted to you for the rest of our lives."

"Mariano, I'm sure some of the snoops here in town, and believe me I can name you several, are going to have their version of where the child came from, but don't worry, they can't prove anything. Like I said, you don't have to worry about anything. Just stick to your story.

Don't worry," says Doc.

Then he pauses for a moment, then he says, "I'll tell you what, this is what you can do for me.

After the new church is built, save a permanent seat for me in the third row on the far-right side, where I'll sit every Sunday, when I come to your service."

"Agreed, I'll even have your name written on it," says Mariano.

✦ ✦ ✦

The next day, Father Luca comes into the mercantile building late. Thomas has already opened the office.

"Good morning, Father, yeah running late today," Thomas says.

"Good morning, Thomas. It sure has started out as a hectic day," replies Father as he's reviewing several papers laying on his desk.

"Where is Adela today? She's got a few errands to run?"

"No, Thomas, a serious thing happened yesterday. I had to take Adela to see Doc Murphy yesterday evening. She had a really high temperature, and her throat was all inflamed, she couldn't even drink water to take an aspirin."

"Is she bad off?" Thomas interrupts Father Luca.

"No, she's not really bad, but bad enough. After a thorough examination, Doc told me she has strep throat, and is very contagious. We're not sure where she may have contracted it. Doc told me since we've been working around each other, I should be on alert that I might get it as well. So Doc thinks it would be best for a lot of us since it would be difficult for her to take care of herself to stay at his house for three or four days until she is much better. Doc has this Mexican woman that comes in to help out when he's busy."

Thomas says, "Father, you don't look too good yourself. Maybe you should go home early and get some rest. Will you be ready for service tomorrow?"

"Yes, I'll be ready for service tomorrow. I have to announce the planned start date for the new church."

Father Luca gets comfortable at his desk and begins to write what he will be preaching about at the service tomorrow. He needs to emphasize about the construction of the church and the top-quality lumber and the best stone available. People will come from miles away to see the church.

He needs to invite Mr. Notary to come to the front, and he'll talk about the timeless efforts it took to secure loan papers, purchase all the building materials, and permits, with wonderful looking prints all coming together in preparing the church's construction.

Then Father Luca's mind jumps to tonight. *It would take too long to hook up the buggy and go to Doc's house to visit with Adela and Victor and get back home and get a decent night's rest to be ready for tomorrow's service. I'll have to wait until Sunday night to see Adela and Victor.*

✦ ✦ ✦

The next day at the mercantile building, everyone's arriving for the church service. Buggies, wagons, horses all jogging for a good parking spot and people walking, dressed in their Sunday best, all arriving for service. The parishioners squeezing in between bales of hay, bags of corn, beans, potatoes, horses' harnesses hanging from the walls. The seniors are working their way up to the front where there are wooden planks, stretching between bags of potatoes, sitting in the front row, where Father Luca will be standing on the apple crates. A few children have found a few seats on the counter up where the cash register is located. Ethan is busy trying to help people find seats, almost giving up the idea because of so many are arriving.

There were a couple women sitting on a couple burlap bags of beans talking about what they think Father Luca will be talking about. One tells the other woman, "If he tells us for some reason, we don't have enough money again, and we're going to make some structural modifications, I'm getting up and walk out of here, and you better follow me."

Ethan, standing in the front, address everyone, "Has everyone found themselves a seat? We have a couple open areas over to my left." Several people weave their way over in that direction, fusing around as they finally settle down. "Everyone is comfortable?" Ethan asks. "Service will be starting in five minutes."

Father Luca comes out of his office carrying his Bible, squeezes past a few people as he dodges the horse harness hanging on the wall. He steps high onto the apple crates as Ethan holds his elbows for balance, and continues to stand beside him through the service.

"Hello, everyone," Father Luca says, and everyone enthusiastically replies good morning. "I hope everyone is comfortable. It's such a beautiful day. Please, let us pray."

+ + +

Sometime later after Father Luca finishes his sermon, he asks his congregation, "Would anyone like to express thanks to God for a recent event?"An older woman in the back of the room stands up and says, "Yes, I would like to say something."

"Please go ahead," replies Father Luca."My husband has been deathly ill for almost week, with a high temperature. I thought he was going to burn up, I just kept putting cold presses all over him, trying to cool him off. He was so miserable, he asked me a couple nights ago if I would stop his misery. I couldn't believe what he asked me. There's no way I would take his life."

"No way," she repeats herself. "Doc came by several times and couldn't figure out what was his ailment. It will be a week he hasn't been able to sleep. I prayed for him every night, and every day. And Lord behold, last night, his fever suddenly broke. He is sleeping right now, he hasn't been able to sleep and was so exhausted. The poor man was ready to die. I don't know what he had, and I hope no one in town gets what he had. He would have come to church today, but he was too exhausted to pray and thank God."

"What is his name and your name?" asks Father Luca. The woman says, "His name is Vernon, and mine is Concetta."

"Please, let us pray for Vernon and Concetta." After the brief prayer, Father Luca says, "Amen. Are there anyone else who would like to thank God?"Another woman standing off to the side of the building says, "Yes, I would like to thank God for bringing Father Luca to this town, and for he has made this town to what it is today. He is the sole instrument of bringing a church to this town. I want to thank God for bringing him here."

"I support that thought about Father Luca," a man standing by the bales of hay says. Another woman says the same, and suddenly everyone in the building are saying, "Thank God for bringing Father Luca to Denver."

Father Luca standing on the apple crates is blushing, not knowing what to say. He finally says, "Please, please, thank you. I'm so humbled to your thoughts. It wasn't just me that brought the church to Denver, it was all of you," he says as he pauses and looks out over the packed room.

"It was all of you, you were the ones who has made it happen. I just helped it along. Our first church, many things didn't work right, but now we have a plan, and we've got it right this time.

Our new church, will be built with designed, sculptured sandstones, the interior big enough for everyone to pray in and space for visitors coming from other parts of the land. You will be very proud of it." The congregation began talking and showing excitement with the person sitting beside them, talking to people sitting in front and behind them.

"Now, now, please give me your attention," says Father Luca with his hands up in the air, trying to calm and quiet the congregation down. After everyone stopped talking, Father Luca says, "It gives me great pleasure to introduce a very fine man, who everyone knows. A person who has devoted his life and donated money in making this idea come true, of building a modern and beautifully designed church. Please welcome Mr. Notary."

Mr. Notary comes to the front of the building, choosing not to stand on the crates, fearing he might break through the boards. The congregation claps their hands with enjoyment as Mr. Notary begins, "Thank you. I have lived in this town long before it was a town, my parents moved here long ago, way before there was a train. They worked hard and suffered many times, but they endured and succeeded. They grew a family and bought a lot of land and sold some of it to the railroad when they came here. With the good money, my family prospered, my father built a wonderful house, he sent his children to school and became a well, successful businessman in town. They had everything except for one thing, they had no place to pray. A few people come by here and planned to build a church or someplace to pray, and nothing happened. Father Luca came here from New Jersey, a very faraway place. He was young, and he tried, and he succeeded, he stayed, and look what is going to happen in a week from now.

"We are going to have a super wonderful church, a place everyone can pray in. Sometimes I think that if things could have changed many years ago and Father Luca was here thirty years earlier, my parents, bless their souls, would have had a place to pray in to God. But one mustn't look back in life. Sometimes it can be very depressing. I know this is right, and we are all going to move forward and help build one of the most beautiful churches in the state and country. Tomorrow, the surveyors will be staking the directions to start digging the trenches to build the foundation forms. After the foundation forms are built, they will start mixing the cement and pour the foundation. Then after that, they have to let the cement dry or cure or something like that. I'm not familiar with the word they use. The sand stone blocks will be arriving at the train station sometime in the near future, we'll get updated information the closer to the shipping time.

"Each church service, we'll keep you informed as the time nears. Then at that time, everyone will be needed, to move, dig, carry anything that is needed. In a couple of weeks, the expert masons will be here to start laying the walls. If anyone has any questions, see me in half an hour in the front of the mercantile. We won't be taking any questions now. We have to vacate Ethan's store so he can start to put it back together. Father Luca told me to tell everyone the service is over, thank you."

Everyone began milling around as Ethan was standing in the corner of the room talking with a couple men and several ladies from the church committee as they glance over several times at Father Luca as he was talking with several parishioners. It appears they were talking about him.

✦ ✦ ✦

Several hours later, Father Luca sitting in his office going over papers dealing with the new church, Thomas comes in. "Good afternoon, Father, your sermon today was motivating. It gave everyone a purpose of living here in town."

"Thank you, Thomas. I'm glad you liked it. Like I said, it's the people here that makes it all work.

Mr. Notary's information about his family history was inspiring, made you think that history was standing in front of us, as the next generation was planning the new church to further his family ties in this town."

"And yes, Father, the timeline of construction inspired all the parishioners, and they are ready to work. Oh, Father, your horse and buggy will be left out in front. I notified the stable boy, and he'll take care of the horse upon your return."

"Thank you, Thomas. I'll put away the buggy when I return, which I don't think it will be too late. Stable boy doesn't have to stay. I want to pay a visit and see how Adela is feeling."

"Give her my wishes for a quick recovery, Father. I was just thinking, that woman you spoke to at service this morning, about her husband having some kind of illness, be careful it doesn't spread to you. Is Doc sure she has strep throat, which I know is very contagious, maybe she has that other strange illness. Be careful."

"I will. Thank you, Thomas, for your concern, I will be very careful."

CHAPTER 27

It's a cool night, the moon shining brightly, as Father Luca leaves his house driving his buggy to Doc Murphy's house. It's a Sunday night, most people in town has gone to bed early, tomorrow is a working day for most. As his horse clops along the dirt road, Father Luca starts feeling it might be too late to see Adela and his son, Victor. If they are asleep, he doesn't want to wake them. He'll just take a quick peek.

He's starting to think Doc's an interesting man, with some very interesting stories. He'd like to get to know him better. He had vowed a secrecy under his Hippocratic Oath of keeping the birth of his and Adela's son's birth a secret. "For that personal feeling from Doc, and his oath to his practice as a doctor, I will devotee my life to Doc!" he says out load.

As he rides for a while longer, he can sense there's no noise, the air is fresh and deathly quiet, no sound of anything except the horse trotting, and the buggy wheels makes a few squeaks as they hit several low spots on the road. His mind starts drifting in no particular direction when his thought stops on, *Maybe, just maybe, I might be able to talk with Doc about my deep secret.*

Can I trust him? I don't have anyone to talk with about what should I do. I don't think he's a religious man, maybe it might not matter to him, or he might not want to get involved with my problem. He has told me he knows of many people with secrets, some might even mean life or death if they were revealed here in town. Then his thought disappears from his mind, just as fast as it appeared.

"Doc's house's just down the street," he says to himself as he pulls around the corner and parks at the back of his house. Father Luca walks up to the back door and notices there are no lights on in the house. He knocks on the screen door and waits for a couple of minutes, then he knocks again. After a few minutes, Doc comes to the door.

"Hello, Father Luca," he says as he opens the screen door. "Come in," he says as he's lighting a small lantern.

Father Luca then realizes that Doc may have been asleep. "Doc, did I wake you up?"

"Well, Mariano, why don't you come on in. Here, let me light another light." Father Luca gets in the house where there is more light and sees Doc standing with a robe on, his hair is messed up. "No, no, Doc, I'm terribly sorry for waking you up. I didn't realize it was so late."

"No, it's all right. I'm used to sudden surprises. You never know when there is an emergency."

Then Doc asks Father Luca, "You're not here for an emergency, are you?" as he's looking closer at Father Luca. "No, Doc, I'm fine. I was going to take a peek at Adela and Victor, see how they are!"

"Well, they are doing real good and happy. They have been in bed for some time, and it's dark down there in the hall. Don't you think it would be a good idea if you come back tomorrow and make a visit? You don't want to wake up the little one, who, I might say, is doing real fine."

"I understand, Doc, I truly do, and I'm really sorry for disturbing everyone."

"That's all right, Mariano. We'll see you tomorrow, early evening."

Father Luca goes outside and gets into his buggy, feeling slightly embarrassed, and heads back to his home in town.

✦ ✦ ✦

The next day Father Luca got to the mercantile a couple minutes late with several things on his mind. As he was unlocking his office door, Mr. Notary comes walking up to his back and politely greets him with, "Good morning, Father." The surprise greeting jolted Father Luca, and he jumps, almost dropping several file folders he had in his arms.

"Oh, I'm sorry," says Mr. Notary, realizing that he surprised Father Luca. "Oh, that's all right," replies Father, turning around with a pleasant smile. Mr. Notary says, "I was here in the building picking up a few things to take home when I saw you. Last Friday, I was over at the bank, and everything is moving along, and the bricks should start arriving in about a month. We probably can start digging the trenches to lay the foundation in a couple of weeks. This Sunday, you can make the announcement so the town folks can start planning. The surveyors are almost done. Oh, how is Adela doing? I spoke with Thomas and he said she's real sick."

"Yes, Doc said she has some kind of strep throat that's very contagious. She's staying at Doc's place until she gets better."

"Wish her well for me, next time you see her."

"I will."

+ + +

Three days later, it's Sunday service. The road in front of the mercantile crowded with all type of wagons, buggies, horses, people dodging between them getting to the mercantile as all the drivers of the units tying up to the hitching posts. All churchgoers, dressed in their Sunday's best, are squeezing into the already packed mercantile building, no standing room left inside, only outside in front on the wooden walk there's room for the late comers. The large barn doors in the backside of the building closed to keep out the larger animals.

Father Luca is standing on the apple crates with Ethan, standing by his side in the back of the building, listening to everyone talk as he's smiling to everyone. Thinking to himself, as he looks out across at all the faces of his parishioners, *Oh god, how lucky of a man I am.* Then he begins, "Fellow parishioners, I wish you all well today," getting attention. Everyone immediately stopped talking, so quiet you could have heard a pin drop to the floor to listen. Father Luca is ready to speak. "Such a wonderful and blessed morning. Please, everyone, bow your heads and let us pray."

+ + +

Sometime later, after the service was over and before anyone started to leave, Father Luca says, "People, I spoke with Mr. Notary and he gave me the latest news about the construction of the new church. Oh, such a wonderful good man, Mr. Notary is here this morning, I'm sure he is?"

"Here I am, Father," a man's voice coming from the right side of the building in the standing crowd. Mr. Notary, not a tall man, could hardly be seen. For the crowd being so thick, it would take too long to get up in front of the congregation.

Mr. Notary decided to make his announcement from where he is standing. The crowd around him manages to spread out a bit, giving the man a few extra inches to speak. "Ladies and gentlemen, it gives be pleasure to tell yeah, the loan has been approved on the new church, and the buildings sand stone blocks and additional material will be arriving in one month by train. The surveyors are almost done. They have marked the ground with lines and stakes where we can start building the foundation for our new church. We have tentatively set the time after service next Sunday to start digging the trenches for the foundation. Other men who have carpenter experience will be instructed by the engineer on how to build the wooden part of the foundation. So bring your tools, and we start to work after service next week. If you have any questions, see me after we leave the building. Otherwise you probably won't be able to find me." He gives a small chuckle.

Everyone begins edging their way to the exit in the front of the building when Mrs. Silverstone whispers something into Mr. Notary's ear. "Oh, everyone, just one more thing I need to say. Don't leave as yet," he sort of yells to the congregation trying to get their attention. "There is one more announcement, which will give me great pleasure to announce. Bishop Mangini, Mother Cabrini, Ethan, myself, and the church's social committee, managed by Mrs. Silverstone standing right here beside me. I have also received a mighty fine letter from the railroad supporting our idea. We have had several meetings and have decided who we feel will be the perfect recipient, and that person's name at the date we feel should be on that corner stone." He takes a pause.

Suddenly, Mr. Notary hears someone call out, "Father Luca!" Then another person calls out Father Luca, and another, and another. Mr. Notary puts his hands up in the air, calming the people down. "Now this is going to be a big surprise, we haven't had a situation like this in our town before.

With the coming of the new church, it's customary a person who has put in more work into getting the church built, then any other person or persons, his or her name will be put on its cornerstone in a brass plate. Their name, the name of the building with a date of completion, future generations will be able to see history. This announcement is going to be a very big surprise to that person I'm momentarily going to announce. I'm going to let Mrs. Silverstone announce the name. Please, Mrs. Silverstone."

Mrs. Silverstone begins, "Ladies and gentlemen, this has been a great secret our committee who has been working on this presentation for some time. We have already commissioned the foundry to make the brass plate, which is not finished at this time. So now I have the great pleasure of representing our committee to announce the lucky person whose name is..." She pauses for a moment, then she says, "Father Mariano Luca, congratulations for your honor."

Father Luca, still standing on the apple crates, heard his name and couldn't believe what he heard.

Everyone standing around him started talking at the same time to him, congratulating him, shaking his hands many times. Suddenly, he's overwhelmed with emotion as he drops to his knees still on the apple crates. As Ethan holds his shoulder for balance, he begins to pray with tears coming from his eyes. The people around him started to get on their knees and began to pray with Father Luca. All of the parishioners in the mercantile building were on their knees, praying with Father Mariano Luca, a very emotional time for him and everyone at that service.

For several minutes, Father Luca was saying a prayer, a private prayer, then raising his head, he says, "My family, please let us pray." Several minutes later, Father says, "Amen," repeated by all the parishioners, as everyone stood up. Ethan carefully assisted Father Luca off the apple crates. Congratulations started coming, shaking his hands as they praised him, thanking him, telling him they are looking forward to start work on the new church the following week. Thomas has squeezed through the crowed to congratulate him, saying, "Father, such a wonderful honor, something you can cherish for the rest of your life," as he gives Father Luca a nice hug.

✦ ✦ ✦

Several hours later, after the church service and the celebration is over, the mercantile building empty, Father Luca gets back to his office, still so excited, he doesn't know what to do. He begins to talk to himself, "God, I was a bad man at the beginning, I was sneaky, I lied, I did things that I should not have done, I was disloyal to the church, but I hope you will forgive me." Thomas had told him earlier that he will be by in a couple of hours to leave the horse and buggy so Father Luca can visit Adela and Victor. Then he sees an envelope addressed to him lying on his desk.

Sitting down he opens the letter, it reads, "Congratulations, I knew you would be something big one of these days. You are a winner. Come early for dinner, but not too early, the two cooks have a lot to cook. Dinner will be waiting." Looking at the letter for a moment, he says, "Who is this from? How did they get into my office?"

"Yes," he suddenly says. "It's Doc who brought the letter, he must have given it to Thomas, who put it in the office."

+ + +

The sun has gone down, Thomas came by and left the horse and buggy. Father Luca is keeping himself busy trying to finish what he's been working on for the last several hours, and has finished it now. He wants to stop by his house to clean up a bit before heading to Doc's place.

Checking the time, he's getting hungry and it's time to leave.

A short time later, Father Luca parks his buggy behind Doc's place. He ties up his horse and knocks on the screen door. "Come on in," he hears Doc's voice. "My hands are full, I'm in the kitchen." Father Luca opens the screen door and comes into Doc's house, bringing a bottle of wine.

"Hello, Doc," he softly says as Doc comes out into the living room with baking mittens on, and he says, "Mariano, the glasses are over there." He points toward the glasses kept in the cabinet. "I'm getting the biscuits out of the oven right now."

As Mariano is busy opening up the bottle of wine, he suddenly hears, "Congratulations, you handsome guy." He quickly turns around as Adela is standing there with something in her arms wrapped up in a blanket, her long black hair hanging down over both shoulders, with a big beautiful smile.

"Hello, Adela, you look so beautiful this evening." He gives a little kiss on her cheek. Adela says, "I would like to introduce you to your new beautiful little boy, Victor."Mariano opens up the corner of the blanket to peek at the cute little guy. "He's beautiful, but he's so small."

"What do you expect, he's only four days old," she says and smiles at him.

"You and Doc go ahead and eat. I'm going to take him back in the room and will probably stay for a while to make sure he won't wake up. I'll eat later, don't worry."

Doc has brought out the cooked stake, mash potatoes with gravy, and lettuce salad. "Well, is that's all you're going to say?" says Doc as Mariano starts to sit down at the table.

"Doc, it's a wonderful looking dinner, and I'm sure it's going to taste just as good as it looks."

"I spent a lot of time on it, it better taste good, although I got a few suggestions from Adela. She must be a good cook. Mariano, would you like to say a few words?"

"Sure Doc, just a few, I'm starving today. May the Lord bless this wonderful meal, and the people who put it together, Amen."As Mariano and Doc eats their meal, Doc says, "I think in about two days from now, Adela should come back to work. I will keep Victor here and in about two days later, I'm going to bring Victor to your office door in the mercantile before it is opened. I'm going to write a letter, using my other hand, so no one will recognize my handwriting, a note from a destitute family who had a newborn child and cannot support the child. They want the church to take care of the child. The poor family are all packed up and on the way out of town. I would like to have Adela discover the child in a box, but we need to have a witness. Have Adela come in when Thomas is opening up or maybe Ethan when he is opening up. Someone will contact me and I will come and look the child over. While I'm looking the child over, Adela can volunteer taking care of the child. Then maybe a couple weeks later, I will help her fill out paperwork for adoption of the child. What do you think?"

"Doc," says Mariano, "while you were telling me all those ideas, I could see in my mind that it will work. It's a good idea. Doc, I want to express my deepest appreciation for your ideas and help, and I hope you will not be punished in any way for helping us, if our plan doesn't work. If we fail, both Adela and myself will have to leave town forever, and I don't want that to happen."

"That is going to be just about the only way you are going to be able to keep Victor. I'm afraid you're right, Mariano. The town would not accept the child as being yours. You two are a wonderful couple, you just can't express your affection in public. I think you two will succeed in life, and I wish you both all the happiness in the world."Now, tomorrow night, come by and pick up Adela and take her home, and she can come to work the next day, feeling a little tired. After the sun is down, pick her back up at her house, and both of you come out for another meal and visit with Victor. Then the next day, I'll bring Victor in to town and leave at your door. We have to be very careful no one see's me. Victor will be in a small wooden box covered with a towel, and I'll leave a note on the towel. If someone sees me with the box, I will have to abort the drop-off for another day. Then we can have another meeting."Well, we are done eating, and Adela must be asleep with Victor. You go ahead and go home, I'll get the dishes. She'll eat something later after she wakes up. You've got to get up early for work tomorrow, and you have a bit of a drive to get home as well."

"Thank you very much, Doc. Like I said, I owe my life, Adela's life, and our son's life to your commitment as a doctor and as being an honest, trustworthy human being."

"Thank you, Mariano. Good night, and god bless you. Drive safely."

CHAPTER 28

The next day Father Luca couldn't focus on any work in the office as he keeps thinking his name will be immortalized on a brass plate and fixed to the cornerstone of the new church to be seen by everyone for eons to come.

Getting frustrated. he begins to ask himself, *What did I do to deserve this divine prophesy? Oh, if the people of this town really knew my haunting secret, even Adela, the mother of my child, Victor. Even Doc, the man who has promised a lifetime secret about my wife and child.* Then suddenly he thinks, *I should not accept this honor, I can't accept it. It would go against everything I believe in.* Then he stops talking as he begins to think what did he do to get here, representing a man of God's faith. The lies he had told, being dishonest to the woman he sold the property to in Trenton, dishonest to Bishop Mangini telling him he is a priest, and dishonest to everyone who believes he is a man of God, and everyone he has talked to about building the old and the new church.

Father Luca's thoughts are interrupted as Ethan came to his office door and taps on it and says, "Father Luca, the service yesterday was fabulous, and I want to personally congratulate you on your honor. I'm sure you are going to get many visitors today, for congratulations, which are in an outstanding order."

"Thank you, Ethan, the honor was really so unexpected. I was thinking about it, and I can't accept it. There's nothing I have done to deserve it. If anyone who should get the recognition, it should be Bishop Mangini." Ethan cuts in.

"Hey, wait a minute, Father, you deserve everything the people of this town has said about you. You don't have to be a saint before we like you. Just being who you are, the honesty you project, no one asked where you came from, it doesn't matter. What really matters is what you do today, tomorrow, and for the future of this town. You have shown a true person and a priest who loves this town and everyone in it. You have gotten the people to believe in themselves, and that included all those railroad workers who now come to our town and brings happiness and prosperity that creates wealth. You are the man and the priest of this town."

"Ethan, thank you very much for those kind words. You are the first person who has really told me what you just said, and it feels really good to hear those words."

"I wasn't trying to lecture you, Father. I just wanted to tell you what I've been hearing from the town folks, they do a lot of that when they come in here to buy things. These little old women sure do a lot of talking. All I have to do is listen."

"Like I just said, I want to thank you very much for your honesty and telling me like it is, and being a great friend."

"Well, Father, I have a wagon to load, and I'm going to have to go. One of these days, we can have a much longer talk, when I'm not so busy. But today, I had to take a break and personally congratulate you."

"Thank you, Ethan, and have a wonderful day."

"I will, bye for now."

Father Luca, after talking with Ethan, feels more at ease now, as he begins to start writing the plan for next week's service. Then he hears an older woman clearing her throat, as she's trying to get Father Luca's attention. He looks up and see's two women from the church's community committee standing at the door. One of the little older women is holding a pan covered with a pastry towel, and she says, "Father Luca, we both," she motions toward the other little older woman, "had made a wonderful cherry pie, and we want to leave it with you."

"Thank you very much, what a lovely looking pie," he says as he gets up and walks over to the women.

"Oh, it smells so yummy," he says. The other woman, sort of shy, quietly says, "We brought alone a plate and a fork for you."

"Thank you so much, ladies, but I just ate a while ago, but I'll take it home and eat it with dinner this evening. And I will definitely let you know how delicious it tasted."

"Oh, would you please," says both women almost in unison as they both got excited after Father Luca told them how delicious it will taste."Father, enjoy the pie tonight, we must go, and we are sorry to have disturbed you. We'll see you at next week's service."

"Thank you, ladies, and I will enjoy the pie tonight."

+ + +

The day has finished, Father Luca cleaning himself up at his house, getting ready to have dinner at Doc's and see his lovely Adela and son, Victor. Several hours later, Father Luca is at Doc's back door, knocking on the screen door. He hears Doc's voice call out, "Come on in, the door is open."Father Luca walks in the house caring the cherry pie. "Doc, I brought something for you," he says. Just as he was turning around, to his surprise, Adela is standing at the kitchen door. "Well, hello, stranger," she says. Father Luca, stunned for a second by the surprise, quickly smiles, "What a surprise!" he says. He rushes over to her, giving her a big one-handed hug as he still has the pie in the other hand."Mariano," she says, "be careful. You have a wonderful-looking pie in your other hand."

"Oh, yes," he says as he hands her the pie. Adela holds the pie as she's looking at it. "Are you taking up pie-baking? If you are, you did real nice work."

Mariano replies, "This morning, two friendly senior women came to the office with this pie. They even brought a plate and fork for me to eat at the office. They were very lovely and cute too. They congratulated me for the honor of having a plaque with my name, date, and church's name on it fixed to the cornerstone of the new church."

"That is so wonderful, Mariano. I'm so proud of you. I wanted to congratulate you later this evening while we're eating. Doc had told me today about your honor."

"Guys, we are ready to eat," Doc says as he comes out of the kitchen carry a large plate with meat and vegetables on it.

"My that's a good-looking pie," he says as he glances at it in Adela's hands as he passes her on his way to the table. "I think I know those two little old women. They are always making pies for any function, ceremonies, parties, you name it, and they will be there with a pie, and they are damn good. They have been living together for I think about fifty years, both of their husbands had died long time ago, and they have been together ever since. If I'm correct, one of them husbands were killed in an Indian raid, right here in Denver. Now thinking about that, I think that is when the big push of settlers was coming here. Now maybe my dates are a bit mixed up, but that's all right, it makes a good story. Now, let's all sit down to the table. "Oops, I forgot the gravy."

"No, Doc, you stay right there. I'll get it," says Adela, as she goes into the kitchen.

Doc looks up at Mariano. "That woman is a terrific woman. Treat her nice, and you will be a happy man forever."

"Thanks, Doc," Mariano quickly says as Adela comes out of the kitchen with the gravy and the biscuits.

"I got your biscuits, Doc."

"I knew I was forgetting something else."

Halfway through the meal, Doc puts down his fork and knife and says, "I've been deeply thinking. Mariano, tonight you take Adela home, just like we talked about the other night. Adela, tomorrow, you come to work, look a bit tired because you are recovering from a bad case of strep throat, maybe even go home a bit early. Now in two days, I'm coming to the mercantile, using my key, don't need to worry about someone might suspect me or something. I think there must be twenty people here in town who has a key to the mercantile building. Ethan lost count a long time ago of who has a key to his building. I will be there real early before anyone, and I'll bring Victor in this cute small wooden box, with a towel over the top. I will leave Victor at your door." He looks at Mariano. "It has to be a church, that's where people leave babies when they don't want them anymore, and since we don't have a church, your office is the representation of a church."

Doc leaves the table and comes back with a pencil and a piece of paper. "Now, I'll will write the note now, so we get the wording correct when I'm ready to write it. Here we go." He begins to write, "Father Luca, it gives me a sad heart to write this letter, knowing that I will be giving away part of my heart and soul. We cannot keep this beautiful boy. We are poor, and it's getting worse, and we have to move. We're not sure where we are going, so please do not try to contact us. Find a wonderful family for my boy, and God bless him. What do you think?"

"I love it," says Adela, "but it is so sad."

"Yes, it's supposed to be sad," says Doc.

"I will write up the note tomorrow, probably using my left hand, so no one will recognize my writing. I think I must have written some kind of prescription for almost every person here in Denver in the last forty years. I'll put the note under the towel for whomever finds Victor. By reading the note, they will know why the baby is there. I have seen many notes in my days, and I think this will do. Mariano, you need to time your arrival at the same time that Ethan has arrived so he can be a witness to your discovery of Victor. Adela, come in shortly after that while Ethan is still there. Have someone come to my office, and I will come over and take the child to my office for a physical, letting everyone know we are all concerned about his health. In front of Ethan, talk to me about the child and tell me you have been thinking about adopting a child. We need a witness so there won't be any thought that the child is from you two. I don't know why I said that, I think I'm the only one that knows."

"Doc," says Adela, "there is something on the back of my mind, and it just won't go away. About two weeks before my delivery, I was in our office, and Sister Anna was doing some filing for Mariano, who was not there. When just out of the clear sky, she asks me how I'm doing, which she has never said that to me, ever. Then she asks me, how do I feel, tired? Very strange questions to ask me when I wasn't even talking to her. Well, that morning before coming to work, I was sick at my stomach, probably from the pregnancy, and wasn't really feeling good. I don't remember what I said, but I got these strange feeling that she knew I was pregnant, even with me wearing all those bulky dresses and blouses."

"That does sound a bit odd. Did she say anything else on other days after that?" says Father Luca, looking at Adela, who replies, "No, I'm not sure if she did any filing again with just the two of us in the room. I don't think so."

"Mariano and Adela, I don't think you have to worry about the nun. She was probably making a polite statement, thinking that you weren't feeling well, and maybe even looking like maybe you should go home. Don't worry, there's nothing she can prove. Well, let's finish dinner. I can't wait for that cherry pies," says Doc.

✦ ✦ ✦

Sometime later after the dishes are cleaned and put away, "Guy's," says Doc, "I want to thank you very much for helping with the dishes. You didn't have to do it, but thank you."

"Got the hot water boiling for tea. Let's sit in the other room," says Adela. Doc addresses Mariano, "Next time you see those little old ladies, tell them I have a birthday coming up, and their cherry pie sure does sound great for a present. You can't tell them I ate a slice tonight, thought it was wonderful. Also tell them I remember eating one of their pies at the last picnic we had at church. Maybe they might take a liking to make a pie for me."

"I will, Doc."

After eating the rest of the cherry pie with their hot tea, it was time to go home. Mariano says to Adela, "Sure would like to take a peek at Victor before we go."

"Sure, he is wonderful tonight, hasn't made a sound."

Adela and Mariano walk down the short hall and peek into the dark room at Victor, as Doc takes the plates into the kitchen.

"It sure is dark in there, can't see anything," Mariano says.

"It's supposed to be dark in there, otherwise he'll be making a lot on noise," says Adela quietly as they walk back to the living room.

"Yeah, I suppose so," he mumbles.

Doc is reviewing the plans just to make sure everyone is on the same sheet of music. "Now remember, I'm not bringing Victor tomorrow morning but the following day, early in the morning. Timing is very important."

Adela and Mariano thank Doc for a wonderful dinner and plan to see him in two days.

✦ ✦ ✦

The two are riding along in their buggy down the dirt road heading home, feeling very happy.

The horse's hoofs hitting the dirt the only sound to be herd, the moon shining brightly, Adela snuggles up close to Father Luca and gives him a little peck to his cheek and says, "I love you, Father Mariano Luca."

Father Luca stops around the corner of Adela's little house and helps her out of the coach and walks her to her door.

"What a wonderful evening this has been. I just hope everything will turn out OK," says Adela.

"It will. I'm just so happy that you and Victor are all right. So many things have been in the back of my mind, I think sometimes I'm going mad. A couple more days, and we can live sort of a normal life, all three together. I just can't tell you how happy I am since Doc has helped us. I owe him with my life."

"Yes, thank God for his help."

"Well, I must go now, got to put away the horse and buggy."

"Good night," says Adela as they kiss.

CHAPTER 29

The next morning as Father Luca unlocked the office door, Thomas had brought Adela and came up in front of the mercantile in their buggy.

"Thank you, Thomas," says Adela as he assists her out of the buggy, and she comes into the mercantile, saying, "Good morning," to one of the female workers, and she heads to the office. As she's almost to the office, Ethan sees her and he walks up and says, "Good morning, Adela. You look mighty radiant this beautiful day."

"Thank you, Ethan, it's a wonderful day. I'm just a little tired trying to get my energy back."

"Yes, I know, I had that bad stuff one time, as it'll grab ya and never let go. I know exactly how you feel. Don't work too hard today, maybe a half day would be a good idea."

"I'll talk it over with Father Luca. Thank you."

"Enjoy, talk with ya later." Ethan leaves.

"Well, good morning, Adela," says Father Luca as he slightly holds and quickly releases one of her hands. She walks by his desk and heads to her chair on the other side of the desk in their office.

"Adela, could you write a letter to Mrs. Silverstone thanking her for the lovely bread that her committee baked for the service last Sunday?"

"Father, which paper shall I use, the note paper or the formal paper?"

"I think we should use the formal paper. She likes to be seen and being in her leadership role of the committee. Also you might put it in a professional envelope."

+ + +

As noontime approaches, Adela tells Mariano, "I have made arrangements with Thomas to pick me up at twelve thirty and take me home. I don't think I should work a full day on the first day back to work. I also asked Thomas to leave the buggy in front of the mercantile after work for you."

"Are you coming over after work? I can fix something simple for dinner."

"Yes, I'll be there."

"Hello, Father," Thomas says as he walks into the office. "Are you ready, Adela? Got the buggy in front."

"I'll be ready in just a few minutes. I'm finishing up this letter for Mrs. Silverstone. Mariano, I'll drop the letter off at the post office for Mrs. Silverstone. Bye, bye."

+ + +

The next morning, it's the special day, Father Luca timed it perfectly, arriving at the same time as Ethan as he's opening up the double front doors to the mercantile. Father Luca pauses to say to Ethan, "I just can't believe how beautiful these days has been this last week."

"Yes, Father, it's really amazing. But don't be fooled, the weather will change very quickly sometime, and will get blazing hot. That's when lizards begin to beg for water."

"My, that does sound hot," says Father Luca as both men start walking down through the mercantile, heading toward Father Luca's office. Father Luca looks toward his office and says, "What could that be, a box at my front door?"

"Yeah, maybe more of your little baking ladies have brought you another present."

Father Luca bends down and picks up the box using both hands, when suddenly something moves inside.

Father Luca, showing a surprised look, yells, "It moved!" He almost drops the box, although his movement was intentionally done to make it look realistic. Ethan slightly jumps backward when Father Luca told him something moved inside, thinking that maybe someone was playing a trick and put some small animal in the box. Ethan, showing a little alarm, slowly reaches over and raises the corner of the towel to take a peek. Suddenly his eyes got big as he gasped, "My god, it's a baby in there!"

"A baby!" Father Luca yells. "In this box!" He franticly looks around to set the box down, and he turns around and sets it on the checkout counter. Quickly, Father Luca removes the towel off the box. He looks down into the box and sees his beautiful little Victor smiling back at him, and he almost loses it and starts to get chocked up. Quickly to control his emotions, he steps away and looks at Ethan and says, "Who's baby is it?"

"I don't know," replies Ethan. Both men look at each other, as Ethan says, "What do we do with a baby? Is someone here in the building shopping and forgot their baby? No, that can't be. I just opened up one minute ago. In a wooden box, who carries their children in a wooden box?" says Ethan as he raises his voice. Changing his tone, Ethan says, "I think this child is abandoned, someone left this child."

"Hey, what is this?" Ethan says as he sees a folded sheet of paper tucked in beside the baby. He pulls it out and opens it as he says it's a letter. "Father, listen to this." He begins to read it, "To Father Luca, it gives me a sad heart to write this letter, knowing I will be giving away part of my heart and soul. We cannot keep this beautiful boy. We are poor, and it's getting worse, and we have to move. We're not sure where we are going, so please do not try to contact us.

Find a wonderful family for my boy, and God bless him."

Father Luca, doing better now as he's controlling his emotions, says, "I experienced this one time when I was in Trenton, New Jersey, and found that the first person that needs to be contacted is a doctor to make sure the baby is not sick or might die. Doctors have that intuition about women, on who has given birth and who has not. Maybe he might know who's baby it is?"

"Your right, I'm going to have someone go and get Doc."

✦ ✦ ✦

As the hour passes, Father Luca sits in his office with Victor trying not to get attached with him right now, as Victor lays in the box surprisingly not making a fuss, waiting for Doc to arrive.

Ethan's busy going all over the mercantile as he pokes his head in the office every few minutes and asks if the Doc has arrived.

"Hello, Mariano," says Doc Murphy as he rushes into Father Luca's office, carrying his doctor's bag.

"I heard you have an unexpected visitor here." He glances at Mariano and gives him a wink. Doc pulls out a towel from his bag and starts wiping his hands as he asks Father Luca speaking loud so the several people standing outside of the office could hear him, "Father, where did you find this child, and was anyone with you?"

"Yes, Ethan and I were walking to my office. Ethan had just opened the mercantile this morning, and there was this box in front of my office door."

"Did you notice anyone you didn't know around here this morning?"

"No, I hadn't even opened my office, as I was talking with Ethan."

"Oh, I see," replies Doc, and reaches into the box and lifts the baby up into the air without the blanket he was wrapped in. He feels around the baby's body, examines his arms and feet, making sure there are no problems with the child.

Father Luca, looking at his Victor, has to look down so he wouldn't chock all up.

Doc, putting the baby back into the box, mumbles, "Everything seems normal, all clean, looks strong, and healthy." He gets out his stethoscope, hooking the two ear pieces into his ears, and lightly presses it to the little baby's chest. "Heart sounds fine."

"Father," says Doc, "I think it would be a good idea if I keep the little one at my place for the time being, until we can decide on what we are going to do with this little guy. It will give me some time to look around, maybe someone on the outskirts of town had the child. I'll get back with ya later." Doc picks up the box with the little baby in it and leaves, heading back to his office.

+ + +

That evening at Adela's little house, Mariano and Adela enjoys a wonderful dinner as they talk about what happened that day at the mercantile.

Mariano says, "Doc did an amazing job in pretending he didn't know Victor. He looked so professional, holding the cute little guy up in the air, looking him over, and then listening to his little heartbeat. It was hard for me to hold back as I watched."

Mariano suggests to Adela, "Tomorrow evening, let's go to Doc's house and start filling out the papers to adopt Victor. Just thinking about it today, when I looked into the box and seen our little Victor, pretending it was a baby being given away, I almost lost it. It was so hard for me to hold a straight face. I felt like picking him up and telling everyone it is my child."

"I know it must have been hard, Mariano. But the end is not too far away."

✦ ✦ ✦

Several days later with the help from Doc, Adela got herself a nice baby carriage with a cover to protect Victor from the sun. And she began to walk around town pushing her baby perambulator with her son, Victor, talking with ladies as she shopped.

Doc had turned in the paperwork to a friend of his who worked in the court house, getting the adoption papers pushed through the sometime lengthily process. Doc had pretended to have dug through all type of files, newspaper articles for any information about any woman giving birth to a child in town this last month, and could not come up with any birth. The adoption was blessed by Father Luca, the priest of the town, and Adela become the proud legal mother of Victor.

Thomas, in his spare time, started to transport Adela and Victor to different parts of the town, and she would walk back home pushing the buggy.

Father Luca started to come over to Adela's house more often, like several times a week, for dinner and to play with Victor. Slowly he started to feel that he was married to Adela, and he didn't have to hide the secret from the townspeople. As he was sitting around her small room talking with Adela, as Victor sleep peacefully in his crib, he said, "I was thinking back last month, when Mrs. Silverstone and her committee with the recommendation of the church's parishioners chose me to lay the cornerstone of the new church, with my name on the attached historical brass plate. I was almost overcome by emotions, just like the day Ethan and I found Victor at the office door. God, so many wonderful things have been happening to me lately, I wish that I could include you in some of those things. You have to pretend to have your child by an adoption, when in your heart, you know Victor is yours. God, I wish I could change things, but it's impossible."

"Mariano, you are such a wonderful man. I'm blessed to have had your child. Maybe someday, we can leave this town and start over, but society will not allow us to do that. I have noticed, your emotions are becoming strong with Victor. I know you would love to have him call your name, or say daddy when he starts to speak, but that cannot be. We will not be able to live together."

"I know, Adela, I've thought about that many times. I guess we'll just live the way we are for the time."

Then impulsively, Mariano gets this urge to tell Adela that he is not a real priest, everything about him is a lie, there is no hope for them. When suddenly something strange happens, sweat suddenly beaded on his forehead, he opens his mouth to speak and nothing comes out, no noise, no words. What is happening to him, he asks himself, and he starts to panic. *What happened to my voice?* He closes his eyes and tries to relax.

"Mariano, are you all right?" Adela asks.

Mariano's face flushed white, slightly looking disoriented, he looks at Adela and says, "My voice, what." He's realizing he can talk again. "I can talk now!" he says, smiling.

Mariano, pausing for moment as he rubs his face a couple times, says, "Wait, just a moment, I have to clear my head. I suddenly had this revelation about something I should do with Victor. This idea came from, I don't know where, it just popped into my mind. I don't know where it came from."

Not understanding what Mariano is trying to say, Adela says, "Mariano, I'm totally lost in what you were say and doing. It's not making any sense. Are you feeling all right?"

"I know, Adela, it's hardly making any sense to me as well."

"Are you getting a fever?" she asks, as she puts her hand on his forehead. "You feel a little warm, but not hot."

"I'm all right," Mariano says. "There was something like, I don't know where it came from, something like a command I heard." Mariano stops talking.

"It told you what?" Adela said as she begins to get a little nervous with Mariano and his actions.

"This voice, or maybe it wasn't a voice, but something told me that I should get a lock of hair from my son, Victor, and lay it under the cornerstone of the new church."

Adela is sitting there for a moment as she thinks about what Mariano just said. "There was a voice or something that told you this?" she says.

"Yes, it really sounds eerie."

"So this voice," says Adela, "or an afterthought suggestion that sounded unbelievably strange, but the idea sounds like something we want to do to celebrate the birth of Victor."

Mariano quietly says, "It sounds like something we can do, it won't be difficult. I can have a clip of Victor's hair in my pocket and slip it under the block when the workers slide it into place.

Adela agrees as she's thinking, *We can tell Victor after he's old enough to understand what we had done. His hair will be with the church for as long as the church is standing, which could be hundreds of years."*

"Yes, let's plan on it," says Mariano.

CHAPTER 30

Nolan, the old friend of Antonio who had changed his name to Father Mariano Luca just before he moved from Trenton, New Jersey, to Denver, Colorado, is still hanging around town.

He's making a few dollars digging in the foot hills looking for gold, but competition is furious with a lot of guys getting shot trying to steal other prospector's claims. As he sometimes thinks about it, he's still bitter about the gold he found in the railroad tunnel and hadn't been back to dig out the rest. The possibilities of getting back into the tunnel without the railroad's approval is none, too many security guards, so he's trying to forget the idea. Playing cards is a way he's making a few dollars now, but that might change if something else comes along. He's decided he won't being going back to Trenton. There's a lot more opportunities of making more money out here in Denver than back home.

He hasn't been back to see his buddy Antonio for some time. He feels a bit uncomfortable talking with him since he became a priest. Antonio just doesn't seem to be the old Antonio he knew when they worked together back home. They don't have the same things and ideas to talk about anymore.

It's Saturday, Nolan is sitting in a card game having a few beers in a salon on the other side of town. He has hooked up with a couple drunk drifters, one guy named Turk, who doesn't say much, the other guy the leader of the two, named Seblizki. Needing a fourth player, Seblizi snagged a guy name Gianno, a big man who just came into the salon.

"So your name is Gianno, that's Italian, isn't it," says Seblizki as he slurs his words to the new guy at the table.

"Yeah, that's right."

Finishing his bottle of beer and ordering another one, Sebliziki continues, "Well, what is an Italian doing in Denver? It's a long way from home."

"I came here to make money, digging for gold."

"It looks like you wouldn't have any problems digging in a hole."

Gianno didn't like the smartass comment Seblizki had made. "What part of the world did you dig in and your friend crawled from?" Gianno asks sarcastically. Turk hasn't said a word, as he continues to drink his beers and look at his cards.

Seblizki is drunk as he replies, "Oh, we came from New York area, too damn people there, and not enough women," as he slightly laughs.

Gianno asks, "Are we going to play cards, or are we getting all friendly?" and Seblizki began dealing the cards, not saying anything.

After playing cards for a while, Sebliziki begins mumbling again and says, "Does anyone know of a man who came from Trenton, who's a priest or something like that. Maybe he's not a priest?"

No one says anything, as they continue to play cards as Seblizki drinks another beer. After playing for a while, he begins to talk and mumble again, "You know, this priest isn't a real priest at all, he's a phony, you know that, and if I kill him, I can get five hundred dollars, you know that." As he continues to ramble, no one at the table says a word as they continue to play cards.

Nolan doesn't want to get in a conversation with this drunk, and he's starting to think he needs to get out of the game before trouble might start. He has won several hands and has made some money off these guys, and it might be the wrong time to leave the game, so he has decided to stay in for a while longer. The drunk starts to talk gibberish again, not making a lot of sense as he says, "There's a building, or that is it's a church or maybe it is both," as he mumbles a description. "This place tomorrow, we get free wine. It's popular, but maybe it's a salon?" as he directs his question toward Nolan, who replies, "No, I don't know of any place."

"You haven't heard of this place," he raises his voice as he looks around at the other players slurring his words. "I thought everyone should know this place. I just heard about it yesterday, no maybe it was yesterday morning, no, someone told me, and me and my friend are going tomorrow for free wine." He points his thumb toward his buddy Turk.

As Nolan continues to play cards, he's thinking about what the drunk just said. *A man from Trenton, New Jersey, and phony priest. What was this five hundred dollars dead about?*

Nolan is thinking, *Does any of this might implicate Antonio, alias Father Luca? I need to warn him about this drunk.*

Now he's thinking more about what the drunk had just said. *What is he talking about five hundred dollars dead? If I tell Antonio and I'm wrong, then we can have a nice meeting, maybe we might have a few more of those nice beers we had last time at his office. But if I'm right, Antonio will be in serious trouble.*

+ + +

The next day, it's Sunday service at the mercantile today, everyone has arrived early dressed in their working clothes. It's kind of strange looking at the appearance of the parishioners, not in the Sunday's best, but dressed in old, worn clothing ready to work. The women are busy talking with each other about what they are cooking and bringing for the workers for lunch and dinner. Ethan is busy making arrangements of where they're going to put up the tables for the meals and tables for the card players.

Ethan tells a couple workers, "Let's bring those wooden planks out of the building and use the bags of potatoes and the other burlap-filled bags for seating at the long tables. Just bridge the wooden planks from bag to bag. It works perfectly.

We'll keep the card tables inside." Ethan spots two of the workers moving the apple crates to the side of the room, and he stops him and says, "Hey, wait a minute, don't move those crates. Move them back to where they were. Those crates are what Father Luca stands on during service. If he didn't have them, people in the back might not be able to see him."

In front of the mercantile, many wagons and buggies were tied up at the hitching posts from the parishioners going to the service. They're parked there until the service is over, filled with shovels, picks, saws, hammers, sledgehammers, tools to be used in digging the trenches for the foundations of the new church. After service, the owners of these wagons and friends will head to the area of where the new church will be built about three blocks way. They will work until dinner is ready at the mercantile and return for a festival.

Most of the townspeople have experience digging in the hard dirt using their picks and shovels.

The diggers will follow the lines that were staked out by the land surveyors. They will dig long deep trenches several feet wide in the hard dirt, followed by the wood carpenters who will build wooden framework in the trenches, extending several feet higher than ground level, for the cement to be poured later. Inspectors follow the carpenters with their plum bobs, making sure the walls of the foundation are straight.

Service is just about ready as everyone has found a seat somewhere in the mercantile, the late arrivers standing since some of the seating has been moved outside for the tables to eat on.

Ethan, standing in the front of the barn-like room is instructing the parishioners, "Please, everyone, the service will start real soon. Everyone must find a seat or stand."

After several minutes, there's still a loud buzz of people talking, moving around, still trying to find a seat, and some are just having a nice conversation with their neighbor. Ethan decides if he doesn't get control, the church service will be running very late. He needs to make an announcement. Ethan, a big man, puts both hands into the air and announces, "Please, please, the service has started." Everyone got quite quickly. Father Luca comes out of his office wearing his frock, carrying his Bible with the underlined phrases. He works his way toward the front. He slowly weaves in and out of people and round several potato bags with parishioners sitting on top of them as one man got up to give him room to get by, heading to the front of the big room. Getting close to the front, he spots big Ethan and heads in his direction. There he gets up on the apple crates with his assistance. He stands on the apple crates, smiling as he looks out at all the people, seeing many new faces, and many faces he recognizes. Then says, "My family, I'm very happy today that so many of us can come this morning. It is such a wonderful and meaningful day today." He pauses as he looks at all the excitement on all the faces, young, old, black, white, brown, big, small, beautiful, and...everyone are equal. Father Luca put both hands up into the air and says, "Today, it gives me great pleasure to announce that we are starting construction on our own beautiful stoned church."

Everyone starts clapping, and they continued to clap for five minutes. After the applause has stopped, he says, "Bow your heads and let us pray." After the prayer, he begins to read a few scriptures he had underlined in his Bible and spoke for a while about hope. He tells everyone, "Today will be a short service. Just working on the new church will be a prayer from yourself, to God, and that everyone here who works today is blessed."

✦ ✦ ✦

The service is over, and everyone rushes in different directions. The women are busy getting the tables organized and started cooking the meat for dinner. The men are out in their wagons heading down the street to the open lot, where the new church is going to be built on. Ethan and his group of workers are organizing the seating inside and outside of the mercantile.

Rory, the railroad supervisor, at his camp in the foothills has loaded ten workers in two wagons with tools and are running late for the Sunday service. But they're ready to dig ditches and help build the wooden foundation for the new church. These workers are looking forward to eating a great home-cooked meal with free wine. They have been eating the same old meals almost every day and are getting tired of them. A couple workers are looking forward of getting into some serious card games, with people who have money.

Ethan has approved a waiver for the railroad workers where they don't have to be at the service in order to be served free wine after the service. These workers have been selected by their company to represent their railroad. They will be observed under the watchful eye of their supervisor, Rory.

Seblizki and his buddy Turk has finally arrived at the mercantile on their horses. Seblizki says to Turk, "This looks like the place, a lot of buggies, horses, and wagons. Let's tie our horses around the corner." They walk into the building, not saying a word to anyone as they walk around, looking for a place to sit. They spot several tables in the back part of the room that had been set up by Ethan's workers for card games. Pulling out several chairs, they sit down.

Sebliziki looking around, he nudges Turk's boot under the table to get his attention. "Nice-looking place. We should have found this place a long time ago. Look what we have been missing," he mumbles to Turk, who hasn't said a word. Sebliziki pulls out a pack of cigarette and lights one, handing the pack to Turk, who does the same, as they look around wondering where they get their free wine.

Sebliziki stops an attractive young woman worker as she passes their table carrying an armful of table covers and asks, "Hey, honey, where do we get our free wine?" Pausing briefly, she asks, "Were you here for the service?"

Pausing for a moment, as his brain's dead from too much beer, he replies, "Oh yeah, I remember that. Yes, of course, we were, honey, we were in the back here, up front was too crowded."

"You are early, we won't be giving out the wine until we start eating. That won't happen for about another hour or so, after the men return from working on the church. We are still setting things up."

"Yeah, well thanks, honey, for the information," mumbles Sebliziki as he's trying to smile.

"Your welcome," she says as she hurries off.

"Now that is a cute dame. I'm going to get to know her," growls Sebliziki as he watches her walk away.

"I can't wait for a couple of hours."

Looking at Turk, he asks, "Did you see a salon when we got here?"

"Nope, didn't see nothing," replies Turk.

"Let's get out of this place," says Sebliziki as he's getting upset.

"I need to find a drink," he grumbles as both men stagger out of the mercantile heading to their horses. After riding for about five blocks, they started to think there are no salons in this part of town, then they stumble onto one located in an alley and started to drink.

✦ ✦ ✦

Nolan has arrived on his horse and rushes into the mercantile, heading to Father Luca's office, finding his office door locked. Wondering what is he going to do, he stops someone walking by.

"Excuse me," Nolan asks, "do you know where I might find Father Luca?"

"Oh sure," replies the man. "Father Luca was invited by several businessmen and the ladies committee group to go over to where they are working on the foundation of the new church. They all left in several wagons and should be back in about two hours, for dinner. We are very lucky, the railroad has sent several wagons full of workers here to help out."

"Thanks for the info," replies Nolan.

Nolan's thinking, *I don't want to interrupt Father Luca and all his guests, and maybe my warning might turn out to be nothing. That drunk at the card game was wasted and probably got everything twisted in his brain with all those beers he had drunk, and he'd never be able to find this place. Hanging around here's not a good idea. I don't know anyone. Now, there's that ongoing open card game, several miles away at Mitch's salon, and I can get into it and make some money before it gets too late.*

✦ ✦ ✦

Several hours later, all the railroad workers have finished work and are on their way back to the mercantile in their two wagons, followed by four wagons full of businessmen, women from the committee group, and Father Luca, all happy and talking about everything looking for a wonderful dinner.

"Dinner is now being served, find your seats," Ethan announces as he walks around telling everyone. The dinner is being served at the long tables outside in the back side of the mercantile, with its large back doors opened. Everyone has seated, and the volunteers are bringing out the food to all the tables. People who don't want to seat outside are sitting at the tables set up inside in the big room. Several volunteers are walking around with large carafes of wine, pouring everybody's glasses.

CHAPTER 31

"**L**et's go find game and get some free wine," Sebliziki mumbles to Turk as they leave the salon they have been in for several hours drinking. After riding for some time, making several wrong turns getting lost, they eventually make their way back to the mercantile. Not finding a place to tie their horses, they drop the bridle reins to the ground and make their way into the building. Dragging their drunk feet, the two head to the same table they were at many hours earlier that's still open and crash down into their chairs. Rory and several of the railroad workers are playing cards next to the table where Sebliziki and Turk decided to sit. There are several other tables in the area, where cards games are going on. Sebliziki pulls out a deck of cards out of his trousers and drops them on the table. Looking at Turk, he grunts, "We have to find two players, we can't play by ourselves."

Turk nods his head.

As they sit looking around for another player, a woman walks up carrying a large carafe of wine and asks, "Are you two interested in a glass of wine?"

"Well, hell yes, we are, we're almost dried out," Sebliziki replies, slurring his words. Trying to smile at the woman, he says, "We are looking for several card players, do you want to play with us?" Sebliziki belches out his words.

"No, thanks, but if I find someone, I'll send them here," she says as she pours them two full glasses of wine.

"Yeah," mumbles Seblizki as he drinks all of the glass of wine the woman poured. "Oh, can we have a refill?" he asks the woman? "Sure, you must be very dry," replies the woman as she refills his glass.

As the two drunks are drinking, trying to find two players, a man walks up and asks, "Is this a closed game, or are you looking for two players?"

"Sure, we're looking for a couple players, and you can play with us. All we need is one more." Sebliziki is slurring his words again.

As the three players are sitting, smoking their cigarettes, drinking their free wine, they keep looking around for a fourth player. Just then, Father Luca comes walking by their table.

"Hello, Father," Sebliziki says as he smiles, which was rare.

"Hello, men, how are you doing?" replies Father Luca. "Did you enjoy that wonderful meal, it was excellent, wasn't it?" he asks.

"No, we were late."

"Oh, you're new here. I haven't seen you before."

"This the first time, haven' t come in this part of town before. I'm wondering, we need a fourth player. You need to play several hands, it sure would help our morale a little, until another player comes." Sebliziki managed to spit the words out of his mouth.

"I'm not sure, I don't play very well."

"We can show you. Just a few hands until someone else come by."

"Well, maybe," says Father Luca as he pauses looking at the three players. "OK, just a few, then I must go."

"That would be great," said the third player who just joined the game himself.

Sebliziki says, as he begins to shovel the cards, "Let's play five card draw, you can throw everything away if you want to. It's OK." He looks around at all the players, and they all looked with blank expressions. "We're not going to use money the first two hands so Father here can understand the game," he spits out the words.

Father Luca is thinking, he knew how to play cards back when he was Antonio, and not a priest in Jersey, but he can't let them know that now. He will make a few stupid mistakes, and they will ask him to leave the game.

As they began to play the first game, Father Luca makes a few stupid mistakes, and Sebliziki gets mad. "Hey, Father, you really that dumb? Why did you throw that card down? That is not the way I had shown you."

They played a couple more minutes when Sebliziki mumbles, "Father, I know you can't be that stupid. Where are you from? I know you are not from here, you sound like you're from New York or around there. Are you from New York?" Father looked surprised that the drunk almost guessed the state he is from and didn't say anything.

"Oh, you looked surprised, but I don't think you're from there. I know, you are from Jersey." The wild guess surprised Father Luca, and Sebliziki saw his startled look on his face. Sebliziki is starting to get agitated because Father Luca is not answering his questions, and he thinks he's really dumb.

"Yeah, well, ya know, I'm from New York, and I have heard a lot of you dumb people from New Jersey. Where are you from, what church did you preach at?"

Rory, sitting at the table next to theirs, says, "Hey, mister, you can't talk to our priest like that. Why don't you leave? You are drunk as shit."

"I'll talk the way I want to, and no one is going to stop me," mumbles Sebliziki. He continues with his tirade. "This stupid Father can't play cards."

Father Luca stands up from the game and says, "I'm sorry if I made a few mistakes. I told you at the beginning, I'm not a good card player, and I'm leaving the game."

"Hey, Father, why don't you sit your ass back down? We haven't finished," says Sebliziki when he suddenly gasps. "Hey wait, what happened to that money I had on the table?" He starts looking around the table. All the players started scanning the table. Looking for the missing money, they look under the table. No one can find the money Sebliziki claims he had.

Suddenly Sebliziki starts jabbing his finger at Father Luca, saying, "I think the father here is a crook and a thief, and I think he just stole my money," and jumps up from the table, almost falling down, knocking cards all over the table as he's struggling to pull his gun out of his trousers.

Finally, he's got the gun out and starts yelling at Father Luca, "You are a no-good thief cloaked in a priest's cloth, and I kill thieves."

Rory, sitting close to their table, grabs Sebliziki's arm that's holding the gun. Sebliziki swings his arm free from his tight grip, spins around, and fires one shot, hitting the big man in his shoulder, knocking him out of the chair to the floor. Father Luca, already standing, shocked and in disbelief, not thinking about his safety, says quickly, "Help me Lord, I must stop this madman." He makes a lunge at Sebliziki, who fires three shots, all hitting him in the stomach. Father Luca, still moving forward in the lunge, grabs the barrel of the gun, twisting Sebliziki's hand around, pointing it back into his stomach, and the gun fires one bullet into his stomach. Both Father Luca and Sebliziki are standing for several seconds before falling to the floor with Father Luca falling on top. Everyone at the card tables are standing, as they stare in shock at all three bodies lying on the floor.

Everyone in the building had stopped what they were doing when they heard the gunshots.

Several men and Ethan come running from the festival's dinner in the direction of the gunshots.

Someone starts yelling, "Call the doc, call the doc!" Doc sitting at the long table with Adela and her son, Victor, in a baby carriage, just finished their dinner, relaxing as they are having a glass of wine.

A woman came running up to where Doc is sitting, yelling, "Three people are shot at the card tables. One of them is our priest, Father Luca, oh Lordy, oh Lordy!" She continues to cry.

Doc grabs his bag and start walking as fast as he can through the mercantile to where the card tables are at.

When he gets there, everyone is petrified, still standing in disbelieving shock. Doc grabs the closest person he's beside, telling him, "Here, grab those table cloths, roll them up in a ball, and press them directly on the wound. Press hard to stop the bleeding. As Doc is giving instructions on what these men need to do, he's pulling off his coat and rolling up his sleeves, looking at all the victims, trying to assess the situation.

"Here." He grabs another man and says, "Watch this man, have him show you what you need to do, you need to stop the bleeding." Doc is quickly talking to a couple of guys telling them, "Get Rory up in that chair," as he points to one. "Help him get his shirt off, and press on the wound to stop the bleeding using one of those tablecloths."

Doc is focusing as he opens up his bag hooking his stethoscope around his neck. He tells another man standing beside him, "Please keep everyone back. I need some room."

Doc, with several other men, slowly rolls Father Luca off Sebliziki, both men are covered with blood. Doc glances up and sees half a dozen men and women all praying on their knees only five feet away. "God Lord," grumbles Doc. "Please, if we can have more help, it would be mighty appreciative," he says.

Suddenly the entire small room is packed with onlookers. Doc is looking around the room for something he can use like a stretcher or something to carry Father Luca on and says, "We need to get something to lay Father Luca on to carry him out to the wagon so we can rush him to my office." Doc starts cutting away Father Luca's frock with a pair of scissors from his bag, to examine the bullet wound. He then puts the scope on Father Lucas chest. "Yes, I have a heartbeat, but it's weak," he mumbles.

"Hurry up with what you found," Doc says loudly. Suddenly, Ethan arrives carrying the door he removed from Father Luca's office. "Doc, I hope this will help," says Ethan.

"Great," Doc replies, and several men clear a spot where they can lay the door down on the floor.

Everyone helps to lift Father Luca up onto the door.

Suddenly a woman screams out, "Oh god, my Mariano!" Everyone briefly turns around and sees Adela standing with her baby Victor in his perambulator, with both hands to her mouth, as she collapses. Two men standing beside her catches her and sets her in a chair, getting her some water. Eight strong men lift the door up into the air and carries Father Luca out through the big double doors of the mercantile to the wagon and slides him in the back.

Doc, kneeling as he listen to Sebliziki's chest for a heartbeat, tries several locations, then he feels for a pulse on his wrist, slides his hand in several locations on the side of his neck, then he raises up his head and slightly shakes it and says, "I can't hear a beat, he's gone."

Rory's been helped by several of his railroad workers as he's walked out to one of their wagons, and he sits on the tail end of the wagon. Doc's still yelling orders as he barks, "While you are there, get some boiling water. Does anyone have some additional clean linen, that I will need?"

Doc continues with orders, calling out as Father Luca's wagon begins to leave, "Get him to my office and carry him into my surgery room in the back and put him on the table. I will be right behind yeah." Doc rushes over to see Adela, and several women attending to her. Thomas has managed to get through the crowd as he's helping Adela. He's got a wet cloth and is applying it to her forehead.

Several men had carried Sebliziki out to another wagon and slides him in the back. There is no rush for him, he has been pronounced dead by Doc.

✦ ✦ ✦

It's night time now, Doc is still at his office, and now he's taken a break, looking very tired as he sits in his comfort chair in the front room of his office. He's finishing a short glass of brandy, and Adela is sitting across from him in another comfortable chair, relaxed after she had finished her glass of brandy. The baby carriage is by her, with Victor in it.

"Mariano is a fine man," Doc begins. "He's helped everyone through the church and through his personal feelings. I tried my best with what equipment I have and my knowledge, but I can't see any hope in his recovery. There are three bullets in a very bad spot, and I can't operate on them. Even if he was in better condition, I couldn't operate. He is extremely weak, and getting weaker very hour. I think you should visit him now while he's still alive. I don't know if he's conscious, but now should be the time to visit." By having the glass of Brandy, Adela has calmed herself down.

Adela walks slowly down the hallway, pushing Victor in his carriage. She stops and slowly opens the door and sees her Mariano laying on the bed, partly covered, looking peaceful as he's sleeping. "My beautiful man," she whispers as she lightly holds his hand as she sits on the edge of the bed. You are a wonderful man, making me happy every time you turn around. I try to remember all those happy times we had together. And oh, how foolish we were in getting secretly married and having a wonderful healthy boy. For a while, I feared that we might lose our Victor, but God helped us. I wished you would have been able to enjoy the pleasures of growing with your little boy. Victor is with me sleeping in his carriage right next to you right now. We both could have been banished from this town, and you losing your priesthood, but it was all worth it while it lasted. We had a wonderful life, and I shall never forget my wonderful Mariano."

Briefly, Adela felt Mariano's hand slowly squeeze her hand for a couple seconds, then she felt it relax and fall open with no other movement. She knew he had heard her, or acknowledged her, but now he is gone. She's deeply thinking, *Maybe Mariano didn't hear everything I said, but in his last dying effort, he let me know he loved me.* Adela came out of the room and saw Doc sitting there. Both looked at each other, and she said, "I think my Mariano is gone!"

Doc got up from his chair and hugged Adela for several minutes. Not saying a word, he walks down to the room where Father Mariano Luca is lying. Using his stethoscope, he listened for a heartbeat on his chest and found none, then moving to another location on his chest, still not hearing any beat. Then he puts his fingers on the side of Father Luca's neck, feeling for a pulse in several spots, and found none. Slowly removing the scope from his ears, Doc stands up and does a sign of the cross over his chest and says, "My good friend, Father Mariano Luca, may God be with you, and rest in peace, Amen."

A little while later, Thomas has arrived at Doc's office to see if he can help and give Adela a ride back to her home. Doc tells Thomas, "Father Luca has just passed." Thomas could hardly believe what Doc just told him, and he started to show a lot of emotion. He excuses himself, stepping outside for a while to be alone as he cries.

Father Luca will be kept at Doc's office as he contacts Andy, the undertaker, who will come over first thing in the morning to see Father Luca and start making arrangements for the funeral.

It's late and Thomas and Adela are getting ready to go home, and Doc's very concerned if they are emotionally all right.

Doc says, "I can throw something together, and you both can stay here for the night. Adela looks at Doc and says, "Doc, thank you for the thoughtful idea, but I couldn't stay here with my Mariano in the other room. I must go home and accept what has happened."

"Good night to both of you, and, Victor, try to sleep," says Doc as he gives Adela a hug and shakes Thomas's hand.

CHAPTER 32

Early the next morning at Doc's office, he's poured himself a mug of stale coffee, standing in the middle of his front room, mentally putting things in order what he has to do today. In between sips of coffee, he's stretching out his body kinks he got after sleeping on the office sofa last night. Walking slowly, he goes into the back room where he has a small stove and began cooking a few eggs and bacon, finding two-day-old biscuits in the cupboard. It was too late last night to go home. Reason why he didn't go home, too long of drive and return early the next day, knowing there's going to be a lot of visitors today.

Doc is finishing up his breakfast when he hears a buggy pulling up in front of his office. Shortly he hears Bishop Mangini's driver, Christopher, call out, "Doc, hello, Doc. Are you here? It's Christopher."

"Yes, Christopher, I'm on my way out," says Doc, and he comes out into the front office and opens the front door.

"Hello, Christopher, how are you doing? It's been a while since I've seen you."

"Yes, Doc, I've been busy with visitors from out of town, and all the meetings with the development of the new church. Isn't it terrible news about the shooting of Father Luca? He was such a nice and understanding man, it's terrible."

"Yes, Christopher, he was a wonderful man, and it's going to be even more devastating for all the parishioners in this part of town."

"Doc," Christopher asks, "is it too early for a visit with Bishop Mangini? He's waiting in the buggy.

He didn't know if you were here or at your home."

"Yes, yes, please have him come in," says Doc.

A few minutes later, Bishop Mangini walks into the room. "Doc, how are you doing, my good friend," he says as he walks into Doc's office, and both men embrace and hug.

233

"It's so tragic, I can't believe it. Father Luca was such a liked man doing so well," Bishop Mangini says with a saddened face. He continues, "Doc, how are you holding up? You must be very tired with all the emergencies and so many patients at the same time."

"Yeah, it's been quite hectic. Andy is going to be by here in a while to do some measuring for the casket. He's going to design a beautiful one for Father Luca."

"Doc, I've had a meeting with Mother Cabrini, and we have decided that Father Luca will be buried right next to the new church. If it wasn't for him, we would not have the construction of the church happening right now. We'll have his grave completely ringed with a fence so it will not be disturbed by the construction of the church."

Bishop Mangini quickly changed his tone of voice from praiseworthy to quietness. He asks Doc, "Can you take me in to see Mariano? I want to have a final and private moment with him before everyone starts arriving."

"Sure, Bishop Mangini, come this way." Doc and the bishop walk down the narrow hall and stops at a door on the left.

"This is his room," says Doc as he turns around and leaves, leaving the bishop alone in the hallway. Bishop Mangini stands at the door for a few moments, says something under his breath, and he opens the door and enters.

An hour later, Bishop Mangini comes walking down the hall, out into the front room, and says to Doc who's sitting in his chair. "I had a wonderful talk with Mariano, and he will be happy of where he's journey will take him. May his soul rest in peace."

"Hello, Bishop Mangini," says Andy, the undertaker, sitting in another chair, who arrived earlier, waiting for Bishop Mangini to come out of the room.

Bishop Mangini replies, "Hi, Andrew, how have you been, my good friend? If you can, I would like for you to make Father Luca as radiant as if he was in real life. He was just a wonderful young man and had so much going for himself in this small part of town. So many people will deeply miss him, and now he is gone. We'll have an open casket very soon, don't have the exact time yet."

"I will," replies Andy.

✦ ✦ ✦

Ethan and Thomas are at the mercantile, reorganizing everything that was moved for the celebration dinner. They're talking about what kind of funeral the town should have and need to get with Andy and Doc to see what they think. Impulsively, Ethan snapped his fingers and said, "I've got a great idea. Why don't we have an open viewing right here at the mercantile, almost everyone in town thinks this is their church anyway. We can have it up close in the front of the building, where they can enter from one side and exit out the other. There won't be any clogged foot traffic."

"Yes, that sounds like a good idea, if it won't interfere with your business," replies Thomas.

"Well, it might, but most of my regular customers arrive in the back, with their wagons."

Thomas agrees, "Yeah, I understand Andy should be able to build the casket today. I also heard that Bishop Mangini will authorize to bury Father Luca right beside the church, and not up on the mesa. I think Father Luca would enjoy that very much."

After they had moved several bags of potatoes to the other side of the room, Thomas says, "Getting that monster Sebliziki into the ground will be no problem. We'll dig a hole and drop him in it. There will be no service."

After a few minutes as the two men move more items, Thomas says, "I've got to get with Christopher about where the bishop has decided to have Father Luca buried."

"Say, how is Rory doing?" Ethan asks. "Rory and part of his working crew are staying over at the hotel and will be heading back to their camp in a couple of days. While the supervisor's resting, five of his men are continuing to work on the digging and the building of the foundation for the church. Those guys are the hardest damn workers I have ever seen."

"I guess working on the railroad definitely builds stamina and puts muscle on your body. Maybe next time, I could get a couple of those guys to move some of this stuff," says Ethan as he's straining to move a piece of a field plow he has in the corner.

✦ ✦ ✦

Early this morning, Christopher stopped by the mercantile and left a drawn map with Thomas of where Bishop Mangini and Mother Cabrini had decided to have Father Luca buried. Andy, the undertaker, got his buckboard wagon out of his garage and has cleaned it up in preparation for the funeral procession to carry Father Mariano Luca's casket tomorrow to the grave site.

Ethan had talked with Andy, Doc, and the bishop, and they all agreed they will open up the mercantile for viewing of Father Mariano Luca in the morning at 10:00 a.m., before the day starts to warm up. The funeral procession will begin at 2:00 p.m., with Andy and the casket in the lead, and proceed to the church's construction site. Thomas had written a note with all the needed information about the funeral and tacked it to the bulletin board in front of the mercantile building, keeping everyone posted about the funeral.

Ethan had moved all merchandise from around the site where Father Luca will rest for viewing.

Father Luca's casket will be positioned at the entrance in the mercantile. With posted signs, people will be able to enter through one door and exit through the other door, which will eliminate congestion. The casket will be put on a low table covered with a plain blanket. Andy will leave his wagon in front of the mercantile until the viewing is over, at about 1:30 p.m.

+ + +

The next day, it's 10:00 a.m., the townspeople are in a line stretched up into the mercantile, and exiting out the other door. The casket of Father Mariano Luca will be open for two and half hours for viewing. A sign posted by the viewing line explains the viewing rules. "There is to be no touching, kissing, or laying flowers on Father Luca. All prayers must be short. And no taking of souvenirs strictly enforced." Hundreds of people are arriving, some of them from out of the city, and some have never been to a service. Some of the mourners had never seen Father Luca, but they are there to show their respect. Many people have been leaving flowers and other small items beside the casket, and many stop and lay their heads on the casket as they are grieving.

Ethan has a worker standing beside the casket to enforce the rules as they try to keep curious people from wanting to touch Father Luca, or wanting to have a souvenir or something.

It's 1:30 p.m., the viewing of Father Luca is over. The pallbearers wearing black dress clothes lift Father Luca's casket and takes it outside to Andy's wagon and slide it into the back, covering it with a dark red cover. Another person gathers up all the flowers that were left with the casket and sitting on the floor and put them into another waiting wagon that will take them to the grave site.

Andy is in his buck wagon with Father Luca's casket dressed with beautiful flowers, waiting to be told when the procession will start. He will be followed by Bishop Mangini, Mother Cabrini, and Sister Anna in their carriage with a sun cover, driven by Christopher. The next buggy has Adela and Victor, Doc Murphy, Ethan, with Thomas driving, followed by the carriage of Mr. Notary and his wife, Carmine, and several other wagons following. There were many mourners riding horses, some walking the five blocks to the new church. Most of the women in the procession were using parasols to protect them from the sun. The funeral procession will go down the street for three blocks and turn on Osage Street, where the new church is under construction halfway down the street.

Ethan has gotten out of this buggy and walks up and tells Andy, "I think everyone is here. Just start off slow and keep the same pace. There are a lot of people walking, and some of them are old and can't walk too fast. You know where the street is. It's Osage Street, make a right and a couple hundred feet on your left. Jeremy and Enrique are already there, making sure everything is in place. They'll direct you where to park the wagon. Most likely you will be parked next to the grave. Bishop will speak from the bed of your wagon. Got any questions?"

"Nope, got everything."

Ethan hustles back to his wagon he's riding in.

There were hundreds of people in the precession, and it slowly starts moving down the road, heading to the lot where the new church will be built. Small groups of people are standing beside the road, all showing the sign of crossing their hearts as Father Luca's casket passes by.

Bishop Angelo Mangini is standing on the bed of Andy's buckboard parked beside the open grave, with a large pile of dirt on one side of the grave. Many wagons and buggies parked close by, and some wagons managed to work their way into the middle of the construction site, messing up some of the dug ditches. Parishioners were standing all around the grave site, some were straddling the deep trenches dug in the rough dirt for the church's foundations, trying to get a better view of the grave. The pallbearers had set Father Luca's casket on a spread-out blanket on the edge of the grave. Everyone is constantly moving around the construction site, trying to get a better view. All the mourners had completely surrounded the grave as Bishop Mangini eulogized Father Mariano Luca.

Off out of the way from the funeral, an old wagon sits full of working tools used to dig grave, Jeremy and Enrique, the grave diggers, sitting on their wagon seat. They could hardly see where Father Luca will be laid to rest because of the enormous crowd of people. The people are standing shoulder to shoulder around the grave as Jeremy says, "I didn't really get to know Father Luca.

Just a couple times he walked by while we were at a grave waiting for the service to be over so we can fill it in."

"Yeah, it's really sad," says Enrique. "He was the only priest we ever had, so sad. I wonder how long will it be until we get another priest?"

"You know, Ethan didn't do that bad," says Jeremy.

"Yeah, Ethan did all right, but he wasn't a priest, and he didn't follow the Bible much."

Jeremy stands up and says as he's swaying his head around trying to get a better look, "The bishop is saying a prayer for Father Luca now, maybe we both should stand." They both stand up."

The pallbearers start to lower Father Luca's casket into the ground, hand over hand as they let the rope slide, all the pallbearers moving at the same time, inch by inch making sure the casket doesn't turn and fall, and the mourners get to their knees, if they can, and start to pray.

After several long minutes, Bishop Mangini says another prayer, and the funeral finishes. Then a line forms as the mourners walk by the grave, getting a handful of soil and throwing it in on the casket as they say a quiet prayer, then walks away. Then some of the mourners start walking up to the grave, and they started saying personal prayers as they stretch their arms out up into the air above the casket. As it lay down in the grave, some were casting more flowers in on and around the casket. There started to be a large crowd jockeying around, looking down into the grave, expressing their personal feelings to Father Luca.

After some time, the mourners begin leaving in their wagons. Some who started walking are offered rides as the wagons and buggies passes by. About two hours pass as the last two mourners that have been praying start walking away.

Jeremy nudges Enrique, "Hey, buddy, it looks like it's our time now." He picks up the reins and commands his horse, and they begin to navigate their wagon over next to the grave.

"Ya know," Enrique, says to Jeremy, "Andy had ordered the headstone and will have it done in a couple of weeks. It's going to be a large stone of some kind, and we'll be needing some additional help to move it and to put it into place. Also to protect the grave site, Mr. Notary got several carpenters who will construct a nice white picket fence around the grave, after the headstone has been put into place."

CHAPTER 33

The next day, Doc's at his office busy with two elderly women who had walked too far in the funeral procession, complaining about their feet are killing them. He's got the two women comfortably sitting in the front room with their feet soaking in a warm pan of Epsom salt to sooth their aching feet. One of the women asks Doc, "That's all you gonna do for us, just soaking in a warm pan of water? I could have done that at home."

"Just keep your feet in the pan, and you will see wonders in a while from now."

Thomas has been at his office in the mercantile, wondering what has happened to the office door that was used to carry Father Luca out to the wagon.

One of the workers at the mercantile told him, "I helped Ethan remove your door to your office for them to carry Father Luca out to the wagon, and I think it's at Doc's office."

Thomas was on his way over to Doc's office to retrieve the office door when he decides since he was in the neighborhood, he'd stop by and see how Adela's doing. She didn't come into work today.

Thomas parks his buggy and knocks on her door, and she come to the door. "Hello, Thomas," she says. "Won't you please come in." She opens the screen door.

"Hi, Adela," he says and gives he a small hug and walks in.

"Are you going somewhere?" he says as he looks around at all the boxes and her luggage carrier lying open on the floor. "Last night, it was impossible for me to get any sleep. With my Mariano getting killed, I was not prepared for that." She began to tear up.

"With my Mariano gone, I'm totally lost, I don't know what I'm going to do. There has been so much going on, I'm totally exhausted, and I'm in too much pain. What can I do?"

241

Thomas, trying to find the right words, he begins, "Well, you can still work here in the church's office. You can do the filing for..." He stops talking, knowing his words are going in the wrong direction. Then he continues, "I can see what you mean."Adela tells him, "I can't bring Victor to the office and try to do work. If I have to go somewhere, I can't be taking Victor with me. My Mariano was everything to me, and now he's gone, I have nothing here."

Thomas sadly says, "Bishop Mangini said he might be able to get another priest but not sure when. What I understand, there was no priest here for many years until Father Luca showed up."

"Yes, Thomas, but I would have to start my life all over again with a new priest, and with my Mariano's spirit still here, right here in this office, I would not be able to handle it. I don't really want to talk with anyone about staying here because they will want to try and change my mind. I thought about this all last night. I think I have to go someplace far away and start life all over. I have checked the train schedule and will be catching the train tomorrow morning at 12:45 p.m. I've had some conversations with several people who told me Los Angeles, in California, would be a wonderful place to start over, and the weather is not as harsh as it's here."I was hoping you will be able to take me and Victor to the bank so that I can withdraw Mariano and my money out of our account so Victor and I will be able to live on, until I get established. I shouldn't take too long at the bank. I would like to be at the station tomorrow at 11:45 a.m., the train here is so unpredictable sometimes."

"Yes, Adela, that would be no problem at all. And I will definitely miss you."

+ + +

The next morning, Thomas arrives at Adela's house and begins to load all of her boxes and luggage into their buggy. He helps Adela and Victor into the buggy. As the buggy starts traveling down the road toward the bank, Thomas asks, "Adela, have you thought about what you are going to do when you get to Los Angeles?"

"It's a big city, and there are many opportunities of finding a good-paying job. I haven't decided on anything yet. You see I also have a child to take care of."

Thomas is waiting in the buggy with Victor outside the bank when Adela comes out, and he helps her into the buggy. Thomas gets into his seat and glances over his shoulder and asks, "Are you settled in, have you got everything?"

"Yes, everything went smoothly," she replies.

✦ ✦ ✦

At the train station, Thomas gets a train porter to help him with all of her boxes and luggage.

The porter, using his hand dolly, carries all her luggage into the station. Adela at the ticket window confirms and pays for a one-way train ticket to Los Angeles. Sitting in the waiting room with Victor sleeping in his carriage beside her, Adela says to Thomas, "I may come back here someday to visit my Mariano. I couldn't tell you when. Right now, I would say no, but over time, things will change."

"Thomas," Adela asks, "there is one thing I would like you to do for me, but the request is really from Mariano. Late last night while I was packing, I came across a small towel neatly folded up with a ribbon wrapped around it. I don't remember folding a towel so neatly and tying a ribbon around it, until I opened it up. What I saw in the towel quickly brought back fond memories. One evening shortly after the birth of Victor, while both of us sitting around my house, Mariano had this wonderful idea. He commented that since Victor being born with a lot of hair, and Mariano was selected to lay the cornerstone on the new church, maybe we could take a snip of his lovely hair and put it under the cornerstone when it is laid." She hands the towel to Thomas.

Nervously, Thomas holds the small towel and opens it up. "Wow," he says as he takes a look at the little snip of black hair. Not touching the hair, he carefully holds the towel up close to his eyes, getting a better look. "It's so small, very pretty," he says.

"Yes, I'll do it. I will get with Bishop Mangini tomorrow and make arrangements for when the time comes for the laying of the cornerstone. We will make sure that it will be put under the cornerstone when it is laid."

"Thank you very much, Thomas. I know Mariano will be very happy looking down at the splendor when it happens."Oh, Thomas, has Bishop Mangini decided on a name for the new church?""I'm not sure. Bishop Mangini was talking with Ethan and Mrs. Silverwood about having a public debate to choose a name. Someone had made a suggestion about having a drawing, but that idea got shot down. They said drawing is not the majority of a town, just a lucky thing, which could turn out to be a wrong name."

"Yes, I agree with that idea. Drawings are not good for names," Adela says.

Thomas suggests, "My best idea would be a vote from all the parishioners, but I guess I'll just wait and see. I think Bishop Mangini already has a name, I'm not sure if it's the final name. It's got something to do with a church's name back in Italy many years ago. The name right now its Mount Carmel Church. Maybe it should be called Mount Luca, or something like that."

"Mariano would have loved that," says Adela as she looks down for a moment, showing sadness on her face, then she quickly raised her head up, trying to show a smile.

"I think I should get aboard the train now, got to find a nice seat to watch the scenery."

"Adela, a lot of people here are going to miss you very much, and I hate to see you go."

"If they do name it after my Mariano, please let me know. Once I get settled in wherever I go, I will write you a letter with my address."

"That would be wonderful," Thomas says.

Thomas gives Adela a long hug as she gives him a light kiss to his cheek and says, "Goodbye, my friend. We had a wonderful time working together, and I truly will miss you. Tell Doc, for what he did for me and my Mariano, I will never ever forget him. And big Ethan, and his mercantile building, what a wonderful man he is. He worked so well with my Mariano, his building was the backbone of the town, where everything happened. Tell them all I truly will miss them." She starts tearing up, and she pushed Victor toward the exit of the train station to where the train is waiting. Adela, pushing Victor, enters the train and finds a seat, and the train slowly pulls out of the station as she waves.

The end of the story of
Father Mariano Luca
The Usurper